LONE OAKS
CROSSING

Don't miss any of Janet Dailey's bestsellers

The Calder Brand Series
Calder Brand
Calder Grit
A Calder at Heart

The New Americana Series
Blue Moon Haven
Hope Creek
Paradise Peak
Sunrise Canyon
Refuge Cove
Letters from Peaceful Lane
Hart's Hollow Farm

The Champions
Whirlwind
Whiplash
Quicksand

The Tylers of Texas
Texas Forever
Texas Free
Texas Fierce
Texas Tall
Texas Tough
Texas True

Bannon Brothers: Triumph
Bannon Brothers: Honor
Bannon Brothers: Trust
American Destiny
American Dreams
Masquerade
Tangled Vines
Heiress
Rivals

LONE OAKS CROSSING

JANET DAILEY

ZEBRA BOOKS
Kensington Publishing Corp.
www.kensingtonbooks.com

CHAPTER 1

Jo Beth Ellis had never been a quitter and she wouldn't start today.

"This morning's events were unfortunate. I'm sorry this happened to you."

Jo, her bottom lip bleeding, stood by a window in the principal's office of Stone Hill High School, ignoring the somber drawl of the man behind her and the silent vibrations of the cell phone ringing in her pocket (one she never had time to answer—even during her planning period) and stared out at the parking lot that bordered the front of the school. A cool September breeze rustled the thorny hedges along the cracked sidewalks, and the Kentucky sun struggled to nourish life, glinting off the metal hoods and rearview mirrors of parked cars, barely piercing the shadows covering sparse tufts of grass hidden between the brick wings of the school.

For a place that was intended to be a safe, nurturing environment, the landscape lacked warmth or welcome. Inside, the atmosphere was worse: hallways reeked of bleach and floor wax, profanities echoed against cinder blocks behind locked classroom doors, and voices of harried administrators crackled through static-laden two-way radios clipped to the hips of patrolling campus security officers.

The place had become more of a prison than a high school.

Heart pounding, Jo closed her eyes and tried to remember her first day as a teacher, six years ago when she'd been an energetic twenty-one-year-old college graduate. The day she'd marched up that sidewalk and into Stone Hill High School, head high and smile wide, eager to make a difference in the lives of students she loved, to help them improve their futures and achieve security.

But the realities of teaching were far different from the ones she'd been led to envision in college, and thoughts of quitting—along with the realization that she'd thrown away what amounted to a decade of her life—were stronger than ever.

Only, there was no way she could walk away and abandon the same student body to whom she'd committed herself faithfully years ago. How many other adults had abandoned these children when they had been needed the most? And hadn't she told her students to stick with it countless times over the years? To keep trying? To not give up? She couldn't let them down—especially not now . . . not when she'd sacrificed her relationship with what was left of her own family for them.

Earl. She thought of her grandfather, whom she'd left behind for her career, mucking stalls, grooming horses, and carrying the full weight of their family horse farm, Lone Oaks Crossing, alone. She thought of him, exhausted, ending each day in an empty house, a shot of bourbon and a view of dark pastures his only comforts.

An ache spread through her, stealing her breath.

"Perhaps," her principal, Dr. McKenzie, continued, "employing a more effective de-escalation technique would have deterred Natasha from striking out at you. Next time—"

"Next time?" Jo winced as the act of speaking split the wound in her bottom lip more deeply. She touched her tongue to it, tasting blood, and faced him. "Twice wasn't enough? Natasha has attacked other students and teachers like this before—all through elementary, middle, and now high school. And what else was I supposed to do? Ask her mid-swing to have a seat, give her a talking stick, then tell her to share her feelings? And what about the other thirty-two teens in the class, sitting there, with nowhere to go, having to watch that play out?"

She spread her hands, searching for words.

"Our kids are exposed to violence every day in this building," she continued. "Not to mention the amount of quality instruction incidents like this cost their education. The interventions you've dictated to us aren't working. The entire schoolwide behavior plan hasn't been working for years. I have no voice, no autonomy—not even in my own classroom. Our kids—especially Natasha—need more help than we're giving them. As it is—"

"As it is"—McKenzie leaned forward in his seat and rested his elbows on his wide desk—"Natasha's mother is threatening to sue the district and you, personally."

"For what? Natasha attacked a female student half her size from behind—unprovoked—in my classroom." Voice catching at the images the memory conjured, Jo inhaled a shaky breath. "She was slamming the other child's head into a cinder block wall. If I hadn't stepped in, that child might've walked away with more than just a bleeding forehead and bruised eye."

He picked up a pen. Twirled it between his thumb and forefinger. "I instructed you, as well as the entire faculty and staff, at the start of the year not to intervene in fights."

"I pulled Natasha off the student, stepped in front of her to protect the other child, and Natasha took a swing at me." Oh, dear God, her lip throbbed. "That's what happened, from beginning to end. The other child's blood is still on the wall. Check the classroom camera, it's all there."

He frowned. "We already have, but that's not the point. You're not allowed to restrain students. Stepping in is someone else's job. Our administration is dedicated to ensuring a safe environ—"

"Then where was the safety officer? Where were you? I hit the emergency call button." She shook her head. "If a shooter enters the building, I'm expected to step in front of a bullet to save a child, but if that same child is attacked by a peer, I'm supposed to simply stand there and watch the child be beaten to death? If I fail to act in the first scenario, I'm crucified. In the second scenario, if I do act, I'm in danger of being sued. Do I need to ask for permission before I'm even allowed to protect *myself*?" A mirthless chuckle broke free of her chest. "And when, in the midst of all of this, am I supposed to be able to teach?"

Sighing, he put down the pen. "You're a great teacher, Ms. Ellis. One of our best. Admittedly, today was a bad day. But one bad day shouldn't make or break an entire career."

"But it's not just one bad day," she said softly.

There had been so many, and increasingly more every year. More violence, more anger, more arguments, more blame, more politics, more chaos, more confusion, more criticism . . . but always less time and support, fewer resources. The more she spoke up about the toxic school culture and working conditions and the more she asked for help, the more she paid for voicing her concerns— personally as well as professionally. Every day inside these walls, students' and teachers' safety, well-being, and futures were gambled. And today, a typical Monday at Stone Hill High School, had been no exception.

Something wet plopped onto her collarbone. She looked down and a second drop of blood fell from her lip to join the first, rolled over her skin, then settled against the collar of her blouse. The white cotton absorbed it, the stain spreading.

Oh, dear God. Here she stood, bleeding in her boss's office, as he blamed her for being physically assaulted on the job. This was no way to make a living . . . and certainly no way to live.

"I can't do this anymore," she whispered.

"Then do it for the kids," he said quietly.

McKenzie stood, tugged a tissue from a tissue box on his desk, and handed it to Jo. "As punishment, I've suspended Natasha from school for the rest of the week, but she'd like to speak to you before she leaves today." He crossed the room and opened the closed door of his office. "Natasha, please come in."

There were hushed voices and footsteps outside the door along the corridor of the school's main office, then a tall, blond girl sauntered in and crossed her arms over her chest. Another blonde, who appeared to be in her late thirties, propped her fists on her hips, and stood on the threshold of the room, glaring at Jo.

"Natasha," McKenzie said. "Don't you have something to say to Ms. Ellis?"

The teen narrowed her eyes at Jo and remained silent.

"Natasha," he prompted again.

Natasha's lip curled as she locked eyes with Jo. The sheer hatred in the girl's gaze made Jo shudder. "Sorry you got your lip busted. Next time, stay out of my way."

McKenzie's chest lifted on a sharp inhale. "Natash—"

"She ought to be fired." The blonde in the doorway—Natasha's mother, Jo presumed—stabbed a finger in the air, aimed toward Jo. "She had no right to put her hands on my child. Had no idea what that other girl said about her. From now on, I expect this woman to report to me every day on Natasha's progress—academically and otherwise. And if Natasha sees fit to take care of gossip again herself, that woman had better not interfere."

"If an incident occurs in Ms. Ellis's classroom, Mrs. Bennett," McKenzie said tightly, "Ms. Ellis has no choice but to address it, just as she did in this instance. And district leadership has also decided to leave it up to Ms. Ellis as to whether charges will be filed against Natasha for striking her in the face." He leveled a look at Jo. "Though I'm sure that's not what Ms. Ellis wants. She, like district leadership, cares deeply for all students, and I don't think she'd want one unpleasant mistake to mar a student's permanent record." He paused, holding Jo's gaze, then asked, "Do you, Ms. Ellis?"

Jo lifted her bloody chin. "Or the school's record?"

He blinked, then stared back at her. "Excuse me?"

"You mean, you don't want to mar the school's record either."

He didn't answer, and he didn't have to. McKenzie had a family to support. Everything he did was in support of his efforts to boost Stone Hill High's public image and ensure he kept his position—a position that paid triple the salary of the average classroom teacher who worked tire-lessly in the trenches.

This was McKenzie's first year serving as a high school principal. Prior to his current position, he'd taught U.S. History and coached football for a few years before being promoted. McKenzie was a good guy, but an inex-perienced and ill-prepared leader, which, over the years, had become the rule rather than the exception in public education as more and more experienced educators left the profession.

Jo looked at Natasha again, her eyes searching the younger girl's face as a residual trickle of sympathy moved through her. She'd noticed Natasha on the first day of class seven weeks ago, the girl's stony expression and disdainful gaze having caught her attention, raising the hairs on the back of her neck.

Natasha, like so many other students at Stone Hill High, was hurting—that had been easy to detect. No teenager her age became so hardened, angry, and cynical without external influence of some kind. But despite re-peated—and exhaustive—attempts, Jo had failed to reach her. And even now, Jo, lip split and dignity stripped, still found herself wanting to reach out, to strive to make a connection of some kind. To prove to Natasha that some-one did, in fact, care.

"Natasha," Jo said. "Hurting someone else won't solve your problems, and the only reason I teach—have ever taught—is to educate, protect, and support students like you in a healthy way. If you need help, I want to help y—"

"I'm not listening to this, bitch." Natasha spun around, pushed past her mother, and stalked out of the office. "Let her press charges. I don't give a damn."

Natasha's mother shot Jo one more hard glare, then left, too, following her daughter down the corridor.

Jo stood silently for a few moments, her breaths coming in tandem with the painful throb in her bottom lip. Her mouth had begun to swell and the adrenaline that had shot through her veins for hours had subsided. She felt heavy suddenly, as though her limbs were made of dense concrete.

"I won't file charges." She removed her classroom keys, which were attached to a lanyard, from her neck, then lifted the lanyard over her head. "And I won't be back."

McKenzie's mouth opened, then closed, soundlessly, as she handed him the lanyard and keys as well as the unused tissue he'd given her earlier. He stared down at them then lifted his head, a stern gleam in his eyes. "You signed a contract, Ms. Ellis, and we're not even two months into the current school year. If you leave now rather than honoring your obligations for the full year, I'll be obligated to report you to the Professional Standards Board for neglecting your duties. Your teaching certificate will be suspended or, possibly, revoked. And there's a financial penalty for breach of contract."

Jo shrugged. What did it matter? She'd been broke for ten years. First, she'd struggled to pay her way through four years of college to earn a teaching degree, and for the past six years, her teaching salary had been barely enough to pay for her tiny, one-bedroom apartment and buy groceries, which left her with nothing left over to save. So, what was one less paycheck anyway?

She headed for the door. "I'll mail a check to you to cover my financial obligation for breach of contract. Do whatever you have to do as far as my teaching certificate. I won't need it again anyway."

"Ms. Ellis." His voice changed, the stern bravado fading, a desperate tone taking its place. "You've done an exceptional job in the classroom for six years. You're appreciated and we need you—especially now that we're understaffed. Please don't give up now. We'll sit down and talk. Explore your ideas and find a compromise."

Hmm. If only he'd said that years ago . . . and if only he meant it now.

"Please don't go," he said.

Jo kept walking, shocked by the depth of her apathy. "I'm already gone."

The sun hit her hard when she stepped outside the building, her eyes squinting, her injured mouth tightening painfully against its warm rays. She forced her legs to keep moving until she reached her car, then got in, cranked the engine, and drove away, refusing to allow herself to look back.

She'd sacrificed so much for a thankless job—including precious time she should've spent with Earl, helping to ease his burden at Lone Oaks Crossing—serving gate duty at athletic events, staying hours after school to tutor struggling students and conduct parent conferences, grading lesson plans at night, writing lesson plans on weekends and holidays, holding down a second job and attending professional learning sessions during the summer break. Years of time she could never recover.

Teaching had been a mistake. One she'd rectify, starting now.

Jo drove on, past the apartment complex that housed her meager belongings, through the bustling city limits of Stone Hill and into the rural landscape that lay on the outskirts of the small Kentucky town, her hands and foot sending the car in the familiar direction of her childhood home.

The car ate up the miles toward Lone Oaks Crossing. She hadn't visited in over a year, but the place had been on her mind more often than not recently. She'd have to tell Earl, of course. He'd say he'd told her so, and he'd be disappointed in her—but no more so than she already was with herself.

Soon, emerald hills emerged, rolling peacefully alongside her car, the breeze gracefully bending the lush bluegrass of sprawling fields in an easy rhythm. She rolled the windows down and inhaled, the swift wind cooling her hot cheeks, slowing her pulse.

The loud peal of her cell phone rang through her car's speakers, the computer system connecting the call.

"Hello?" A female voice chimed through the speakers. "I'm trying to reach Ms. Jo Beth Ellis."

Jo licked her dry lips and cleared her throat. "This is Jo. Who is this?"

"This is Sarah Wyndham," the voice said. "I'm a nurse, calling from Lone Oaks Hospital."

Lone Oaks? Home. *Earl.* Jo straightened in her seat. "Does this have something to do with Earl? Is he okay? Has h—"

"Yes, I'm calling about Earl Ellis, but please don't be alarmed. He's resting comfortably now and was very lucky."

"What do you mean? What's happened?"

"I see here"—rustling crossed the line—"that you're listed as Mr. Ellis's granddaughter. Is that correct?"

"Yes."

"I've been trying to reach you all morning. Your grandfather has had a stroke."

Jo's pulse picked up again, her muscles clenching.

"But he's stable now and resting well in room four-o-eight," Sarah continued. "He'll need to stay here for a few days. He'll require an extensive period of rehabilitation, and as you're listed as his emergency cont—"

"I'm already on my way." Jo pressed the pedal harder, the car picking up speed. "But I'm two hours out."

"There's no rush, Ms. Ellis. As I said, your grandfather's resting peacefully now and will be for some time. If anything changes prior to your arrival, I'll call you immediately."

Jo nodded, then, remembering she was on the phone, said, "Thank you."

"You're welcome. We'll see you soon."

The call disconnected.

Thoughts racing, Jo drove for an hour then, tank running low, pulled into a gas station—Jimbo's Pit—and fueled up. A man exited the small convenience store and walked by her car on the way to his, an odd expression crossing his face as he eyed her face, then chest.

Jo looked down at the blood staining her white blouse. Oh, no. She couldn't show up at Earl's bedside looking like this. She touched her fingertip to the dried blood on her bottom lip and flinched. There were two restrooms outside the convenience store, both with signs that read SEE CLERK FOR KEY.

Tank full, she replaced the pump handle and went inside to pay, grabbing salt, bottled water, and gauze before approaching the checkout counter. The clerk, a young man with blue hair, rang up her purchases, bagged them, and handed the sack to her.

"May I have the restroom key, please?" She kept her eyes down but felt the intensity of his scrutiny on her bloody lip anyway.

His hands left the counter briefly then returned, holding a key out toward her. "Ma'am?"

She took the key, then looked up, meeting his concerned gaze.

"Are you okay?" He glanced out the window, then back at her and whispered, "If you need help . . ."

That mirthless laugh returned, bursting from her lips before she could stop it, her eyes burning. "D-do you know I offered someone the very same thing today?"

He tilted his head and his concerned expression changed to confusion.

"No, I—" She backed away, clutching her bag. "No, thank you."

Jo went inside the restroom and locked the door, dumped the salt she'd purchased into the bottle of water, soaked a strip of gauze in the mixture, and dabbed at her bloody mouth. She hissed at the sharp sting, her eyes welling.

She thought of Earl, ill and alone; McKenzie, short-handed and disappointed; Natasha, angry and full of hate; and her students who sat in a classroom without her. She thought of how she'd failed them all and how she'd failed herself.

Then her fingers stilled against her throbbing lip, and an unexpected surge of determination coursed through her as she realized how much Earl would need her in the coming days . . . and how—even though her life was crumbling around her—she wouldn't fail him again.

"What do you mean you're quitting?" Brooks Moore demanded.

He had spent the past decade of his thirty-two years of life adhering to a strategic business plan he'd infused with one primary goal: justice. A hard-fought objective he'd been on the brink of achieving but that now squirmed in his clenched fist, threatening to slide between his fingers and bolt out of his reach.

"I can't believe you're doing this to me now," Brooks said. "We're only nine months away from the Derby." The fall breeze tugged at the resignation letter he held, fluttering the crumpled corners against his knuckles as he eyed the older man who stood in front of him. "Your reputation for loyalty is unblemished. That's the reason I hired you in the first place."

Rhett Thomas, sharp-eyed, thin-lipped, and hard-bitten—a testimony to thirty years spent navigating the corrupt underbelly of horse racing as a trainer—stepped closer on the porch of Brooks's three-story colonial-style home and met him head-on. "Is that the only reason?"

Brooks cut his gaze to the left, past Rhett's stocky physique, to the eight hundred acres of sunlit Kentucky land that housed his custom-built home, state-of-the-art stables, and bourbon distillery buildings. He'd undertaken a risky venture—blending bourbon, thoroughbreds, tourism, and his ultimate life's goal into the thriving business of Original Sin—but his plan had been solid and successful . . . until now.

Gritting his teeth, he faced Rhett again. "I hired you because you were known as the most highly skilled and devoutly loyal trainer in the business. Both of which I witnessed myself throughout your two-year tenure in my stables, training my thoroughbred. And now, at the eleventh hour, you tell me you're walking." An unexpected pang moved through Brooks, cutting deep, twisting his mouth. "I thought we were in this for the long haul. I thought we'd established some level of trust between us."

Rhett nodded. "We have. You've been a great partner, Brooks. I'd even go so far as to say you've been the best partner I've had in my three decades in this sport."

"Then wh—?"

"You're also in this for the worst reasons." Rhett gestured toward the lush bluegrass, massive oaks, and rolling hills extending beyond them. "Look at what you have. Look at how much you've achieved at such a young age. You've got more here, deeded and thriving, than all your ancestors combined. More than most men could accumulate over ten lifetimes." His tone softened. "Forgive me, Brooks. But your father didn't know when to stop . . . and neither do you."

Brooks bristled. The words were a familiar refrain he'd heard often over the years, but he'd discovered that no matter how much time passed, the wound that festered inside his soul was still as fresh as the day it had been inflicted.

His father had never walked the straight and narrow path—no, not Deacon Moore. He'd developed a gambling habit in his twenties that had morphed into an addiction over the years, and beset by vices and tremendous losses, he'd struggled to remain loyal to his wife and son. Deacon had gambled and lost his life savings, but he'd always safeguarded the deed to Moore family land, especially Rose Farm—a gorgeous stretch of Kentucky acreage where healthy thoroughbreds were bred, and which would serve as a financial safety net for his wife and son.

The Moore family business had thrived for generations until seventeen years ago when Deacon's gambling losses had left him vulnerable, and the Harris family—Spencer Harris, in particular—had wielded their wealth and power and connived their way into stealing the only financial asset Deacon had left. Months after losing Rose Farm, Spencer had taken the Moore family home as well. Deacon, devastated and destitute, had succumbed to his demons and taken his own life, leaving Brooks and his mother, Ada, grief-stricken, homeless, and the target of ridicule.

One month after that, Ada had died from heart failure (a broken heart, Brooks recalled a nurse whispering) and he'd been placed in a local foster home, where he'd spent three years nurturing the rage inside him. Anger with a purpose, he'd discovered quickly, made a man stronger than tears.

It'd taken Brooks years to rebuild and surpass his family's wealth—thanks to a blend of luck, risk, and hard work that would've shocked even his own mother . . . if she'd lived to see it. Still, no amount of money could buy a good family name, sincere respect, or entry into the social circles of the local elite. A sphere Brooks had to enter to gain access to Spencer and hit the other man's pride, power, and wealth where it would cause the most damage.

Brooks clenched his jaw as he scanned the expansive grounds of his estate, then smiled tightly at Rhett. "I think it's obvious I'm not careless with money."

"I never said gambling was your addiction." Rhett's gaze roved over his face for a moment, and then he sighed. "Look, I'm not doing this on a whim. Fact is, I don't have much choice in the matter."

Brooks narrowed his eyes. "Who didn't give you a choice?"

Rhett looked away, lifted his face into the cool breeze rustling the bluegrass, and closed his eyes. "Brooks—"

"What's he holding?"

Rhett remained silent.

"What's he holding, Rhett?" A rueful smile lifted Brooks's lips. "Or maybe I'm wrong? Maybe our enemy isn't the same after all?"

Rhett ducked his gray head, opened his heavy-lidded

eyes, and stared at his worn boots. "I'm not a young man, Brooks," he said softly. "I'm not a rich or influential one either—never have been. I'm two years away from being able to afford to retire and, hopefully, have a long, peaceful stretch of rest in front of me to spend with my wife and grandkids. My time is the second most valuable asset I possess."

"What's he hol—"

"My name." Rhett lifted his head and glared. "Spencer Harris has my reputation in his palm, threatening to crush it if I continue working with you. If it were just my loss, I wouldn't care. But it's my family's. My sons are in this business, and as talented as they are, they're set to climb as high as they aim—but not without a decent rep. In this business, word-of-mouth makes or breaks a man, and my boys—as hard as they've worked for what little they have—don't deserve to have their livelihood stripped from them by that bastard because they share my name."

Brooks held out Rhett's letter of resignation. "All the more reason to see this through with me. You've trained Another Round since his birth—you know what he's capable of, and so do a lot of others betting on this sport—including Spencer. That's the only reason he's doing this. He knows what a Derby win will bring. Spencer won't be able to touch us when we wi—"

"*If* we win." Rhett shook his head. "You of all people know nothing in horse racing is a sure bet. Luck plays its part no matter what we do."

Brooks held Rhett's gaze. "Another Round will win."

"I hope he does," Rhett said. "I truly do. I just can't take that chance with you. I hope you can understand."

The finality in his tone hollowed Brooks's gut, a sensation at odds with the surge of admiration that coursed through him. He shoved the resignation letter in his pocket and spun away, bracing his hands on the porch rail and eyeing his stables in the distance.

"You're a good man," he forced between stiff lips, "and I won't fault you for doing what you think is best for your family. Stop by the main office on your way out. I'll instruct my secretary to have your final check ready at the front desk. It'll include a hefty bonus—enough for you to start that retirement and spend your time with your wife and grandkids now, if you see fit."

"Thank you, Brooks. You've always been a generous man." Rhett's footsteps, heavy and slow, receded, then paused several feet away. "I also know you well enough to know that you're not giving up without a fight. Spencer's gonna do everything he can to impede your progress. And even if I'd stayed, I don't know that my help would've been enough. You need a great trainer—one far better than me."

Brooks watched as one of his employees led a small group of tourists along one of the trails leading from the stables to the stillhouses. The sun, which had shone strong throughout the day, was beginning to slide lower in the sky, and the tourists, the fifth tour group today, would've already been given a personal introduction to a few of his thoroughbreds and were now on their way to tour his distilleries and sample his best whiskey.

The unique blend of horses and bourbon on one estate had enabled Brooks's business to thrive. The only element that could substantially enhance Original Sin's value would be the prestige of having a Derby winner born, raised, and trained on the estate. Another Round, Brooks's soon-to-be three-year-old thoroughbred, fit the bill. But now, with the Derby only nine months away and qualifying races already underway, Brooks had no trainer to see him through to the finish line.

"You need a trainer whose horse has won before," Rhett said.

A rueful laugh burst from Brooks's lips. "I've already been down that route. No one at that level will give me the time of day on account of my name—or rather, lack thereof—and the fact that they know of my rivalry with Spencer and want no part in it." He glanced at Rhett and managed to smile. "Not that that's the only reason I hired you. You're an excellent trainer."

"I know the best there is. Someone who's trained a Derby winner. Someone who's beyond Spencer's influence and whose hands are clean. Someone with integrity and honor."

"Who is he?"

Rhett's mouth twisted. "She."

Brooks frowned. "No woman is on record as having trained a Derby winner."

"No. She wouldn't be." Rhett dipped his head. "She's never been officially named as a winning trainer—she's only served as an assistant and only for one Derby race. But everyone on the backside knew she was behind that win. The woman behind the man, so to speak. And lucky for you, you know the man. Her grandfather's your neighbor, Earl Ellis. The guy that owns Lone Oaks Crossing."

Brooks recalled the name of both the man and the property, but he'd only seen him once, from a distance. Five years ago, the day the construction crew had broken ground on Brooks's house, Earl had appeared between the oak trees that divided their properties and watched from afar for over an hour as the crew worked. Eventually, Brooks crossed the field and introduced himself.

Earl, his tan, leathery skin creased with age and a world-weary expression on his face, had given his name, shaken Brooks's hand, and said one thing before he clucked his tongue to the mare he was mounted on and rode back to his home.

What you got right there's a dream. Best keep your eyes open and hold it tight.

"I only met him once," Brooks said. "And I haven't gotten a good look at his land. Just saw the outskirts from a distance when I broke ground here."

"Lone Oaks Crossing used to be a breeding and training farm but it's run-down now," Rhett said. "Earl's best days as a trainer have been behind him for quite a while, I'm afraid. Ever since his granddaughter left, really. Now he just boards horses occasionally to make ends meet." He reached into his back pocket, withdrew a tightly folded paper, and held it out. "Her name's Jo Beth Ellis. She has the touch but left the sport and Lone Oaks some time ago. Hasn't trained a horse in years, from what I've been told. Been teaching at a high school across state instead."

Brooks strode across the porch, took the paper, and unfolded it. Two phone numbers, the name of a local hospital, and a hospital room number were scrawled on the page.

"That first number," Rhett said, "which won't do you any good right now, belongs to Earl, and the second to one of his friends, Frankie Kyle. I gave her a call earlier, trying to track Earl down, and she told me he had a stroke sometime early this morning. She was still at the hospital with him when we spoke."

Brooks frowned. "How's he doing?"

"Good, from what Frankie told me, though she said he'll have a ways to go before he's back on his feet. She also mentioned that Jo's on her way into town to see him." He gestured toward the paper. "Earl's room number is on there in case you decide to give it a go. I expect you'll find Jo there if you go tonight or first thing tomorrow morning."

Brooks grimaced. "A hospital isn't an appropriate place to pitch a business venture."

Rhett nodded. "I agree. But it's an opportunity to introduce yourself, and it may be your only chance to snag a word with Jo. She didn't leave the sport on very good terms and, from what Frankie told me, doesn't make it out this way often. You have a lot of convincing ahead of you."

Brooks looked at his stables again, his hopes sinking. Until now, everything had played into his hands. He was so close to success—*so close!* But without a trainer, his plan was shot. And Spencer, who'd taken advantage of the weaknesses of others, would ruin more lives.

"To beat Spencer, you need Jo," Rhett advised. "You either go all in now or fold."

CHAPTER 2

When Jo arrived at Lone Oaks Hospital, the sun had just begun to dip below the horizon, casting long shadows of trees across the half-empty parking lot. She barely noticed the hour as she hustled inside, anxious to see Earl after the long drive. She clutched the collar of her bloodstained blouse higher on her neck.

Inside, the long halls were quiet, save for rhythmic beeps and the low murmurs of doctors and nurses. Jo followed the signs on the wall to locate the room number the nurse had given her. The door had been left open a few inches and she pushed it wide, carefully not making any noise. She halted midstep at the sight of Earl, pale and still, sleeping in a bed.

"Oh, my sweet Jo." An older woman, slumped in a chair beside the bed, shoved to her feet, crossed the room, and wrapped her arms around Jo. "I'm so glad you're here."

"Frankie." Jo sank into her embrace and breathed her

in, her lips trembling as the familiar scents of hay, horses, and lumber—*home*—enveloped her.

Frankie, now sixty-five years old, was Earl's oldest friend and a retired veterinarian. She was also the woman who'd stepped in twenty years ago when Jo's mother had abandoned her, leaving her in Earl's care. Having never known her father, Jo had been left at Lone Oaks Crossing with Earl when she was seven years old, and Frankie had always been more like a mother to her than her biological mother had ever been.

If looks were anything to go by, Frankie hadn't changed much over the past few years. Brown hair mussed, cheeks dirt-streaked, and jeans and T-shirt well-worn, Frankie was still as laid-back and real as ever. She'd never stood on ceremony and never bit her tongue—especially when it came to Earl.

Jo hugged her tighter. "H-how is he?"

"He's okay. They've run some tests and the doctor will have more information for us tomorrow." Her hand smoothed over Jo's hair, her whisper tickling Jo's ear. "He's been asking for you."

Jo turned her head, rested her opposite cheek on Frankie's shoulder, and studied Earl's features. "He's able to talk?"

"Some," she said softly. "He gestures to get across the rest." Frankie's chest vibrated slightly against Jo, an amused tone tinging her voice. "His mind's working good, though. He managed to give a male nurse the finger when the guy had trouble sticking a needle in his vein for the IV."

A grin sprang to Jo's lips despite the lump in her throat. "Leave it to Earl. He never did like having to lean on others for help." She slipped out of Frankie's arms and kissed her cheek. "Thank you for staying here with him.

I'm usually not able to answer my phone at work, and I didn't realize the hospital was c—"

"Girl, what'd you get into?" Frowning, Frankie gently gripped Jo's chin with two fingers and lifted her face, tilting her head one way then the other. "You're bleeding."

"I was." Jo stepped back and tugged the jacket collar higher against her chin. "It's stopped now and it's not important." She looked at Earl, her throat constricting. "Are we allowed to stay here with him tonight?"

"One of us can. But I don't think either of us should."

Jo glanced at Frankie in surprise.

"The nurse will be in around nine tonight to give him another round of meds," Frankie said. "She told me he probably won't crack open an eyelid after that until sometime tomorrow afternoon, and after the day we've had, I'm wore slap out," Frankie said. "And you look like you need a better night's sleep than a hard-backed chair and frequent vital check interruptions would provide."

"I'd like to stay with him."

"Then stay tomorrow night." Frankie jerked her chin toward Earl's motionless form. "He needs his rest, too, tonight. And he's more likely to be alert tomorrow. That'll give you a chance to go home, clean yourself up, and get a decent night's rest."

Jo nodded. "You're still practical as always, I see."

"Yep." Frankie, her eyes heavy and tired, smiled. "Sit with him 'til your nerves settle, then come on back to the farm. Fall's creeping in and it's cool out. I'll get a fire started in the pit, and we'll sit around it a while, give you a chance to relax under those stars I'm sure you've been missing."

"Thank you, Frankie."

"Don't stay too long," she said over her shoulder as she walked out of the room. "Earl needs his rest."

Jo stood still for a moment, visually scanning Earl, his wiry seventy-three-year-old physique draped with a sheet, an IV leading to the back of his thick-veined hand and a nasal cannula, providing oxygen, positioned in his nostrils. Deep creases bracketed his chapped down-turned lips and heavy crow's feet fanned out from each of his closed eyelids.

The months since she'd last seen him had changed him; his body showed his age more than it ever had. Nine years ago, she'd known, even at eighteen, that Earl's many years of hardship and long days of training horses on the farm were taking a toll on his health, which made her decision to abandon her short-lived career in training thoroughbreds all the more difficult.

She'd loved training—she truly had—but the dark side of racing, of gambling a horse's life for money, had eventually been too painful for her to continue.

Pursuing a career in teaching had felt like the perfect next step. Training was teaching at its core, which was one of the reasons she'd loved it so much. She also knew firsthand how challenging life could be as a child without a sense of security, safety, and encouragement—an experience she wanted to diminish as much as possible for other children who might be suffering as she had in the months after her mother had abandoned her. Earl, Frankie, and the tranquility of Lone Oaks Crossing had transformed her life for the better over the years and she wanted to do the same for others. But in order to transition into teaching, she'd need a college degree—something that couldn't be had in the little town of Lone Oaks—which meant packing up and moving away.

Earl had taken it hard. He'd homeschooled her at her request during the last two years of her high school career in order to mentor her in the sport they both loved, fully expecting her to partner with him and operate a joint training venture after she graduated high school. And when a thoroughbred she'd helped Earl train won the Derby a month prior to her high school graduation, Earl's excitement over the new business he'd proposed had only intensified.

Her own excitement, however, had diminished after witnessing the horrors of racing first-hand. From that point on, she could not, in good conscience, continue participating in the sport. It had been painful breaking the news to Earl, and even more painful for Earl to accept. He'd argued against her new career path, pointing out her natural talent at training, stressing how rare her gift was and how much he needed her at Lone Oaks Crossing. Jo had expected her choice to leave home to be difficult for him given the way her mother—his daughter—had abandoned them both years prior with no word since. But to his credit, he'd eventually accepted her decision, wished her well, and supported her move.

Now, seeing him like this, she regretted leaving him—and Lone Oaks Crossing—more than ever.

Jo walked over to the bed and sat in the chair beside it. Reluctant to disturb him, but needing the physical reassurance of touch, she reached out, smoothed her fingers over the back of his hand, then curled her hand gently around his, cradling his palm.

His mouth parted and a faint groan escaped his lips.

She leaned closer and brought her face to his, her mouth near his ear. "I'm here, Earl," she whispered. "I've come home."

Another hoarse moan rose from his chest; then his wrinkled eyelids lifted, one after the other, and his eyes focused on her face. His chest lifted as his mouth opened wider, pulling in air.

"Don't talk," she said. "Just rest."

"I . . ." He scowled, then blinked hard, his lips contorting as he struggled to speak. "W-will if . . ." He struggled for a moment, then exhaled heavily, his chest sinking.

Wet heat filled her eyes, but she forced herself to smile. "You will if you want to? That's what you're trying to tell me, isn't it?"

His bleary eyes returned to hers and one corner of his mouth hitched up.

"See?" She squeezed his hand gently. "You don't need words. I know you well enough to know what you're thinking."

His gaze left hers and roved lower, focusing on her bottom lip. The scowl on his face melted away, deep creases of pained concern taking its place on his face. "Wh—wh . . ." He stopped trying to speak and lifted one shaky hand to point at her wound instead.

Still smiling, she touched her injured lip with the tip of her tongue and shrugged. "Just another day on the job in my profession." Her breath caught. Well . . . her former profession. But now was neither the right time nor place to share that news. "Don't worry. It's nothing. It doesn't matter."

Earl, his mouth twisting again, turned his hand over in hers, his gnarled fingers weakly squeezing her thumb. "Y-you . . ." He struggled, then mouthed the word soundlessly: *matter*.

Smile fading, Jo held his gaze, watching as his eyes grew heavier each second until they eventually closed, his soft, rhythmic breaths the only sound in the room. Then she lowered her head to the bed, her forehead touching Earl's strong shoulder, and, for the first time that day, allowed the tears to fall.

* * *

Brooks stood outside room 408 in Lone Oaks Hospital, staring at the numbers tacked to the wooden door, and shifted the flower-filled vase he held from one hand to the other.

"May I help you, sir?"

He glanced over his shoulder at the woman—a nurse, judging from the scrubs she wore—and shook his head. "No, thank you. I'm just here to . . ." *Intrude in a stranger's life during a vulnerable moment for opportunistic gain like a heartless jerk?* ". . . visit a friend."

The nurse smiled in return, her eyes lit with a warm spark he'd seen many times over the course of his life. "You're Brooks Moore, aren't you? Owner of Original Sin? A friend and I toured your estate recently. It's absolutely beautiful."

He nodded, recognizing the cajoling tone. "Thank you."

When he'd first opened Original Sin, many locals had been skeptical. Lone Oaks, a rural town about sixty miles outside of Lexington, sustained several tourist destinations for either bourbon or thoroughbred seekers, but none of the tourist hot spots combined the two. Most believed undertaking both would dilute the quality of one or the other. Original Sin, the first estate in Lone Oaks to offer tourists the two local attractions in one scenic location, had succeeded beyond everyone's expectations—including his own—generating a level of status and wealth the local business community hadn't foreseen. As a result, he was recognized—and propositioned—in multiple ways nowadays.

"I hope to visit your estate again soon. Maybe for a private one-on-one tour," the nurse said, a teasing note entering her tone. "You sure I can't help you with anything?"

"No, thank you."

"Well, if you need anything, please don't hesitate to let me know." She gestured over her shoulder. "You can find me at the nurse's station." Her smile widened as her gaze roved over him from head to toe. "Just ask for Jenny."

He dipped his head, recognizing the invitation in her tone though he wasn't in the mood. Women, he'd had. Money, he had. It was power he was after now. And, according to the inside knowledge Rhett had shared with him hours earlier, he needed Jo Beth Ellis to earn the respect and access he craved.

"Thank you," he repeated tonelessly to the nurse as he turned away. He waited for her steps to fade before nudging the door in front of him open and entering the room.

Inside, an older man lay on the bed, sleeping. *Earl.* Brooks recognized the craggy features of his tan face. A pang moved through him as he studied Earl's sinewy frame and frail hands, lying still on the bed. He didn't know Earl well—at all, really—but he could clearly recall from their first meeting how the older man's body held all the hallmarks of outdoor labor, grit, and determination. To see him like this now, ill and vulnerable, unsettled Brooks more than the sight of a stranger should.

Beside Earl, long waves of what Brooks could only think of as honey-colored hair the same shade as his finest double-barrel bourbon spilled across the mattress. A slim woman slept there, her arms folded on the bed, her head resting on her forearms, and those beautiful strands of hair obscuring her face.

Brooks hesitated, glancing down at his boots, then back at the door, weighing his options. He could wake her, he supposed, but only an insensitive jerk would do that. He winced, realizing he was already one for barging in here, unannounced and uninvited. Best to rectify that mistake before he made it worse.

Moving quietly, he walked slowly across the room and set the vase he carried on the window ledge. His business card was tucked into a thin plastic holder buried inside the blooms. Perhaps if he waited until tomorrow afternoon, called, and asked to speak with Jo Beth Ellis, the timing would be more appropriate and she'd be receptive to speaking with him. Then maybe he wouldn't come across as a completely insensitive ass.

Satisfied with his decision, he cast one more glance at the bed then headed for the door, stepping silently across the linoleum floor.

"Are you a friend of Earl's?"

At the soft voice, Brooks halted, mere inches from the door, then faced the bed again. The woman sat upright now, her pale hands pushing her long hair back from her face as she stared up at him. She had the darkest blue eyes he'd ever seen—so dark and rich, they took on a black hue when the light hit them just right. But her mouth was what held his attention, the dried blood on her lower lip and the bloodstain on her blouse at odds with her pretty features, business-style slacks, and sensible shoes.

"My grandfather," she said in quiet tones. "Are you a friend of his?"

Brooks nodded, then focusing on her words, shook his head. "No." He spoke softly, too, so as not to disturb Earl. "I'm his neighbor. May I ask how he is?"

A fleeting gleam of dry amusement moved through her eyes. "You may." Her gaze turned somber again as she looked at Earl, still sleeping in the bed. "He's doing well, from what I've been told, but we'll know more tomorrow. It seems to have been a minor stroke."

"That's good to hear." He walked across the room and

held out his hand, unable to tear his attention away from her face, the warm, clear intensity in her gaze so unique it stirred a curious attraction deep within him. "I apologize for disturbing you."

Carefully keeping his expression blank, he lowered his eyes to her mouth, tracing the bow of her bottom lip, then lingering on the wound marring it. A spark of anger lit in his gut at the sight, a strange surge of protectiveness sweeping over him. Where had she gotten that? And—he glanced at the bloodstain on her business blouse—in work clothes? Had she been mugged? Attacked by an abusive husband? Boyfriend?

"I'm Brooks Moore," he said quietly. "I own the property to the east of Lone Oaks Crossing."

She stood and gripped his hand. "Jo Ellis. I'm his granddaughter." She returned his stare, a wry expression crossing her face. "You want to know where I got it. The busted lip, I mean."

He blinked, unsettled by her blunt insight. In his business, people rarely shared their thoughts so openly, and even if they did, they cloaked them in a shroud of deceit or calculated persuasion. He'd mastered bluffing years ago, easily masking his emotions during all his transactions. Her quick assessment of his thoughts left him feeling vulnerable.

"The thought did cross my mind," he said. "Though it's none of my business."

"You're right." She released his hand. "It's not."

Disappointment lowered his shoulders, and he missed her warm, gentle grip immediately, the air cold against his empty palm.

She has the touch . . . but left the sport and Lone Oaks some time ago . . .

Brooks, recalling Rhett's comment, flexed his fingers

against the odd sensation she'd left behind on his skin. The whole length of his body tingled, and he eyed her graceful hands as they rested by her side. She was an attractive woman, but he'd ignored the sexual advances of women for over two years now, choosing instead to focus his energy on building his business and learning the intricacies of dealmaking on the front and back sides of the track.

That's all it was. Sexual attraction—lust—pure and simple. Something there was no room for in the successful business partnership he hoped to forge with her.

"Black-eyed Susans?" She stood by the window now, staring down at the bright blooms spilling over the tall vase he'd brought.

He shoved his hands in his pockets and rocked back on his heels. "Yes." He hid his smile. "Thought I'd bring something to cheer Earl up."

She raised one eyebrow as she scrutinized his expression then gripped the glass vase with both hands, lifted it, and tilted her head. "Pretty heavy for a vase of flowers." She set it back on the ledge, sifted her long fingers delicately through the blooms, then withdrew a bottle of bourbon from the vase.

He'd been right. Her long waves of hair matched the rich, amber shade of bourbon perfectly.

"Original Sin?" she asked, reading the label.

"My brand. Sweet, smooth, double-oaked, and ninety proof. Crafted in my distillery." He cocked one eyebrow. "Like I said, I brought something to cheer him up."

She gave him a pointed look—one he found more endearing than stern. "I think there's a hospital policy against alcohol."

He grinned. "No doubt."

Lips curving, she lifted the bottle of bourbon. "Thank

you for this, and your visit." She glanced at Earl, the amusement fading from her expression. "I'll tell Earl tomorrow that you stopped by. I'm sure you understand that he needs his rest tonight."

"Yes, of course." Brooks glanced once more at Earl, who still slept peacefully, then walked to the door. He paused on the threshold, hesitating, then looked back at Jo. "I wish I could mention this under better circumstances . . . but there's something I'd like to discuss with you later this week, if you have the time. A business proposition, of sorts."

She studied him, then crossed her arms over her chest and frowned. "I can't imagine how I might be of help to a distillery owner. And this is hardly the time for a pitch."

"I know." He gestured weakly toward the hospital bed. "As I said, I apologize for intruding, but the matter is time sensitive, and it has the potential to benefit you and Earl as much as it will me. Especially Earl," he whispered. "I imagine Earl is going to need time to recover, and with him off his feet, Lone Oaks Crossing will take a hit in terms of incom—"

"Thank you for the visit, Mr. Moore."

The hard finality in her tone sank his hopes.

"It's Brooks, please." He held her gaze. "I know you think I'm opportunistic—and I am to some extent—but I have my reasons. Personal ones tied to my family's past. I promise you, what I have to offer you and Earl will carry you both through this hardship in many ways. Most especially, financially." He pointed at the flower vase. "My business card's inside the vase. Please feel free to call me anytime."

At her silence, he left, shutting the door quietly behind him. The nurse—Jenny, if he recalled correctly—smiled at him expectantly as he walked past the nurse's station, her bright expression dimming when he continued by silently.

Brooks frowned at the irony. Here he and Jenny were, both offering their services to a stranger, hoping to get a return on the investment. He'd already disappointed Jenny, and he had a sinking suspicion that Jo would disappoint him.

Dear God, he needed this win. And if the reputation Rhett touted were true, he also needed Jo.

Brooks slid his hand in his pocket, gripped his cell phone, and picked up his pace, praying with each step he took that she would call.

CHAPTER 3

"So, tell me about this Brooks Moore," Jo said. "What's his deal?"

Seated outside in a chair by a fire pit on the grounds of Lone Oaks Crossing, Jo brought a bottle of bourbon to her lips, tilted it back, and swigged another shot of the strong alcohol. She winced as the amber liquid burned the wound on her bottom lip but relished the numbness it left behind.

Frankie had been right. Two hours of drinking bourbon, peering into a crackling fire, and sharing a casual conversation beneath a Kentucky night sky had been a much more welcome alternative than spending the night in a hospital room—especially when Earl, medicated, was sleeping peacefully for what the nurse promised would be the duration of the night.

Jo held the bottle out, closer to the bright flames, and struggled to focus her bleary gaze on the label: ORIGINAL SIN.

Her lip curled. Though cliché, the phrase suited Brooks Moore perfectly.

Hours earlier, she'd awakened in Earl's hospital room, surprised to see a stranger standing there. Brooks had been standing by the window, his back to her, his big hands setting the vase of flowers he held onto the window ledge. The dim lighting in the hospital room, combined with the bright glow of security lights in the parking lot had cast his frame into shadow.

Brooks's impressive height, the strong curve of his jaw, wide-set shoulders, and lean muscular length had been unexpected, imposing, and more appealing to Jo's senses than she'd been comfortable admitting. But no amount of sheer physical attraction, soulful brown eyes, or sex appeal could distract her attention from his carefully guarded expression.

"I mean, I know the man makes spectacular bourbon, is over six feet of rock-solid muscle, and has more sex appeal than God should give any man," Jo said, "but tell me the important stuff."

Frankie, seated in a chair next to her, grinned and held out her empty shot glass. "In my world, baby girl, that *is* the important stuff. And my Lord, this liquor's phenomenal."

Jo smiled and poured her a shot, her aim a little off. "We should feel bad, you know." She stared at the bottle again. "He brought this for Earl, not us. And here we are, downing it like it's water."

"After the day we've had, I think we've earned it. Besides, it won't do Earl any good at the moment. The nurse gave him his meds hours ago, so he'll be snoring away 'til morning."

Jo nodded, though the action didn't ease the guilt that

still lingered in her heart. After Brooks had left the hospital room, she'd stayed by Earl's bedside for another hour, holding his hand as he slept, regretting the years she'd spent apart from him and Lone Oaks Crossing. He hadn't stirred or spoken again, and when the nurse arrived to administer his evening round of medicine, she waited a little longer, hoping he'd open his eyes, look at her, and smile the way he used to years ago when he'd been strong and healthy.

But he hadn't.

As she'd stood there, watching Earl sleep, it had become very clear that things were different now. Earl's immediate future—and possibly long-term future—would be very different from the one he'd hoped for or expected, and it was more important than ever that she be here for him—and Lone Oaks Crossing.

"Besides," Frankie said, jerking her chin toward Jo's lap, "it's not like Brooks handed over a bottle of his prized liquor with no strings attached. Though I'm guessing you figured that out already."

Jo propped the liquor bottle against her middle and turned the man's business card over and over between each of her fingers until it dangled precariously between the ring and pinky fingers of her right hand. "Yep. I had an inkling."

During Jo's short tenure as a teacher, sly glances and hidden intentions had become easily recognizable to her. She'd known from the moment she laid eyes on Brooks that he wanted something from her . . . but that he was holding something back, something he knew she might not be receptive to. It had been clear to her that Brooks had been uncomfortable about showing up uninvited, unannounced, and possibly unwelcome.

"I do believe the man thinks I'm in need of rescuing."

Jo smirked and ran her tongue gently over the puffy swelling in her lower lip. "Not that I can blame him for that. I mean, I do look a tad beat-up."

Frankie's grin faded and her eyes, barely visible in the dim firelight, narrowed on Jo's face. "You still haven't told me how you got that busted lip."

Jo tugged her bloodstained collar closer to her chin, leaned back in her chair, and stared up at the sky. Her blurry gaze roved over what seemed like millions of stars glowing in the velvet darkness spread out above them.

She'd forgotten how bright the stars were here. The balcony of her apartment in Stone Hill offered an unimpeded view of the night sky, but the light pollution caused by the streetlights and garish neon signage of the booming city limits drowned out the glow of the stars, and the revving of engines and honking of horns along the streets below shattered the peaceful stillness of every evening.

Here, on the grounds of Lone Oaks Crossing, there were no streetlights or car headlights to dilute the beauty of the moon and stars, and no sounds to disrupt the serenity of the night's stillness, save for the soft whisper of the fall breeze, the comforting crackle of wood set ablaze, and the occasional hoot of a barred owl in the distance. There was room to breathe, to think, to heal.

Oh, man. How could she have forgotten how beautiful it was out here? And how had she managed to ignore how much she'd missed Lone Oaks over the years? How much she had missed Earl? And home?

"Jo?" Frankie's concerned tone intruded upon her reverie. "What happened to you today?"

Jo closed her eyes, the thought of the day's events dampening the soothing buzz in her veins. "I got hit." She folded Brooks's business card into her closed fist and rolled her head to the side, meeting Frankie's gaze. "A student I've been working with attacked another student in my classroom. When I tried to break it up, she clocked me in the mouth."

A humorless smile lifted Jo's lips. She took another swig of bourbon, held the bottle up high against the sparkling sky, and struggled to clearly enunciate the words she shouted, "For thirty-seven K a year, you, too, can get assaulted by angry teens, vilified by parents, and demeaned by society." A scornful laugh burst from her lips. "Oh, yeah." Her tongue felt thick, making it hard to form the words. "And insulted by your administrator while you stand bleeding in his office."

Frankie frowned. "What happened to the kid?"

"Nothing of significant consequence." Jo downed another shot. "No such thing as discipline anymore. Just talking. And more talking. By people who don't really know what they're talking about." She stared down at the bottle. Picked at the label with her fingertip. "I'm never asked for my input or considered in any of the decisions that are made. Our district leaders—most of whom haven't set foot in a classroom in years—announce their politically influenced decrees from their peaceful office while we and our students continue to struggle to survive in the classroom . . . sometimes literally."

A hollow opened in Jo's gut, her hand trembling around the bottle of bourbon. "Do you know, after that kid socked me in the mouth . . . the first—and only—person to ask if I was okay, was a gas station attendant at Jimbo's Pit? That's how little I mattered at Stone Hill High School." She looked at Frankie and tried to still the wobble in her lips. "I've thrown away ten years of my life on people who barely see me as human, Frankie."

"Oh, no," Frankie said softly. "I wouldn't say that. You've helped many children. You got four years of col-

lege education, six years of experience teaching, and
from what Earl has told me, you were one of the best
teachers at that school. Why don't you take a look at a
school closer to home? One with leaders you trust? I bet
if you apply to a school around here, they'd scoop you up
so fast—"

"I quit." Jo pressed the rim of the bottle to her lips,
took another shot of bourbon, and closed her eyes as the
liquid scorched a path down her throat, the bitter burn
masking the ache in her chest. "For good."

Frankie was silent for a moment, then asked, "Are you
sure that's what you want to do?"

"It's what I should've done years ago."

They sat silently for a while, staring at the fire, listening to the logs pop among the flames and the breeze sift
through the branches of nearby oak trees. Jo turned her
head slowly and scanned the expansive grounds of Lone
Oaks Crossing. It was difficult to see much detail beyond
the flames of the fire, but the bright glow of the crescent
moon overhead bathed the farm's rolling hills in silvery
light. The shadowy outlines of the oak trees lining the
property were visible, the branches of which were beginning to shed their leaves, and fresh bales of hay were
stacked along the center of a thirteen-acre hayfield that
lay beyond the fire pit. The outlines of a multistall barn,
two outbuildings, and a modest two-story house were
also just visible in the distance.

Two decades ago, when Jo had been left here as a
child, Lone Oaks Crossing had been bustling with guests,
ranch hands, and horses. Trainers and horsemen eager for
the next winning thoroughbred would line up almost
every day at Lone Oaks Crossing's entrance and ring
Earl's phone incessantly for a chance to buy the best foal
bred on the farm. Reservations for training sessions had

always been fully booked, every stall in the barn occupied by a thoroughbred, and every paddock populated with yearlings and trainers hard at work. In the past, the potential for Lone Oaks Crossing's success had been unlimited.

Now, however, the silent grounds, abandoned paddocks, and empty stables were testament to a failing business and a dying dream. A monumental shame.

Jo returned her attention to the fire, the hot flames spitting orange sparks high into the air. "I should've stayed."

Frankie sighed. "You grew up." A sad smile appeared. "Had it been up to me and Earl, we would've kept you a little girl forever. But time passes and circumstances change. You wanted to find your own way in the world and to do that you had to leave."

"But I should've come back sooner. Maybe then things wouldn't have fallen apart here." She licked a drop of bourbon from her lips and continued staring at the blazing fire. "How bad is it?"

Frankie was quiet for a moment, then sighed. "By my estimate, Earl has about another month or so until foreclosure."

Jo closed her eyes and focused on the heat radiating from the fire pit, her face and neck scorching with drunken anger, shame, and regret as she pictured Brooks's guarded features. "Brooks knows, doesn't he? That's why he swooped in today. He does believe we're in need of rescuing. What's he after—our land?"

"No. He's got more than enough of that. But he ain't just in the bourbon business. He's got a top-notch thoroughbred on the other side of that tree line and, from what his former trainer, Rhett, told me on the phone this afternoon, he's on the hunt for another one."

Jo glanced at her and frowned. "Another thorough-bred?"

Frankie, her own gaze growing heavy and unfocused, shook her head. "Trainer. Rhett told Brooks about you. 'Bout your win at the Derby nine years ago."

"It wasn't recorded as my win," Jo whispered. "It was set down as Earl's . . . and Sweet Dash's."

"Mmm-hmm." Frankie's tone softened with affection as she spoke of the thoroughbred they'd once loved—and lost—nine years ago. "Sweet Dash was one of a kind. But everybody who circulates behind the scenes in the sport knows which trainer was really behind Sweet Dash's win. And Brooks wants that trainer."

"So, I can lead his colt to the same fate Sweet Dash met?" Jo stared down at the bourbon bottle, now almost empty, and scowled. "Don't care how good his liquor is. I have no interest in training again."

"I know. I told Rhett the same thing on the phone today." Frankie's fingernail tapped against her shot glass again. "But no one around here had any doubts that Earl was already in need of money and now . . . well, his debts are only gonna build from here on out. Brooks, I'm sure, is aware of that and looking to capitalize."

Eyes heavy, Jo struggled to focus on the thoughts swirling in her foggy mind. "H-how much will it cost to keep foreclosure at bay?"

Frankie named a figure.

"Astronomical!" Jo sagged back against her chair and rolled her eyes at the heavens. "You're not giving us a fair shot, are you, Big Guy?"

Frankie laughed. "Ah, but that's not His job." She lifted her shot glass in the direction of the glowing moon. "Ain't that right, Big Guy? You just keep that eye of yours on us and give us a nudge now and then to help us through the pain, yeah?"

A wispy cloud, the only one marring the sky, drifted over the moon, dulling its shine. "I should never have left Earl," Jo whispered.

"You're here now. That's all that matters." Frankie held out her shot glass and Jo obliged, pouring her another shot.

The bottle was empty now, and the liquor had loosened Jo's tongue. "Thank you for being there for Earl today when I wasn't," she said. "You always loved him so."

For as long as Jo could remember, Frankie had been at Earl's side, and though Frankie and Earl's relationship had never been clearly defined over the years, the two had been a permanent fixture in Jo's life.

When Jo's mother, Amy, had succumbed to the lure of drugs and drifting, she had taken off with her boyfriend—one of many at the time—and had left Jo, then seven years old, on the front stoop of Earl's house at Lone Oaks Crossing. Jo couldn't remember much from that time of her life, but she did remember Earl scooping her up in his arms, hugging her tight, and that Frankie had been there, too. Right by Earl's side . . . and Jo's, too.

Jo could remember clearly that Frankie had been the one to tuck her in bed that night, kiss her forehead, and reassure her that although Amy had left her behind, Jo's mother still loved her. Earl, following Frankie's lead, had done the same.

Throughout her childhood, Jo had been awakened by Earl in the morning, served a home-cooked meal for breakfast by Frankie, and then escorted by them both to the end of the driveway to be helped onto the school bus. The pattern had remained the same over the years until Jo reached middle school and then, her junior year of high school, after she'd worked as a groom in Earl's stables for five years, she'd asked to be homeschooled in order to apprentice with Earl as a trainer. Though Frankie still maintained her own home five miles away from Lone Oaks Crossing, she'd still been there for Jo every day: cooking breakfast with Jo every morning, helping Earl lead her through her school lessons, and then assisting Jo with her duties as an assistant trainer.

Jo knew Frankie loved her as much as she would have loved a daughter of her own—had she been blessed with a family. And Frankie had always loved Earl.

"Earl knows I'm a patient woman," Frankie said. "He's never been interested in marriage—he's always been up-front with me about that—and I've always given him the space he needs. Not my ideal relationship, but I'll take it over not having him at all. I love that damned man too much to give him up. Just means my future looked different than I imagined it when I was a younger woman with pretty family portraits dancing in my mind."

Jo nodded. Her mother, Amy, hadn't been the only one to abandon Earl. Decades ago, when Amy had been around twelve years old, Gena, Earl's childhood sweetheart and wife, had tired of eking out a living on the farm and had left Earl, too, leaving him to raise Amy alone.

Like mother, like daughter, Jo mused. No wonder Earl had developed a fierce disdain for commitment.

Frankie drummed her fingers against the shot glass in her hand, her nails tinkling against the glass. "Tell me, Jo. What's your next move?" she asked. "You got a lot of years ahead of you, God willing. What's your plan for 'em?"

Sighing, Jo leaned her head back against her chair and stared up at the sky again. The heavens stretched out before her, a vast sparkling canvas of possibilities. Her stomach dipped as a dizzy sensation spiraled through her, and the world swirled slowly around her, out of her control.

"My plan?" Jo rolled her head to the side and met Frankie's inquisitive expression. "The Big Guy frowns on those things, doesn't He? Has plans of his own?" She tipped her head back again and breathed deep, embracing the messy swirl of emotions and liquor-induced buzz moving through her, giving in to the weightless floating sensation that drew her eyes to the sky. "I'm quite tempted to wallow. To just lie down and let my misery smother me."

She stared up at the stars and forced her gaze to focus on the small visible sliver of the moon protruding from behind the wispy cloud.

"But that'd mean wasting the air in my lungs," Jo said. "The only valuable thing I still have besides my time. So, I'm staying. I'm going to find a way to revive our business, make Lone Oaks Crossing a welcoming place for Earl to heal . . . maybe even others who need a quiet, peaceful retreat to find themselves again. And I'm going to do it under my own steam—not someone else's."

Lord knew, her ideas and ambitions had been stifled for long enough under the heavy weight of regulations, politics, and restrictive scrutiny that had permeated Stone Hill High School.

"Earl will need help when he gets home." Jo glanced around at the silent fields that sprawled around them in all directions. "More help than I can give, and still clean this place up at the same time. I'll need extra resources— an extra set of hands, materials—to breathe new life into this place so I can support Earl. But I'd need money to pay for the extra set of hands to take care of the grunt work, and right now, between what I owe Stone Hill school district for breach of contract and breaking my apartment lease, I'm beyond broke." She shook her head. "I'd need time to earn money boarding horses so I can pay a farmhand . . . but I'd need a hand to clean up the stables to get more boarders. So, you see, it's a vicious cycle. A conundrum, if you will." The word *conundrum* sounded funny on her slow tongue. She smiled. "A conundrum."

Frankie sighed, staring into the flames, watching the embers scatter toward the heavens. "I could call in a favor or two. Maybe bring someone in to take a look at our finances, prepare a strategy, and tell us wh—"

"No." Despite the alcohol-induced fog swirling in her mind, Jo answered immediately. "No one does anything for nothing nowadays and I don't need a boss," she said. "I need a loan. Unfortunately, that means going to where the money is, and I can tell you right now, there's no bank in the state that'll take a chance on me in my financial situation." She looked down, unfolded her fist, and watched the firelight flicker over the pristine white business card in her palm. "I assume Brooks has money?"

Frankie hiccupped. "A butt ton." She hiccupped again. "And a mighty fine butt, I might add."

Jo grinned, the drunk, dreamy look on Frankie's face even goofier than she'd expected. "His butt, I'm not interested in. His money . . . now that's another matter. I'm assuming he's got connections along with the money and, hopefully, some influence over owners needing to board. He might have the ability to send some new business our way."

Frankie's brows lifted. "And the training he wants? How you gonna talk him out of that?"

Jo shrugged. The combination of Brooks's scintillating bourbon in her blood, Frankie's comforting presence beside her, and the soothing Kentucky night sky made any obstacle seem surmountable. Or, at the very least, gave her the gumption to tackle it head-on.

"He called himself a neighbor," she said softly. "So, I'll give him a chance to be neighborly."

"May I see your guest pass, ma'am?"

Jo, seated behind the wheel of Earl's truck, nudged her sunglasses higher on her nose and studied the security guard who stood beside her truck. "I don't have one."

His eyes narrowed on her face then traveled over the beat-up truck she drove, his nose wrinkling. "A reservation and guest pass are required for entry, ma'am."

Jo glanced at the gated entrance to Brooks's impressive estate. The twenty-foot-wide wrought-iron gate, complete with custom Western Red Cedar inserts and a decorative emblem (*OS*, for Original Sin, she assumed), practically screamed money . . . and more than likely remained closed to anyone who didn't have a hefty share of their own.

She grimaced, the thought of asking anyone for financial help turning her stomach even more than the lingering aftereffects of her bourbon-induced hangover. But after visiting Earl in the hospital earlier this morning and reviewing with his doctor the steps involved in Earl's long road to recovery, she'd found herself in deeper debt than she'd estimated last night. Earl, she'd discovered, had no health insurance. He'd sacrificed it years ago to save the money he would've used for premiums to help keep the farm from going completely under. Earl was scheduled to be released from the hospital in three days and physical therapy needed to begin immediately. Without insurance, Earl's medical costs would far exceed any amount she'd be able to secure on her own in such a limited time frame.

Twenty thousand and two boarders. Jo sucked in a steadying breath. *Just get twenty thousand for Earl's physical therapy, two new horses to board in the stable, and figure out the rest later.*

"I'm here to see Brooks Moore, please," she said.

The security guard raised one cynical eyebrow. "Do you have an appointment?"

"No, but if you let him know I'm here, I'm sure he'll see me."

"Mr. Moore accepts guests only by prior appointment and Original Sin's gates open only for customers who've made a reservation and purchased a guest pass." He waved an impatient hand as he glanced behind her truck. A line of cars had formed behind her. "Please move on, ma'am. You can take a right and follow the paved drive back to the main road."

Jo lifted one hip, reached into her pocket, pulled out Brooks's business card and presented it to the security guard. "I spoke with Mr. Moore last night. Please give him a call and I'm sure he'll see me."

He shook his head and held up a hand. "Ma'am, I got people wait—"

"Call him." She lowered her sunglasses and met his eyes over the rims, trying her best to appear earnest rather than desperate. "Please. It'll take you less than a minute—a minute that can make or break me."

He sighed, glanced once more at the line of vehicles forming behind her, then shook his head as he headed for the nearby security booth. "Your name?"

"Jo Beth Ellis."

His steps paused, his expression flaring with recognition of the name as he glanced back at her before entering the security booth. He stood in front of the window of the booth, studying her as he tapped the Bluetooth earpiece in his left ear. He looked down at a set of security screens, his hands typing into a laptop as his mouth moved. Moments later, he tapped the Bluetooth earpiece again, walked out of the booth, and gestured invitingly with one arm toward the wide, decorative gate as it slowly slid open.

"Welcome to Original Sin, Ms. Ellis. Please follow the paved road past the stables and distillery to the next gate. When it opens, continue following the paved road until you reach the main house. Mr. Moore will be there to welcome you."

Jo tossed the business card in the passenger seat, nudged her sunglasses back into position, and nodded. "Thank you."

She transitioned the parked truck back into drive, guided it through the open gate, and began driving along the wide paved road that wound through the grounds of the estate. When she reached the top of the first hill, the whole world seemed to sparkle. The bright morning light of the Kentucky sun poured a golden hue over rolling pastures and dirt tracks, massive stables, white distillery buildings, brick walkways lined with limestone walls, and white fencing that seemed to stretch for miles and miles.

Jo craned her neck as she drove, gazing from left to right, surveying the smiling guests as they strolled along the brick paths and the impressive thoroughbreds that galloped along dirt tracks snaking over the lush grounds, their riders putting them through their daily training.

"Oh, sweet heaven," she breathed.

This could've been Earl's—every inch of it—had things

turned out differently . . . namely, if Sweet Dash hadn't stumbled on the dirt of the Pimlico Race Course and if Jo hadn't walked away from the sport days later. Instead, acres away, just beyond the dense line of strong oak trees in the distance, Lone Oaks Crossing was gasping its last breath, almost in decay.

Gripping the steering wheel tighter, Jo drove on, keeping her gaze fixed dead ahead, slowing as she reached the second gate, then passing through it as it opened. She drove around the wide circular drive that surrounded a large fountain and parked in front of what the security guard had termed "the main house."

"House?" She cut the engine and leaned across the passenger seat, her eyes widening as she stared at the massive structure looming above her. "Mansion, more like."

The white, three-storied colonial-style home with its elegant double-door entrance, exterior stonework, stunning columns, and multiple balconies had to be at least thirteen thousand square feet if she estimated correctly from her vantage point. And then there was what she assumed was a guest house attached to the side of the huge structure—a beautifully constructed dwelling in its own right, almost as impressive as the main home.

Sunlight glinted off the glass panes of one of the ornate front doors as it swung open and Brooks emerged, striding confidently across the front porch and down the stone walkway toward the truck.

"Get it together." Jo exited the truck, shut the door, and smoothed her hand over her loose hair. "Ask, don't beg," she reminded herself quietly. "And don't look desperate."

"Welcome to Original Sin, Jo." Brooks, smiling, rounded the front of the truck and extended his hand. He looked even taller than when she'd met him yesterday, his muscular physique clad in an expensive business suit and boots. "I was hoping you'd call, but a visit is even better."

She cleared her throat and shook his hand. "Sorry about not giving you notice, but I prefer to discuss business in person rather than on the phone. I hope this isn't a bad time."

"No. Not at all." He glanced down at her hand in his, remaining quiet and still for a moment, then covered their clasped hands with his free one. "How is Earl? Have you been by to see him today?"

His hands were strong and sturdy, and the heat of his big palms warmed hers in the cool fall air, enticing her exhausted, still hungover body to lean in his direction.

She disentangled her hand from his and stepped back. "Yes. I just came from the hospital. That's the reason I stopped by to see you. I know you have something you'd like to discuss with me, but there's something I'd like to discuss with you as well. I'll be honest and fair, and I hope you'll be the same."

His eyes roved over her face, then narrowed on her sunglasses. "That's the only way I operate." He motioned in front of him, toward the entrance of his home. "After you."

Jo hesitated, noting the glint of affront that briefly hardened his expression at her words. She glanced over her shoulder at the sprawling acres of lush luxury, looking up at the refined mansion, then staring up at the polished man before her. Hands trembling, she dragged them across the baggy jeans she wore, feeling more out of her element than ever before.

Maybe she *should* have called first. Scheduled this meeting at Lone Oaks Crossing or perhaps, more neutral territory? As it was, she was in his domain now . . . and at the whim of whatever neighborly goodwill he might or might not possess.

What would a man of his obscene wealth and social stature do with someone like her—a poor neighbor and insignificant trainer—if he managed to rope her into training for him?

She'd become a tool for whatever he had planned, that's what. If she allowed it . . .

Twenty thousand and two boarders. Ask—don't beg.

Jo eased past him and walked inside.

CHAPTER 4

Brooks stood in his home office, watching Jo move from one wide window to the next, gazing out at the grounds of Original Sin, the dark sunglasses she wore hiding the expression in her eyes.

"What do you think?" he asked softly.

She stilled, her back to him as she answered. "Exquisite. That's the word that comes to mind. This place is big enough to comfortably house several families rather than one. Do you have a big family, Mr. Moore?"

"No. It's just me, although I should include my employees as I view them as family. And it's Brooks, please."

"Brooks." She faced him then, removing her sunglasses, her eyes meeting his. "I'm sorry if I offended you earlier. It wasn't my intention."

He tilted his head and took her in. The buffalo plaid shirt and faded jeans she wore had almost swallowed her, the cuffs of the shirt rolled up twice but still hanging to her knuckles, and the hem of her jeans sagging over the tongue and eyelet of the worn tennis shoes she sported.

But she stood tall and confident, her long hair down, spilling over her shoulders and back in shiny, disheveled waves as though freshly washed and dried naturally.

Everything about her seemed natural . . . fresh and frank. And the sincerity in her blue eyes only enhanced the air of candidness that surrounded her.

"I wasn't offended," he said, holding her gaze. "Just disappointed that you may have been given the wrong impression of me."

"How so?"

He smiled. "Well, you don't seem exactly excited to be here, for one. I assume you have reservations about me and what I intend to offer you and your grandfather?"

Her eyes roved over him again slowly. "I said I'd be honest and fair, so I'll be honest now. I know what you want from me, and I'm not interested. But I'm in a bind and I've come to ask something of you. Only, you don't look like the type of man who would offer something for nothing."

His jaw tightened but he forced his smile to remain frozen in place. "What type of man do I look like?"

She studied him once more, then turned away and began strolling around his office. "The kind that likes to be in charge." Her hand lifted as she walked past his wide mahogany desk, her graceful fingertips gliding along its smooth edge. "The kind of man who weighs and measures everything in terms of value and investment." One finger lifted, tapped a page in the small business planner resting on the edge of the desk. "You're a busy man. I'm surprised you had time to meet with me." She'd rounded the desk now, leaned back against it, crossed one ankle over the other and her arms over her chest as she eyed him. "But then again, you wouldn't have given me your business card if you weren't willing to make the time.

You think, given the chance, you'll be able to change my mind and persuade me to take up training again. To join your team and hand you a Derby win. And you plan on using my grandfather's misfortunes as leverage."

Her tone had changed. The pleasant openness he'd admired moments earlier had slowly shifted into a cool, judgmental quality. An uncomfortable ache spread through his chest at the sound of it.

He returned her stare, remaining silent.

"How did I do?" she asked. "Was that about right?"

Smile still pinned in place, he slid his hands in his pockets and rocked back on his heels. "Most of it."

She lifted one dark brow. "Which part did I get wrong?"

He allowed his smile to dissolve as he moved his gaze over her delicate hands, the smooth expanse of her upper chest and graceful curve of her neck, the few inches of bare, creamy skin her oversized shirt revealed. "The part that I always like to be in charge. There are times when letting someone else take the lead provides immeasurable benefits."

That did it. The cold, calculating tone she'd adopted, the one that belied her natural disposition, melted away in tandem with the warm flush that blossomed along the curve of her cheekbones.

"If you want to have even the remotest chance of doing business with me," she said softly, "you'll keep it respectful. I'm no longer willing to sacrifice my dignity for a paycheck."

His smile returned—this time, sincere. The cynical façade she'd adopted was now gone. "I know what you must think of me. What you assumed driving onto my property, walking into my house"—he jerked his chin toward the window—"staring out at the view. I don't play games, Jo. And I'd never seek to take advantage of Earl's misfortune in a way that would harm him, his business, or those he loves. But I do want you on my team. More than that. I *need* you on my team."

She uncrossed her arms, pushed away from the desk, and straightened. "Why? What is it you think you know about me?"

"You love your grandfather," he said. "You returned to him when he needed you, and clearly you're sticking around to find ways to help him. You used to be a damn good trainer. The best, from what I hear. And in a way, you never truly left training behind. From what I'm told, you left Lone Oaks to teach in a high school and, as I'm sure we both know, training is teaching at its core."

Her mouth curved. "You got most of it right."

His smile widened. "Which part did I get wrong?"

"I no longer teach."

He stilled, his attention zeroing in on the wounded swell of her lower lip. "As of?"

"Yesterday," she said.

Ah, that was it. The busted lip, bloodstained blouse, and exhausted expression she'd sported in the hospital room last night. It all made sense now. He wasn't surprised that she had chosen to go the way of so many other teachers before her.

These days, it was impossible to watch the news without hearing about or seeing a clip of violence that had occurred in a classroom. School shootings, student fights, and shouting matches between adults at board of education meetings had become the norm. And at the heart of all the violence, students and teachers were the ones who paid the price.

He frowned, that odd—and unexpected—swell of protectiveness and sympathy welling within him again. "Who was it?"

Her brow creased. "What do you mean?"

"The person who did that to you?" He gestured toward her mouth. "Who was it?"

She looked away. Stared out the window. "One of my students." A wry grin crossed her lips. "She decided to pursue justice on her own terms and, apparently, I got in the way."

Brooks froze then turned his head and followed her gaze to the rolling hills in the distance. "I'm sorry to hear that." His mind drifted to the memory of his father hunched over the TV in the family living room, biting his lip, his teeth drawing blood and fists clenching as his feverish eyes followed the frenzied gallop of horses on the screen. And later . . . Spencer Harris and his father, Victor, knocking on their front door to collect the debt and essentially evict his family from the only home they'd known. "Innocent parties should never be harmed by the conflict of others." He faced her again and peered into her eyes. "Is that why you chose teaching? To set the world right again?"

Her attention drifted over his right shoulder as she mulled over his suggestion. "That's a far too lofty goal for anyone. I was like any other teacher. I just wanted to make a difference. Teach children. Support them in any way I could to help them achieve their dreams and secure a brighter future.

"That's a noble goal," he said softly.

One he wished more people would choose to take on. But, having spent the last three of his teenage years in a foster home, he knew better than most how challenging it could be to take on such a goal, and how easy it was for well-intended people to fall short on their promises. Which was why, once he'd established his business and began breeding thoroughbreds, he began offering a local foster teen a position as groom or stable hand every year. If the kid took to the horses and performed his or her tasks competently, he followed that up with an offer of internship to pursue the equine career of their choice.

Opportunities, he'd discovered over the years, were sometimes hard to come by for youth who were alone in the world and without sufficient financial support. He, himself, had climbed the ladder of success by being offered a helping hand along the way, and he still sought to pay that help forward in whatever way he could.

"Look," she said, "I'm not very good at this."

"Good at what?"

"Asking for help. Trusting someone. I'm used to being the one providing help. Doing things on my own and not leaning on anyone." She shrugged. "It's the way Earl raised me, I suppose. I'm not in need of rescuing, but I'm in a dire enough position to admit that I do need help, and I'm hoping you, as Earl's neighbor, will be willing to assist."

He nodded. "Please go on."

She looked down again and began picking at her nails. "Earl will be released from the hospital at the end of the week. He's doing well but he's going to need months of physical therapy and almost full-time care on a temporary basis." She met his eyes again. "He has no health insurance, and the bills are already piling up. I'm relocating to Lone Oaks Crossing to take care of him, and I have a plan to rehabilitate our farm and restore it to a working one. I'd like to make the place over into a healing retreat of sorts—for people and horses. I just need funds to get started—to get myself and the farm back on our feet so to speak."

"You're asking me for a loan," he said.

To her credit, she didn't deny it or hedge the issue.

"I need twenty thousand dollars," she said. "And at least two new boarders for our stable. The money would be enough to pay for Earl's physical therapy, and two new horses boarding at Lone Oaks Crossing would bring in enough steady income to keep foreclosure at bay. I'm hoping you'll consider loaning me the funds as an investment and possibly sending two boarders my way using your connections. I'll pay you back, I swear. Every cent, plus whatever interest you deem suitable."

Brooks studied the stubborn set of her jaw. "Why not go to a bank? Take out a loan? Why come to me instead?"

She spread her hands, a resigned expression on her face. "Because I just threw away a career I spent a decade building. My teaching certificate is probably being digitally incinerated as we speak. I owe a hefty fine to the board of education for breaking my contract midyear and I'll have to pay a tidy sum to my former landlord for breaking my lease to move back to Lone Oaks Crossing. I was already broke but now, I have less than nothing. There's no bank around that would be willing to take a chance on my financial situation."

"And you think I will?"

"Last night you called yourself Earl's neighbor and said you wanted to help," she said. "I'm hoping you'll decide to do a neighborly good deed."

A neighborly good deed is right, he mused. No one in their right financial mind would sink as much money or energy into such a failing farm, except . . . his plans for a Derby win were founded in risk, so what was one more?

Especially if it tipped the scales in his favor and offered him a second opportunity to entice her into training Another Round. In his experience, just the smallest taste of money and success was enough to woo even the most cynical of minds into tossing caution to the wind in exchange for a shot at a bigger pay day.

"Growing up, were you close to your parents, Brooks?"

He stilled, surprised at the surge of grief tightening his throat. "My mother, yes. My father . . . it depended upon the type of day he was having."

She seemed to hesitate. "Are they still with you? Still living, I mean?"

He shook his head.

Her expression fell. "There's no way for me to prove to you that I mean to work very hard to earn and repay the help you might give me, other than to say, I intend to see this through for my grandfather's sake. I never knew my father, and when my mom abandoned me, Earl raised me. He's the only blood relation I have left . . . and I'll do everything in my power to support him. I don't know if you understand what taking care of him means to me, but I hope you believe me in that regard."

He did believe that. But how could he prove to her—a woman who seemed to want nothing to do with him, aside from his money—that his intentions were just as honorable?

"Yes," he said.

"You believe me?"

"Yes, I'll give you the money."

She visibly sagged with relief.

"And the boarders," he added. "On one condition."

Her slender figure stiffened, a wary look entering her eyes.

"You agree to keep an open mind about me," he said.

"And my business proposition that you train my thoroughbred for the Derby."

Shaking her head, she moved to speak.

"You're not obligated to accept my job offer, Jo. I'm just asking you to think it over. To consider my offer with no expectation on my part that you'll agree. To simply accept my help and consider my business offer of training as you would that of a well-meaning neighbor . . . or friend. One who will be at your beck and call so long as you need me."

Laughter burst from her lips, the act lighting up her pretty features with a pleasing glow. "You? At my beck and call?"

He grinned. "Exactly that."

The humorous light in her expression turned skeptical. "Have you ever been at someone's beck and call before?"

"No." He moved closer and reached out, his attention drifting to her motionless hand at her side, the flesh of his palm almost tingling with the anticipation of pressing against hers again, of feeling that pleasant thrill of attraction from her touch. "But I look forward to the experience of helping you in any way you see fit."

"You're asking me to keep an open mind." She eyed his outstretched hand. "That's all?"

"Yes," he said softly. "In the hope that it will lead you to decide to train again."

"Will you throw in another bottle of your bourbon for Frankie along with the loan?"

His grin widened. "Of course."

Her hand lifted, paused briefly in midair, then slid against his and squeezed. "Deal."

* * *

At the end of the week, on Friday afternoon, Jo stood in the parking lot of Lone Oaks Hospital, sorely tempted to issue her first call for help to Brooks . . . but determined to resist doing so.

"Look, Granddad." She blew an errant strand of hair out of her face and (heaven forgive her) relished the angry scowl on Earl's face as he sat in his wheelchair beside her. He hated being called Granddad—he'd actually forbidden the term decades ago when her mother had abandoned her on his stoop—demanding she refer to him as Earl, instead. "I know in spite of having had a stroke and despite the advice the doctor and nurse just gave us during discharge, you still insist upon proving them all wrong. But I'm telling you, there's no way you're going to make it into the cab of your truck without help."

"Amen." Frankie, standing on the other side of Earl's wheelchair, nodded her head in agreement.

"L . . . lee me . . . lo," Earl grumbled from his slumped position in the wheelchair.

"No, I won't leave you alone," Jo said. "Because doing so means leaving you sitting here in that wheelchair in this parking lot for the foreseeable future. You refused to let the nurse or orderlies help you, so here we are. All you have left is me and Frankie."

She glanced at Earl's truck, parked beside them, in dismay. Oh, Lord. She should've foreseen this problem. Should've known Earl would balk at her and Frankie— two (gasp!) *women*—lifting him into the cab of his own truck. But she hadn't. And here they were.

"I knew you'd give us a little trouble," Jo said, looking down at Earl, "but I had no idea you'd put up this much of a fight."

He'd attempted to stand four times on his own already

and had barely lifted himself two inches off the seat of
the wheelchair before slumping back into it with a pained
grunt and thud.

Sighing, she knelt in front of his wheelchair and covered his balled fist gently with her hand. "I know you
don't want help. I know that if I let you, you'd spend the
entire day and night trying to drag yourself out of this
wheelchair and into that truck on your own, but your
body just can't do it right now." She lifted her hand and
cupped his cheek in her palm. "Your muscles are tired.
They've been through a trauma, and they're wore slap
out. Not forever. Just for right now. One day soon, after a
few months of therapy, you'll be kicking our butts around
Lone Oaks Crossing, but for now, I need you to let us
help you, okay? You got to let us put you in that truck."

His scowl eased as he stared down at her.

"Please?" Frankie lowered her face next to his, squeezed
his shoulder, and smiled, her tone tender. "I put clean
sheets and new pillows on your bed, set up the gas grill
yesterday afternoon, and picked up some fresh salmon
this morning before we came to get you. Everything's
ready and waitin' for you to lie down on your own bed,
enjoy a good long nap, then eat a fresh, home-cooked meal.
But we got to get you home first." She kissed his forehead and whispered, "Please, Earl? We've missed you so.
And we want you home."

His wrinkled chin wobbled. Big tears pooled on his
lower lashes as he nodded.

"Thank you," Jo said softly, standing. "Frankie and I
are going to get you to your feet, then help you lift your
left leg into the cab. Then we'll give you a big push to get
you the rest of the way in." She eased one arm around
Earl's back and one under his left leg, poised to lift, then

looked at Frankie. "On the count of three. One, two, three!"

It took more than three counts, four tries, and five disappointing fumbles, but eventually, they managed it, hefting Earl safely into the passenger seat of the cab, strapping on his seat belt and sighing with relief.

"Good night above," Frankie whispered as they loaded the wheelchair into the truck bed. "How in the world are we gonna manage to get him in the house? We can use the wheelchair to get him across the lawn but there ain't no way we'll be able to carry him up all those steps to get him inside."

Jo secured the wheelchair with a truck bed bungee cord to keep it from sliding around during the drive over the potholes in bumpy dirt roads and pushed her hair back from her sweaty forehead. She lifted her face to the cool fall breeze, a chill spreading along her overheated skin, then looked at Frankie, whose cheeks were as flaming red as her own felt from their recent exertion.

"We'll just have to figure that out when we get there, I guess."

Thirty minutes later, Jo took a right and turned Earl's truck onto the long dirt driveway of Lone Oaks Crossing. He hadn't said a word during the entire trip home. Instead, he'd sat silently in the passenger seat and stared at the rural scenery as it passed, his tired eyes growing heavier with each mile.

"We're here, Earl," she said, glancing to her right.

A slow smile lifted her lips. He was asleep, his tanned, wrinkled cheek pressed to the cool glass of the window, his mouth peacefully slack and hands resting motionless in his lap.

"He's tuckered." Frankie, seated in the back seat of the

cab, leaned over the console and gently brushed a strand
of gray hair behind his ear. "Oh, how he hates this, Jo.
Being weak and vulnerable. But Lord knows, I'm glad
he's home where we can take care of him—whether he
likes it or not."

"Me, too," Jo said softly as she drove slowly up the
driveway.

Despite the afternoon's troubles, it was a beautiful day.
The midafternoon sun shined bright over the quiet acreage of Lone Oaks Crossing. Jo eased her foot off the gas
pedal a little more, taking a moment to soak it all in, to
relish her happiness at having Earl home again, safe and
cared for in the home he adored by people he loved.

It seemed like such a small thing to do—to help nurse
him back to health—but the prospect of being able to return just a small percentage of the love, security, and support that Earl had provided throughout her childhood
flooded her heart with hope and a yearning to set things
right again. To see Lone Oaks Crossing thrive as it once
had, its green pastures full of grazing horses, healthy and
strong, and Earl, confident and in control again, oversee-
ing the daily operations of the renewed working farm.

Jo drove on, past the pastures, around the winding dirt
drive, and up to the modest home Earl had lived in all his
life. The one she remembered fondly from childhood.
She slowed the truck, however, at the site of a large truck
and trailer parked near the stables.

"Looks like we have a guest," Frankie said, easing
even farther over the console, peering around Jo toward
the truck and trailer. "You expecting someone?"

"No." Jo's gaze strayed from the truck and trailer and
moved toward the house, where a familiar man stood at
the foot of the porch steps. He looked out of place, his
muscular form clad in a dress shirt and what appeared to

be custom-tailored jeans, pristine and at odds with the aging two-story house behind him. "From the looks of it, I'd say our new benefactor has decided to pay us a visit."

"With a trailer?" Frankie perked up. "You think he found two new boarders for us already?"

Jo slowed the truck, bringing it to a stop in front of the house, several feet away from Brooks, her eyes meeting his through the windshield. "I wouldn't doubt it. From the looks of his estate when I visited the other day, he's pretty much got the entire world at his fingertips."

Which, she thought uncomfortably, was probably true when someone had as much wealth at their disposal as Brooks had. Days before, after he'd handed her a twenty-thousand-dollar check in his home office and she'd returned to Earl's truck and driven away, she'd still found herself looking in the rearview mirror, gaping in awe at the imposing sight of his mansion and pristine grounds.

"Huh." Frankie glanced at Brooks, too. "Good thing he's on our side then."

And heaven help them if he ever decided not to be, Jo thought.

She cut the engine. "Would you mind waiting here for a minute? I'd like to see what he wants before we try to get Earl inside."

Frankie patted her shoulder. "Go ahead. Earl's snoozing pretty good right now. It won't hurt to give him a few more minutes."

Jo glanced fondly at Earl, then exited the truck, shutting the door softly so as not to disturb him.

Brooks strode across the front lawn toward her, his long legs easily eating up the distance between them. "You have a full truck, I see."

Jo removed the sunglasses she'd donned for the drive home. "I wasn't expecting you." She motioned over her shoulder toward the truck and trailer parked by the stable. "But that trailer's a welcome sight. Were you able to find two new boarders for us?"

Brooks nodded. "Yep. And I think you'll be pleased." He leaned to the side and peered over her shoulder into the cab of Earl's truck. "I'm glad to see you made it home safely with Earl."

Jo's confusion must have shown on her face.

"You mentioned he was being released from the hospital at the end of the week when you visited me at Original Sin the other day," Brooks said. "I called the hospital to check on him and was told he was being discharged today. I figured you might need some help getting him inside and comfortable, so I thought I'd pop over and give you a hand while I was delivering your new boarders."

His chivalrous impulse sent a pleasurable flutter through her middle. She grinned. "It's very nice of you, but that kinda sounds like a man who's trying to be in charge." She grinned wider. "I don't remember giving you a call . . . or a beck."

He smiled back, his flirtatious eyes and the boyish dimple in his left cheek enough to charm any woman. "Maybe not. But I wouldn't say I was trying to take charge."

"Then what would you say?"

"I'd say I'm being neighborly." He leaned in, his soft breath tickling the shell of her ear as he whispered, "I'm doing what a neighbor would do in hopes of becoming more than just a neighbor. Possibly a friend?"

His aftershave was spicy but held a hint of sweetness. It lingered on the air between them, tantalizing her senses.

Jo shook her head, attempting to dispel his intoxicating appeal, and stepped back. "I appreciate you finding and delivering us new boarders," she said. "But I think

Frankie and I can manage getting Earl settled on our own."

She walked away and rounded the front of the truck, saying over her shoulder, "If you don't mind hanging around while I get Earl settled, I'll walk with you to the stables to check out the boarders."

His deep voice sounded at her back as she opened the passenger door. "I don't mind. Take your time."

The door creaked as it opened, rousing Earl, who blinked groggily and struggled to focus on Jo's face.

"We're home," Jo said softly.

Earl blinked several times and stared up at her, seeming to have trouble getting his bearings.

A door on the other side of the truck opened and shut and, moments later, Frankie walked around the back of the truck and joined Jo, looking down at Earl. "Ready to go in, hon? We're gonna get your wheelchair set up and push you across the lawn. Then Jo and I will help you up the steps so you can go inside, have a good nap, and get some decent rest in your own bed for a change."

Alert now but still visibly exhausted, Earl pushed himself up straighter in the seat with trembling arms and nodded.

Jo glanced at the lawn separating them from the front porch steps. The high tufts of dormant grass and shallow holes where opossums had dug overnight seemed much more difficult to navigate in a wheelchair than she'd imagined.

"I don't think the wheelchair is going to be an option, Frankie." Jo looked at Earl. "How do you feel about leaning on me and Frankie and going for a little walk? Do you think you have one more push in your legs today? Enough to help me and Frankie walk you inside?"

Earl narrowed his eyes, a spark of anger flaring. "'Course . . . I can."

Jo smiled. "I figured you'd say that." She nudged the passenger door to open it wider. "All right, Frankie. Same drill as in the hospital parking lot—only this time farther—okay?"

They commenced the same steps they'd undertaken in the Lone Oaks Hospital parking lot, Jo supporting one side of Earl and Frankie the other. He was heavier this time around, his limbs weak from his earlier exertions, and it was a struggle just to slide him to the edge of the truck's seat and set both of his feet on the ground.

Jo's lungs burned and her breathing became labored, but she tried to quiet her exhalations and forced a smile. "You okay, Earl? We can do this. It just may take a little longer than before."

He didn't respond. Instead, he sagged more heavily against her and closed his eyes.

"Earl?" Stomach sinking, Jo kissed his forehead. "What if we rest for a moment, then try again?"

Still, he remained silent, his eyes closed. He looked frailer than ever.

"Jo."

Breath catching on a muffled sob, Jo glanced over her shoulder.

Brooks had moved closer, his dark eyes fixed on Earl in concern, his deep voice rumbling softly beside her. "I'd like to help, if I may?"

"He's plumb tuckered." Frankie's eyes were glinting in the sunlight with tears as she studied Earl's weak form. "I think it's best to let Brooks help, Jo."

Jo eyed Brooks's muscular stature and strong hands, her heart pounding at the thought of releasing Earl. Of entrusting his well-being to someone else.

Swallowing hard against the lump in her throat, she stepped back and made room for Brooks. "Thank you," she whispered. "But take care, please. He's very weak."

Brooks eased past her and touched Earl's shoulder. "Earl? It's Brooks. Your neighbor. I'm going to get you inside, if that's okay with you?"

Eyes still closed, Earl didn't respond. His chest rose and lowered on heavy breaths.

At Earl's silence, Brooks slid one arm around Earl's back and the other beneath his knees, then gently lifted him up into his arms.

Earl was ill and frail now, but his frame was still equipped with a fair amount of muscle and his weight must have put a hefty strain on the younger man's arms. But if it did, Brooks didn't let it show. He simply cradled the older man securely against his chest and smiled reassuringly at Jo as he carried Earl past her and across the front lawn.

Heart pounding harder and hands moving nervously, Jo followed close behind, easing in step behind Brooks as he carried Earl up the stairs. She slipped around them and opened the front door, holding it wide as Brooks carried Earl through it and inside the house. Jo guided Brooks through the living room, down the hallway, and into the first bedroom on the left, pointing at Earl's double bed, which sat on the other side of the bedroom.

Nodding, Brooks carried Earl across the room, then laid him gently on the bed, taking care to reposition a pillow more comfortably under Earl's head. His strong hands lingered, easing Earl's legs out into a relaxed position, then touched the toes of Earl's boots lightly with his fingertips.

"Would you like me to take these off for him?" Brooks asked softly.

"No." Frankie's voice, faint and pained, emerged from the doorway. She walked across the room and joined Brooks by the bed, stilling his hand with hers. "I . . ." She wiped her wet cheeks and set her shoulders. "I'd like to take over from here, please."

Brooks straightened and patted her shoulder. "Of course. I'll leave you to it."

As Brooks eased away from the bed, Frankie moved to the end of the mattress and tugged Earl's boots off one by one, a fresh tear rolling down her face.

"Would this be a good time for me to introduce you to your new boarders?"

Startled, Jo dragged her attention away from Frankie's gentle motions and looked up. Brooks stared down at her, concern in his eyes.

Mouth dry, she licked her lips to speak but her throat was so tight, the words wouldn't come.

"Jo?" Brooks, his voice soft and expression gentle, lifted his hand and smoothed his blunt thumb gently across her wet cheek. "He's okay now. He's settled and Frankie's making sure he's comfortable. Why don't we go take a look at your new boarders and give her some time alone with him? It'll do you good to get outside and breathe some fresh air."

Jo watched as he removed his hand, the tip of his thumb moist, and she touched her hot cheek, realizing for the first time that she had shed tears of her own. Perhaps it was the strong, capable way he supported Earl . . . or maybe it was the tenderness in his touch and tone. Either way, she longed to lean against him, press her wet cheek to his warm chest, and wrap her arms around him, seeking his strong support.

"Yes," she whispered, meeting his eyes, the kindness in them easing her pain. "I think that'd be best."

CHAPTER 5

Brooks had experienced loss before. It was nothing new to him. The same loss was written on Jo's face.

He glanced at her as they entered the stable at Lone Oaks Crossing. The tears she had shed minutes earlier inside Earl's bedroom had dried on her face during the walk from the house to the stable, but the rosy flush of pain in her cheeks and the heavy anguish deep in her eyes remained.

"Thank you for helping Earl," she whispered.

He lowered his head, barely catching her soft words, her sorrowful tone coaxing forth a deep-seated pain he'd buried long ago.

"You were very . . . tender with him." Her cheeks flushed. "I guess I didn't quite expect that."

"I'm glad I could help," he said. "I know how painful it is to see someone you love hurting and be unable to heal them."

She glanced up at him, her long lashes still damp with tears as she surveyed his expression. "You've lost someone to an illness?"

He nodded. "More than once. I've experienced a great deal of loss in my life, actually. More than most people assume."

At an early age, he'd lost his father to gambling and greed. Shortly after, he'd lost his mother to grief and despair. He'd lost his family's money, his family's land, and his family home. But worst of all, he'd lost his childhood. The happy memories he treasured—time spent with a loving mother and father who had once enjoyed spending time with him in a childhood home where he roamed freely, fearlessly, and with hope for the future—had all been tarnished in later years by understanding of his father's weakness and greedy habits, which had been easily preyed upon by others.

After his mother's passing, he'd been declared a ward of the state and placed in Dream House, a foster home in Lone Oaks. The plain, two-story brick building situated in the center of the small town had seemed like a prison to Brooks after spending his first fifteen years on the wide-open, serene acres of Rose Farm. A farm much like Lone Oaks Crossing.

Though he'd only spent three years in the facility, from age fifteen to age eighteen, he'd gotten his fill of the place early on, and by the time he'd aged out and left Dream House, he'd had no desire to ever return.

Not that his experience there had been all bad. On the contrary, he'd been well cared for, provided a warm bed along with an acceptable amount of privacy and solitude when he desired it, and had met a handful of boys his age who'd suffered through circumstances that made his own misfortunes pale in comparison. He'd laughed in that building on several occasions. Had fun even. But on the nights he'd locked himself in the small bathroom of his dormitory and released his grief in private, he'd shed more tears than any teenage boy ever should.

The only person he'd missed from Dream House had been Agnes St. Clair, a woman who'd been his mother's age during their first meeting. He'd taken an instant liking to her sweet smiles and warm, comforting hugs. She'd been the only adult who'd always been there for him anytime he wanted to talk and had compassionately admonished him when necessary during the times he'd acted out. She could never fully understand his pain—no one could—but she'd empathized with him as best she could. Losing a father to suicide and a mother one year later to a heart attack was an experience no boy his age should ever have to endure.

Ironically, the loss he'd known had been all the more painful because he'd been fortunate enough to experience a happier period of time in his childhood. A time full of warm, loving moments that had held such bright hope for the future.

He still carried that loss within him every day. It had set down roots in his heart and branched out, infiltrating every cell of his being, driving him to replace it with something new. Something better. A vision of the life that should have been his.

"I'm sorry to hear you've had troubles," she said as they reached the stable entrance.

He shrugged. "I suppose loss is a part of life, but sometimes good outcomes spring from bad events." He motioned toward her. "Take your situation, for instance. You gave up your career and came back to Lone Oaks to take care of Earl. To support him through what I'm sure will be a very difficult time of healing for him and to revive his farm. I'm sure your presence and intentions are a great comfort to him."

"My presence, sure," she said. "But he's unaware that I know how much trouble Lone Oaks Crossing is in. The last thing he would ever do is to cross that line of oaks separating your property from ours and ask you for charity."

"I don't consider my giving you help to be charity."

"No." A cynical tone mixed with the exhaustion in her voice. "You see it as a potential business opportunity, which is fine with me so long as we understand each other."

She ducked her head as they entered the stable, then walked slowly from one stall to the next, her downcast eyes glancing up occasionally to observe the new horses he'd delivered before she arrived home from the hospital with Earl.

"You brought six," she said, stopping with her back to him. "I only asked for two."

"I know." Brooks stopped as well and leaned against the door of an empty stall. The wood of the frame, cracked and weatherworn, creaked beneath his weight. "I thought you could use more than two, seeing as how you'll need as much income as you can get to fix this place up." He surveyed the six stalls stretching out in front of him, each one housing a new horse. "The two grays on the left belong to a friend of mine from out of the county. He runs a boarding service himself that has more business than he can handle, and he considered it a favor for you to take these two off his hands. The three paints on the right are from a rescue ranch near Lexington. They're full up and needed to clear a couple stalls for new arrivals so I suggested that we board them here until we find suitable applicants for adoption."

Jo turned her head to the side, the waves of her honey-brown hair rippling down her slender back. Her wardrobe had changed. Instead of the baggy shirt and jeans she'd worn on her visit to him a few days prior, she now wore a fitted, faded set of jeans, a long-sleeved Henley shirt, and well-worn boots. "And the chestnut?" The cynicism in her tone deepened. "He doesn't look like a typical boarder."

Brooks smiled, his chin lifting as he studied the two-year-old thoroughbred in the stall on Jo's right. "No. That one's a winner."

Shoulders tensing, she turned slowly and faced him. "He's yours, isn't he?" she asked. "Your colt."

"Yeah." Brooks strode over to the stall. Immediately, the thoroughbred raised his head above the stall door, his damp nose sniffing the air, searching for Brooks's outstretched hand. "Another Round is mine."

"Another Round?" Soft footsteps fell behind him as Jo walked to his side, the sweet scent of her hair prompting Another Round's nostrils to flare even wider. "What inspired you to give him that name? His sire?"

"No." He stroked Another Round's forehead, watching as the horse's soulful eyes settled on Jo. "He doesn't need inspiration from a sire. He stands for something in his own right. He's strong and powerful, fierce and competitive. Capable of going the extra mile and turning things around at the last fraction of a second."

"So, he's a closer?"

Another Round, ears moving toward the sound of Jo's voice, dipped his head away from Brooks's hand and nudged his nose toward Jo.

"He's more than a closer," Brooks said, pride lifting his chest. "He's a natural."

Jo issued a wry smile. "One could say that all thoroughbreds are born for it, don't you think?" She glanced up at him and raised one eyebrow. "Isn't that the reason they're born? The reason you breed them?"

Brooks remained silent for a moment, watching as Jo turned back to Another Round, her eyes following the curve of his head, jaw, neck, shoulders, and body, a grudging light of admiration for his impressive musculature brightening her expression.

"Why did you stop training?" he asked, though he had his suspicions. "What happened to change your opinion of the sport?"

Her expression dimmed again. She lifted her hand and rested it on the stall door, a few inches away from Another Round's nose. "Sweet Dash was the first racehorse Earl and I trained together. Earl was named head trainer and I was listed as assistant, but I had a connection with Sweet Dash from the day he was born. One deeper than Earl could replicate, so he stepped aside most of the time and let me take the lead."

Another Round moved at the tender tone of her voice, his hooves stepping on the shavings of his stall as he moved closer, stretched his neck, and brushed his nose against the center of Jo's open palm.

Brooks smiled. Aside from his strength and talent, Another Round was a friendly, vibrant horse who sought attention.

"Sweet Dash was a natural, too." Jo glanced at Brooks, then returned her attention to Another Round. "He loved to run. Loved to race. Loved the competition." Her hand moved, stroking Another Round's forehead gently. The thoroughbred seemed to crave her touch, nudging his broad head closer to her chest. "We had such high hopes for Sweet Dash, and he delivered on all fronts. He took to the track like it was home. Like he never wanted to be anywhere else. And he was friendly, too"—she lifted her chin toward Another Round—"like this one. When Sweet Dash delivered the Derby win, he was the talk of the town. The champion of the sport. Everyone wanted a piece of him." The nostalgic sparkle in her eyes faded. "We should've stopped there. Should've taken him home after he won the Derby and let him enjoy his life. Instead, we hauled him to the next leg of the Triple Crown." She cut her eyes at him, her hand stilling against Another Round's forehead. "I'm sure you know what happened next. You don't strike me as the kind of man to partner up with anyone without thoroughly researching them first."

Brooks winced. "Yes," he said softly. "Once Rhett gave me your name, I did some searching. I saw what happened in an old highlight clip from the Preakness Stakes. I'm sorry. It's a tragic thing. I can't imagine—"

"What?" Her tone hardened. "You can't imagine a horse like yours"—she gestured toward Another Round—"like this one, stumbling for a fraction of a second during a race? A fraction of a second that's just long enough to shatter bone, take him down, and ultimately, end his life? You can't imagine something like that happening to Another Round?"

An uneasy feeling swirled in his gut as he looked at the horse he'd bred, raised . . . and loved. "I try not to. I try to focus on giving Another Round an opportunity to do what he loves. An opportunity every horse who loves to run should be afforded."

Something in his voice must have hinted at the fears he harbored because her own expression gentled as she stroked Another Round's forehead again.

"No one who loves horses wants to imagine or dwell on the tragedy when it happens," she said. "But it's an undeniable hazard of the sport that's dismissed all too easily in the interest of money, tradition, and fame." She stepped away from Another Round, shoved her hands in the pockets of her jeans, and faced him again. "I appreciate all you've done for me, Brooks, but I have no desire to train again. Losing another horse is just too painful a prospect."

"Oh, but the joy, Jo. You can't deny there's joy in the sport—not just for trainers, owners, grooms, and all those who benefit from the economic impact of the sport, but also for the horses. These thoroughbreds live a good life." A small laugh escaped his lips. "They live a better life than most people do—including me. And there's no guarantee Another Round will meet the same fate as Sweet Dash. Surely you remember what that Derby win was like. What witnessing the magnificence of a thoroughbred's strength, power, and accomplishment brings to those who are a part of it."

She nodded. "Money and pride. Those are the biggest joys most people glean from racing. Years of hard work, dedication, and care for a one-hundred-and-twenty-second bet that risks a horse's life. Win or lose, the typical thoroughbred only has a brief window of luxury before their lives are at stake—on and off the track. There are as many—if not more—horror stories as there are successful tales."

Jo brushed past him and walked toward the stable doors, saying over her shoulder, "As I mentioned before, I appreciate everything you've done for us, but you're wasting your time trying to persuade me into taking on that colt of yours."

Brooks lowered his head, patted Another Round's neck, then strolled slowly behind her. "Nothing I've done—or will continue to do—for you, Earl, or Lone Oaks Crossing would ever be a waste to me."

"And why is that?"

"Because, whether you agree to train or not, I still think we'd make a good team." He picked up his pace, drawing nearer to her. "And I enjoy being around you."

She stopped, her feet freezing in midstep before she turned to face him, her eyes seeking his. "We barely know each other."

He stopped, too, the tips of his boots resting in the dirt mere inches from the toes of hers. "There's more to knowing a person than just exchanging facts or whatever fictional details they choose to present to you. There's a person's disposition, their spirit, their concern for others. I've had an opportunity to see those things in you during the short time since we've met."

He tilted his head, surveying the attractive features of her face, features that seemed all-too-familiar somehow. As though an ethereal ideal he'd harbored secretly in his heart all his life had been breathed to life in front of him. It was an odd feeling—this instant affection for someone he'd just recently met. He'd always dismissed it as a sentimental notion, but now found himself experiencing it firsthand.

"I told you the other day that I don't have a family," he said. "But I used to have one. I used to know what love, loyalty, and devotion should look like. Or at least, what I thought they should look like. I see the way you love and support Earl and Lone Oaks Crossing. You're willing to relocate your life here to care for your grandfather and honor your childhood home." He reached out and tucked a stray strand of her long hair behind her ear. "I'm well aware of who I am to you right now. A man with money. A helpful neighbor, at best. But I'm hoping . . . in time, we may become friends. No matter the outcome of any potential business we may or may not undertake together,

I want to help you and Earl the way I wish someone had helped the family I had years ago. Call it old-fashioned nostalgia for the childhood I lost. Maybe you can understand that?"

She swayed in his direction, just a bit. Enough so that her soft cheek grazed his knuckles as he removed his hand from her hair.

"Yes," she said. "I can understand that, and I know you're going out of your way to help me." She looked up at him, those dark blue eyes of hers peering into him. "Two boarders, Frankie and I can handle. But you've brought six and Another Round's going to need daily attention. A set schedule to keep his heart and lungs strong—that is, if you still plan on racing him with another trainer?"

Brooks nodded. He had every intention of entering Another Round in the Kentucky Derby, but his plan only included Jo, and he'd hold on to hope that she'd change her mind . . . even if the end result was disappointing.

"Then there's no way Frankie and I can be available to Earl every day and also care for Another Round and the other boarders you've brought. At least, not without extra help."

Brooks smiled. Even if she didn't realize it, she was offering him another chance to stick around. "I can fix that."

She shook her head, a grudging smile curving her lips. "You seem to have a fix for everything, don't you?"

"Yeah," he said. When it came to her, at least. Unable to resist, he reached out and smoothed his knuckles down her soft cheek as he eased past her. "I'll be here first thing in the morning, and as soon as it's convenient for you, we'll solve that problem. In the meantime"—he glanced over her shoulder as he exited the stable, savoring the somewhat dazed but friendly look on her face as he spoke his next words—"if you need me, I'm still at your beck and call."

Call it old-fashioned nostalgia for the childhood I lost. Maybe you can understand that?

Jo, seated in the passenger seat of Brooks's truck, stared ahead at the paved road winding in front of them. It was early, the sun rising high in the sky, just beginning to warm the chilly fall air. Brooks had driven up the driveway to Earl's house right at dawn—just as he'd promised yesterday—and as Earl was still sleeping soundly in his bed, she'd left Frankie with him and climbed into the passenger seat. Now she tugged the light denim jacket she wore tighter around her shoulders and rubbed her hands together in her lap to ward off the early-morning chill.

"Cold?" Brooks reached out, adjusted a control on the dash, and tilted two vents in her direction. "Does that help?"

Warm air billowed over her chest and neck, and she eased back against her seat, sighing. "Yes. Thank you."

She glanced at him, eyeing his chiseled jaw, the strong column of his neck and confident set of his broad shoulders. Yesterday, after he'd left Lone Oaks Crossing, she'd had difficulty getting him out of her mind. She'd tossed and turned in bed last night, the memory of his deep voice and handsome features, set in a warm, inviting expression, stirring delicious thrills within her as she'd stared up at the ceiling of her bedroom.

I enjoy being around you.

Her reaction had been ridiculous, really—more like a lovesick teen than a grown woman. The last thing she'd expected to stumble upon when returning to Lone Oaks had been a charismatic, wealthy bachelor like Brooks who had an overdose of charm. One who probably couldn't recall how many women he'd entertained, much less remember their names.

But then again, the words he'd spoken in the stable yesterday had seemed sincere. Heartfelt, even. Like those of an honest, forthright man.

I've experienced a great deal of loss in my life, actually. More than most people assume.

What childhood had he lost? He'd mentioned he had no family now but had acknowledged yesterday that he'd had one in the past. One he seemed to have loved and missed quite deeply, if the sorrow etched into his expression yesterday had been any indication.

It was unsettling to think that of a man of his stature, wealth, and power could have experienced such keen loss and be alone in the world. But, having worked with youth in the public school system, she'd seen her share of children suffering through devastating losses at a young age. She'd consoled children who'd lost family, shelter, security, and their very hope for a successful future. Everything in life could change in an instant, and that daunting prospect was no different for children, no matter their youth and innocence.

She looked at Brooks again, a curiosity she hadn't anticipated prompting her to speak before she could think better of it. "What happened to your parents?"

The question seemed to hit a nerve. His broad hands tightened on the steering wheel, his knuckles turning white. He smiled, the expression strained and insincere. "I see we're beginning the day's conversation with lighter topics."

She looked away, giving him some space, and returned

her attention to the road in front of them. "I don't mean to pry, but you mentioned yesterday that you used to have a family. I just couldn't help but wonder what happened to them."

He glanced at her, his eyes pained as he murmured, "Can we save that discussion for another time?"

"Of course." Seeking a distraction, Jo cleared her throat and rubbed her hands over her jeans-clad knees. "So, where are we going?"

"You said you needed extra help yesterday. So, I'm taking you to get extra help." .

She frowned. "You do remember me telling you that I can't afford to pay any extra hands? I don't know anyone who would be willing to work for free."

His smile fell and an ironic expression appeared on his face. "I wouldn't say the person I have in mind is willing to work for free, but they're obligated to do so."

An easy feeling unfurled in Jo's stomach. "What do you mean, they're obligated?"

"I'm not going to bring some dangerous vagrant into your midst, in case that's what you're thinking." Brooks slowed the truck as they entered the city limits of Lone Oaks, his dark eyes scanning the left side of the road. "I'm simply providing a logical solution to your problem by finding someone who needs to work to fulfill an obligation while simultaneously giving you the help you need." He shrugged. "Room and board, home-cooked meals, and a watchful eye are all it'll cost you."

Jo narrowed her eyes. "A watchful eye?"

He looked at her then, his smile broad and genuine. "Only occasionally."

Brooks guided the truck into a left turn and Jo eyed a large sign they passed at the entrance of the driveway.

"Dream House?" she asked. "What is this place?" She

glanced at the two-story building in front of them. It was all brick, with small windows and cracked pavement out front, which, she supposed, was intended to serve as a sidewalk. "It sure doesn't look like a dream to me."

"It's not." Brooks's tone had changed, taking on a heavy, sorrowful note. "But I hope to change that in the future, starting with giving the place a facelift." He parked the truck in front of the building, cut the engine, and exited, pausing before he closed the door to say, "Hop out. A treasure trove of help awaits you."

Jo made a face, watching as he rounded the truck and patted the hood, motioning for her to join him. She did so, glancing around her as she entered the brick building, then stood in the lobby and thrust her hands in her pockets as Brooks spoke to a lady at the reception desk.

He joined her a moment later, a pleased expression on his face. "Ms. Agnes will be with us shortly."

"Ms. Agnes?" Jo glanced at the reception desk where the woman Brooks had spoken with answered the phone, then glided in her chair farther down the desk to type on the keyboard of a desktop computer.

Two teenaged girls strolled down one of the three halls that were located behind the reception desk, each of them wearing sweatpants and a T-shirt, one of them carrying a basketball.

Covering the phone with one hand, the receptionist called out to the teens. "Girls, be sure you're back by curfew. Don't go galivanting all around and drag in late like last Saturday."

The teens made a face. "Yes, ma'am."

"Wait a minute," Jo said, watching the girls as they left the building, laughing. "Dream House." She frowned at Brooks. "Is this a foster home?"

"Brooks!" An older woman with an exuberant expression and kind eyes walked quickly down one of the hallways, rounded the reception desk, and threw her arms around Brooks's waist, burying her pudgy cheek against his chest. "I can't tell you how happy I am to see you. It's been ages since you visited."

Brooks's demeanor softened, his features gentling and his deep voice adopting an affectionate tone Jo had never heard before. "I didn't mean to stay away so long, Ms. Agnes. I've just been buried under work." He lifted his strong arms and returned her embrace, lowering his head and kissing the top of her gray head. "I didn't mean to interrupt your workday," he said softly, "but you've always come through for me in the past, and I have a friend in need now."

Agnes released him and stepped back, patting his forearms with her wrinkled hands. "Oh, my boy," she said. "You're never an interruption to my day. I wish you'd drop in more often. And I'm more than happy to help your friend."

"This is Jo," Brooks said. "She's the granddaughter of my neighbor, Earl Ellis."

"Oh, my dear." Agnes stepped over to Jo and clasped her hands. "I understand your grandfather had some health problems recently. I just heard yesterday that he was in the hospital."

Jo nodded, the supportive warmth of the older woman's hands around her offering comfort she hadn't expected. "He was, but he came home yesterday."

Agnes's eyes brightened. "That's wonderful news."

Brooks nodded. "That's why we're here. Jo's returned home to take care of Earl and run their family farm. But"—he spread his hands—"as you probably already know, Lone Oaks Crossing hasn't been doing much business lately."

Agnes nodded. "Yes, I've heard that, too." Her brow creased. "And considering that's the case, I wonder if there's enough work to serve the need for the community service hours my charge has?"

"Trust me, there's plenty," Brooks said. "More than Jo and her friend, Frankie, can handle themselves while taking care of Earl, too." He rocked back on his heels and shoved his hands in his pockets. "As a matter of fact, I just dropped off my thoroughbred yesterday for boarding, so Jo already has her hands full and is in need of the extra help."

Agnes's eyes widened. "Oh, is that so? You and Earl used to train racehorses, didn't you? Won the Derby years ago, if I recall correctly?"

Jo smiled. "Yes, ma'am." She cut her eyes at Brooks. "Though I don't have any plans to train again. But Brooks is right that we're pretty shorthanded right now, what with Earl just coming home and starting therapy. So, we'll need help mucking out the stalls and caring for Brooks's colt. Although"—she glanced over her shoulder as another teen sauntered in—"I don't know if any of your charges would be suited for household chores, mucking stalls, or—"

"That's exactly the type of work we look for in terms of fulfilling community service hours," she said. "Steady, hard work that's worthwhile and helps build community as well as a young person's confidence. Brooks has been our biggest advocate. He hires at least one teen every year to help out in his stables."

Jo glanced at Brooks. "You employ foster children?"

"He certainly does," Agnes said proudly. She reached up and patted his cheeks. "He used to live here, so he knows how much our children need support and opportunities to learn new trades."

"You used to live here?" Surprised, Jo stared up at him.

He nodded, his mouth tightening.

"Brooks was only with us for three years, but he's kept in touch over the years." Agnes smiled. "I shouldn't say this, but he was always my favorite. He was so tough on the outside, but an absolute angel on the inside."

Brooks cleared his throat as a red flush suffused his neck.

Agnes winced. "The girl I've picked out for you has a very similar disposition to Brooks at that age but, well . . . she's not all that happy about going to a farm. But I'm hoping the prospect of working with a horse might help."

"What's her name?" Brooks asked. "How old is she?"

Agnes glanced over her shoulder, shrugging her shoulders as she said softly, "Cheyenne Grier. She's fourteen and a tough nut to crack from what I've seen so far."

Jo shook her head, her hands trembling in her pockets at the thought of undertaking a troubled teen like the ones she'd just left behind a week ago. "I'm sorry, Ms. Agnes. I could certainly use the help, but I don't think our farm would be a good match for a challenging teen, especially given Earl's condition."

Agnes held up her hands, her eyes pleading up at Jo. "Please. She just needs a little . . . encouragement." She bit her lip. "Discipline."

Jo let out a heavy breath. No. No way would she take on the type of kid that had just prompted her to throw away her career. "Ms. Agnes, I can't—"

"My only concern," Agnes said, "is that she keep up with her schoolwork. Cheyenne's been expelled from the local high school, you see. All of her assignments are on-line, and the schedule is more than feasible given the workload she carried when attending school in person.

She's bright—really bright. She's just been let down a lot and is very angry." She leaned in, her voice lowering to a whisper. "She's so much like Brooks at that age. Hurt, angry, and ready to fight anyone and everyone."

Brooks looked away, his neck flushing even more as he scanned the empty lobby. Jo studied him for a moment, then faced Agnes again.

"What's the girl's story?" Jo asked.

"She was abandoned as a baby," Agnes said. "Doesn't know her parents or any extended family. She's bounced from foster home to foster home throughout her childhood—seems she just isn't suited to a traditional foster home setting." Agnes shook her head. "She was expelled from school for stealing—she broke in one night and swiped a laptop and damaged quite a bit of property—and she got into a fight with one of her roommates just yesterday. So . . . I'm not sure this environment is suited for her either. That's why, when Brooks called me yesterday, asking if I had anyone needing to complete community hours, she came to mind first, you see?" She smiled tentatively. "I'm hoping that a change of scenery will do her good. Especially one with wide-open space. She needs a place to heal. A place to think and breathe. A place where she can see possibilities instead of pain."

"A place to heal, huh?" Jo shoved her hands farther into her pockets and glanced at Brooks, asking under her breath, "Is that why you brought me here?"

"Wasn't that what you told me the other day?" he asked. "That you wanted to help kids. That you wanted to help them heal and secure the future of their dreams."

Yeah. Jo rubbed her temples. That's exactly what she'd said. "May I meet her first?" she asked Agnes.

Agnes nodded eagerly. "Of course." She spun on her heel

and hustled off, saying over her shoulder, "She's already packed. I'll just go grab her and bring her out."

"Oh, but I'm . . ." Jo's shoulders slumped as she watched Agnes hurry away. "I'm not sure this is a good idea." She frowned at Brooks. "I wish you'd explained to me who you had in mind before we drove out here."

"Why?" He raised one eyebrow. "Would you have agreed to come?"

"No." She stared at the empty hallway Agnes had walked down. "Probably not."

"Then there you go." Brooks sighed. "I know you've just had a bad experience, but there are good kids here, Jo. They just need a fair shot."

"Like you did, you mean?"

He didn't respond.

Agnes reemerged at the end of a hallway and a tall, skinny girl with long brown hair hanging limply around her shoulders lagged behind her.

"Here she is," Agnes said, a broad smile engulfing her face. Her eyes sparkled like fireworks on the Fourth of July, the eager hope etched into her expression a clear clue to Jo that she was definitely getting in over her head with this kid. "Jo and Brooks, this is Cheyenne Grier. Cheyenne," Agnes prompted, tapping the girl's shoulder, "would you please lift your head and greet Ms. Jo and Mr. Brooks?"

The girl raised her head slowly, the movement jostling the limp strands of her hair back over her shoulders to reveal her face. Her features were plain but the sturdiness of her jaw and the deep dimple in her chin seemed to echo the stubborn glint in her expression. The black eye she sported did the same.

Cheyenne's gaze sought Jo's, holding her stare, judg-

ing, and weighing her as much as—if not more than—Jo
had assessed her, the girl's eyes lingering on the still
slightly swollen wound in Jo's bottom lip. "So . . . you're
the chick that wants me to shovel shit."

Agnes gasped. "Cheyenne! Your manners are atro-
cious." She wrung her hands, glancing up at Jo in dismay.
"Cheyenne really is a sweet girl, Jo. And she'll work very
hard, I promise. She just needs discipline and guidance
and . . . and"—she glanced at Cheyenne, the eager hope
in her expression dimming—"she just needs to be given a
chance."

Cheyenne sneered and rolled her eyes.

"Excuse us for just a minute, please." Jo stepped back,
grabbed Brooks's elbow, and dragged him with her, turning their backs to Agnes and Cheyenne, seeking space
from the potential trouble and pressures the teen presented.

"Look," Jo whispered to Brooks, "I know you're trying to help, but this is a disaster waiting to happen. Did
you see the black eye? There's no way that kid'll do anything I tell her."

"Not true," Brooks whispered back. "From what I've
been told, you were a great teacher, and I'll be on hand to
help out. Besides, this arrangement will give you the opportunity to not only gain an extra pair of hands, but also
to give your idea of a healing retreat a trial run. You did
say you wanted to revive Lone Oaks Crossing into a
place where horses—*and people*—could heal."

Jo smirked. "Yeah, but populating my granddad's farm
with foul-mouthed teenagers isn't what I had in mind
when I walked out on my teaching job."

Brooks grinned, the action lending him a boyish air—
a far too appealing invitation for any red-blooded woman

to ignore. "I admit," he whispered, "the kid might be a challenge. But she has the potential to provide security for both of us. Security in the sense that you will have more time to spend with Earl, and security for me, knowing that you have enough help to take care of Another Round properly."

Jo studied his face, searching for any hint of insincerity or ulterior motive, but the man definitely had a poker face.

"Look," he said. "I know you're probably having some painful flashbacks to the job you just left, but this is different. You and Cheyenne have both been hurt by a system that didn't support either of you." He held her gaze, an earnest intensity in his eyes. "Help her out and let her help you. What do you have to lose?"

Oh, sweet Lord. Just about every single thing she had left—including her sanity.

Jo closed her eyes, regretting her decision almost before she made it. "Where will she stay? At your place or Lone Oaks Crossing?"

"At Lone Oaks Crossing," Brooks said. "That way, she'll be ready and available anytime you need an extra hand." He examined her resigned expression, then nodded. "Welcome to your new class of one. You won't regret it."

Reluctantly, Jo faced Agnes and Cheyenne again. The teen was looking at Brooks's boots, a curious—almost excited gleam—entering her eyes as she studied them; it morphed into a frown as she looked down at her own worn tennis shoes.

"You like boots?" Jo asked. That, at least, was one perk she could provide the girl that might entice her to cooperate.

Cheyenne's eyes snapped back to Jo's, her lips pursing as she shrugged. "Maybe. But you should know before you put a shovel in my hand that I can't be bought with a shiny pair of boots."

Jo tilted her head, her attention lingering on the fresh black eye marring Cheyenne's face, her own hand lifting to touch the wound on her lip. The kid might not be excited about working on a farm, but a farmhand needed gut and gumption to work with horses. And, judging from her outspoken comments, the kid was honest, at least.

Jo sighed. "I suppose she'll do."

CHAPTER 6

Two days later, Jo realized her new class of one (as Brooks had put it) was unmotivated, disrespectful, and irresponsible. Not that she'd expected anything different after the introduction Agnes had given her to the troubled teen.

Cheyenne Grier was indeed a challenging kid in need of discipline and guidance.

After Brooks had driven Jo and Cheyenne from Dream House to Lone Oaks Crossing forty-eight hours ago, Jo had tried her best to bond with the girl on at least a superficial level. She'd given Cheyenne a tour of Lone Oaks Crossing, leading her to the sprawling fields, walking with her through the stables and the house, and showing her the guest room where she'd be staying.

Cheyenne had been unimpressed with her new living quarters. She'd stood in the center of the guest room and spun slowly around, frowning deeper as she'd eyed the sparse furnishings. There was one single bed, one nightstand (which had seen better days), a lamp, a small dresser, and a glider that had been used by Jo's grandmother decades ago, its cushion flat and faded.

"Really?" Cheyenne had flung her bag on the bed, propped her hands on her hips, and eyed Jo with disdain. "This is where you expect me to stay?"

Jo hadn't been surprised by Cheyenne's response—the teen hadn't been very amenable to anything Jo had introduced her to that day. But wanting to give the girl the benefit of the doubt and taking her recent hardships into consideration, Jo had continued showing Cheyenne around the house and pointed out the small bathroom down the hall which Cheyenne would use as her own.

After giving Cheyenne the tour of Lone Oaks Crossing, Jo had left her in Frankie's care long enough to run to the grocery store, where she picked up extra food and a few fresh toiletries for the teen. Jo had given herself a pep talk regarding her new teenage farmhand along the way, reminding herself that every child was different and had their own unique personality and needs. Just because Cheyenne reminded her of Natasha didn't mean Cheyenne would give her the same trouble Natasha had—including the busted lip. Cheyenne might very well turn out to be the great help to her that Brooks had suggested.

And surprisingly, the empathy and compassion that she'd thought had completely left her over a week ago when she'd walked out on her teaching job had pricked her conscience. Though her patience and goodwill had been exhausted by the hopelessness of Stone Hill High School, she wasn't completely inured to Cheyenne's needs. She still cared.

The sense of relief that accompanied the realization overwhelmed Jo. She might have abandoned her teaching career, but the innate drive to teach, support, and protect hadn't abandoned her. Maybe, just maybe, employing

Cheyenne would afford her the opportunity to improve a child's life even though she no longer taught in a classroom.

Jo had left the store, her spirits high, and returned to Lone Oaks Crossing with the hope that she might connect with Cheyenne. That Cheyenne might allow her to help turn her life around and, in turn, Cheyenne might help ease hers and Frankie's workloads. Only, when she'd returned to the farm and parked Earl's truck in front of the house, she'd found Frankie sitting on the porch, a newly opened bottle of Brooks's bourbon in her hand and an expression of disgust on her face.

Apparently, Cheyenne had taken it upon herself to return to the guest room after Jo had left. She'd shut the door, locked it, and refused to exit no matter how many times Frankie had demanded she do so. Frankie, struggling to cope with Earl's frustrated shouts at being bedridden and Cheyenne's stubbornness, had reached her wits' end, flopped in a rocking chair on the porch, and taken a shot of bourbon to soothe her nerves.

The next day had not gone any better, and as Jo had quickly discovered this morning, Cheyenne was determined to continue her same pattern of isolation.

"Cheyenne!" Jo, standing outside Cheyenne's guest room, pounded on the locked door for the third time that morning. "Cheyenne? You were supposed to be down at the stables an hour ago."

It wasn't as though the teen didn't know what was expected of her. Jo had gone over the rules in explicit detail during the tour she'd given Cheyenne on the afternoon she'd arrived. The rules were simple—at least to Jo—but it seemed Cheyenne either didn't understand them . . . or more than likely, simply chose to disregard them. The rules, which were as basic as Jo could make them, included: wake and dress at dawn, come downstairs for breakfast, wash the breakfast dishes, join Jo at the stables, and muck the stalls while Jo groomed and turned the horses out to the paddocks. After that, Cheyenne was expected to return to the main house and complete the lessons in her online classes for the day.

Cheyenne had done none of this over the past two days. Instead, she'd holed up in her guest room, save for the few times she used the bathroom and snuck into the kitchen after midnight to rustle up some sugary snacks, from what Jo could gather from the empty wrappers left behind.

In Jo's opinion, Cheyenne's visit had been nothing but a disaster so far. All the girl had brought to the farm for the past two days was disruption and careless disregard for Jo and Frankie. Rather than easing Jo's worries, Cheyenne had increased them.

"Cheyenne, I have a key." Jo retrieved said key from her pocket and turned it over in her palm. "If you don't unlock this door within the next five seconds, I'm coming in."

A muffled snort sounded behind her. Jo glanced over her shoulder at Frankie, who leaned against the wall, her arms crossed over her chest and a humorless smile on her face.

"You think that girl gives a durn whether you got a key or not?" Frankie asked. "She don't give a rat's patootie what you do so long as you stay out of her hair."

Jo dragged her hand over her face. "What else do you want me to do? You want me to call Brooks? Because I can. I'll call him right now, tell him to come pick this kid up, and take her back to the foster home."

Frankie blew out a breath, uncrossed her arms and

shoved away from the wall. "No. I don't want you doing that. Like it or not, we need the kid."

That sentiment was one Jo agreed with completely, like it or not. Earl's physical therapist was scheduled to arrive tomorrow, and Frankie wanted to stay with Earl during the session so she could better support and help him along the way. That meant Jo needed Cheyenne in the stables first thing in the morning to help her muck the stalls and feed and turn out the horses as Frankie would have normally done.

And as long as Cheyenne was bedding down under Lone Oaks Crossing's roof, there was no way Jo would ask Frankie to leave Earl to help with chores. Not when Cheyenne was available and fully capable.

"Here's what I think," Jo said quietly. She turned the key over again in her palm, considering. "I want to give this kid a fair shot for all our sakes, and since I'm not laboring in a school under someone else's direction anymore, I think it's time for some good, old-fashioned tough love."

Frankie smiled—the first smile Jo had seen on her face since Cheyenne had arrived. "Amen, sister. What's the plan?"

Jo narrowed her eyes. "I'm going to unlock the door, we're both going to go in, haul her out of that bed, down the stairs, and out to the stable. She's not going to be allowed back in this house until she's mucked those stalls or chooses to return to the foster home. In the end, we will have given her a chance—it'll be her choice whether she stays or goes."

Frankie, seemingly eager for a bit of payback, rubbed her hands together. "Sounds good to me. Go on. Open up that door."

Jo steeled herself, her resolve wearing thin as a result
of the week's exhausting events, but she managed to unlock the door and thrust it open.

Cheyenne, still sleeping (or pretending to sleep), had
burrowed under the covers, her face obscured by the thin
sheet she clutched over her head.

"All right, Cheyenne," Jo said. "I'm giving you one
last chance to come out of that bed under your own
steam."

Cheyenne did not respond. There was no movement or
sound from the bed.

Shaking her head, Jo crossed the room to the bed,
cursing herself for the millionth time in two days for
agreeing to take on the teen. "You want her head or feet,
Frankie?"

A muffled squeak emerged from beneath the sheet.

"Oh, I'll be happy to take those stinky feet." Frankie
almost skipped across the room—her giddiness completely
out of place but somehow comforting to Jo—flung back
the sheet, and grabbed Cheyenne's ankles before the girl
could wriggle them away.

Jo followed suit, ignoring the shocked anger on Cheyenne's face and getting a good grip under the girl's arms.

"I don't know what you people think you're doing—"

"This is a working farm. We don't sleep all day in this
joint." Jo released Cheyenne's arms and held up a hand,
signaling Frankie to freeze, then looked down at Cheyenne's disgruntled expression. "Are you ready to get out
of the bed without help or not?"

Cheyenne glared up at her, then sank back against the
pillow. "I ain't going anywhere—especially at the crack
of dawn. I didn't ask to be here, I don't want to be here,
and I ain't doing anything you crazy people say. If you

want me out of this bed," Cheyenne said, her lip curling, "you're gonna have to drag me out."

Jo stared down at her. Cheyenne's words were harsh and angry—completely defiant. But her eyes told a different story. The black eye she'd sported two days ago had lightened in color and the swelling had receded (much like Jo's own wounded lip), and the look in Cheyenne's eyes almost begged Jo to act. To call her bluff and see if Jo cared enough to show her attention and follow through.

"You want it, kid? You got it." Jo slid her hands under the girl's arms again, secured a gentle grip on her armpits, then nodded in Frankie's direction. "Up, Frankie."

They heaved at the same time, lifting Cheyenne into the air and carrying her dead weight through the open doorway and down the hall.

The stairs were another story. By this time, Cheyenne's dignity had taken a blow. She began writhing and kicking, her flailing heels and elbows catching Frankie and Jo in sensitive places. But Jo and Frankie managed somehow, sucking up the pain and maneuvering the teen down the stairs, out the front door, and across the lawn. They carried her to the stable, where they deposited her gently—but decisively—on the dirt in front of the stables' entrance.

Gasping for breath, Frankie bent, braced her hands on her knees, and whooped. "Girl, you may look like you weigh five pounds, but you have some muscle in there somewhere under that skin. That, or"—she dragged in a ragged breath—"could be I'm just getting old."

Cheyenne, lying on the ground, propped herself on her elbows and glared up at Frankie. "You're just old."

"Watch it, Cheyenne." Jo dragged the back of her hand

over her sweaty forehead and sighed. "This is your last chance. You get in that stable and you muck those stalls—and you do a decent job of it—or I call Brooks and you go right back to that foster home. It's your choice. Either way, you're not coming back into our house, sleeping in that bed, or eating our food until you've contributed to this farm."

Cheyenne's glare relaxed just a bit—not much, but enough that Jo noticed. "I'll clean Another Round's stall, but I ain't messing with the other ones. Especially the old gray one. She smells like a fart."

Frankie clucked her tongue. "My Lord! You are one crass kid. Do you always talk like that?"

Cheyenne grinned, apparently pleased she'd managed to offend.

Jo looked down at Cheyenne and narrowed her eyes, deliberately softening her tone. "I know you didn't ask to be here, Cheyenne. Believe it or not, neither did I. But I'm here and you're here and we have a decision to make. I need help and I know you can help me if you choose to. There'll be no hard feelings and no more big scenes. If you really don't want to give this a try, say the word and I'll load you up in Earl's truck and drive you back to Dream House—or to Brooks's stables—whichever you prefer. But given our circumstances, we simply can't afford to house a freeloader right now."

Jo expected the girl to spring to her feet, dust off the dirt, and head back to the house to pack her things. But surprisingly, she gave Jo a once-over, did the same to Frankie, then rolled her eyes and shoved slowly to her feet.

"If I scoop the poop out of the stalls," she said, "do I get to pick what I want to eat for lunch?"

Jo glanced at Frankie, who shrugged. "Yeah. I think Frankie can handle that."

Cheyenne stood there for a moment, clearly thinking it over, then spun around and flounced into the stable.

It was progress—albeit very little progress—but Jo would take it.

It seemed peanut butter and jelly did the trick for Cheyenne.

"Poor thing acts like no one fed her at that foster home," Frankie said, watching Cheyenne shove another three mouthfuls of sandwich into her mouth across the kitchen table.

"They didn't," Cheyenne mumbled around a big mouthful of peanut butter and jelly. "At least, nothin' decent. All they ever gave us was rotisserie chicken and pinto beans."

"Oh," Jo said after sipping her sweet tea. "Heaven forbid they feed y'all something healthy. And please use your napkin when you eat, Cheyenne. We use polite manners at the table during meals." Despite the trouble the girl had given them this morning, she couldn't help but smile. Cheyenne had a healthy appetite—as strong and healthy as her attitude, in fact. "Go ahead and eat up," she said, smiling wider. "You worked hard this morning and earned that sandwich. Thank you for that, Cheyenne."

The teen shrugged off the compliment, but her mouth curved up slightly as she chomped into a second sandwich, then wiped a stray glob of jelly from her chin.

Jo meant it when she said Cheyenne had earned her favorite lunch. She'd earned the praise, too. Not only had Cheyenne mucked the stalls thoroughly, but she'd also helped round the horses up from the paddock and return them to the stable. It hadn't escaped Jo's notice that Cheyenne's gaze seemed to linger on Another Round. She'd hovered by the colt's stall as Jo had stroked Another Round's neck and whispered soothing words in his ear, helping him feel at home in his new, unfamiliar quarters.

Jo hadn't asked to board Another Round and she certainly hadn't asked to have Cheyenne as a stable hand or temporary guest, but they both brought a new energy to Lone Oaks Crossing that was reminiscent of the farm's earlier days. And it seemed, at least to Jo, as though Cheyenne and Another Round might pair well together, if Cheyenne decided to drop that stubbornness of hers and open up enough to let Jo know she was interested in getting better acquainted with the thoroughbred.

"So, who's this Earl y'all keep checking on?" Cheyenne asked, taking a gulp of cold milk from the glass in front of her. Milk splashed down Cheyenne's chin and onto the table.

"Please chew, drink, and swallow completely before you speak, Cheyenne." Jo spun her glass of sweet tea slowly around on the table, her fingers tracing the rim of the glass, before taking a sip. Normally, after a morning of hard work mucking the stalls and working on the grounds, a cold glass of sweet tea hit the spot, but with the cool fall wind blowing in through the open kitchen window along with the reminder of Earl's misfortunes, Jo shivered as the cold liquid trickled down her throat. "Earl is my grandfather and Frankie's close friend," she explained as goose bumps broke out on her forearms. "He had a stroke and is having trouble getting around." She glanced at her wristwatch, a shameful sense of dread creeping through her. "Speaking of Earl, it's almost time for us to bring him his lunch."

Frankie reached across the table, grabbed the pitcher of sweet tea, and refilled her empty glass. "And he'll probably be in a great mood when I bring it to him," she drawled sarcastically.

A painful throb began behind Jo's eyes. Earl had become a handful ever since they'd brought him home from the hospital. He hated being weak, hated his wheelchair, and hated relying on her and Frankie even more, which led to frequent outbursts from him every time they entered his room. "Yeah. I'm sure he'll be in fine spirits."

Cheyenne, who'd polished off a second peanut butter sandwich, stared at them with a surprised expression. "He don't like to eat?"

"Doesn't," Jo corrected. "And yes. Earl does enjoy eating. He just doesn't like being served lunch in bed."

Frankie sighed. "He's always been a hard worker and an active man, so being confined to a bed and wheelchair in the house ain't exactly his cup of tea, even if it's only temporary."

Cheyenne smirked. "Y'all can't pick him up out of bed like you did me, plop him in his wheelchair, and roll him down here to the table?"

Jo considered this, her gaze meeting Frankie's. "We've tried once before, but he was a bit more than we could handle. I suppose we could try again . . . but it'd take some maneuvering."

Frankie nodded slowly, then eyed Cheyenne. "Me and Jo might not be able to pull it off by ourselves, but a third pair of hands might do the trick. Might help us get the hang of it."

Cheyenne rolled her eyes, then huffed out a breath.

"All right. I'll help you get the old dude out of the bed and to the table, but only if you let me have another sandwich."

Frankie whistled low and sat back in her chair. "You best not refer to him as 'old dude.' He won't cotton to that."

"Whatever," Cheyenne mumbled.

Five minutes later when they entered Earl's bedroom, he was already sitting up in bed against the pillows, a sour expression on his face.

"I . . . sick . . . this . . . bed." His mouth twisted around the words, his brow creasing more with each syllable as he struggled to speak.

Jo crossed the room and rubbed his shoulder. "I know. We're here to remedy that." She gestured over her shoulder toward Cheyenne, who stood on the threshold of the room, leaning against the doorframe. "Meet Cheyenne, our new stable hand. She's going to help us get you settled in your wheelchair and into the kitchen for a hot, home-cooked meal before your therapist arrives."

Earl surveyed Cheyenne. "Who . . . you?"

Cheyenne returned Earl's scrutiny for a moment, then said, "The help. I've been scooping the poop out of your stable."

Earl eyed Cheyenne warily, a muscle in his jaw ticking. "Don't . . . want . . . no . . . wheelchair. And don't . . . eed . . . you . . . help."

"Too bad, old dude." Cheyenne grinned. "I want another PB and J so you're gonna have to plop your butt down in that wheelchair."

"Cheyenne!" Jo shot her a stern look, though her irritation wasn't quite as intense as it normally would be considering the kid had used the word *poop* when explaining her job to Earl instead of the expletive she'd enjoyed tossing around a couple days ago.

"Here we go." Frankie walked into the room, rolling a wheelchair, and stopped by the side of Earl's bed. "We're gonna get you out of this bed so you can have a nice lunch at the kitchen table, where you can look out the window and get some sun and fresh air on your face. Then, once you finish with the therapist this afternoon, you can lie back down and take a nice nap."

Earl frowned. He lifted one gnarled finger, stabbing it in Cheyenne's direction. "Don't want . . . no . . . h-help from that k-kid."

Cheyenne, returning Earl's glare, cocked one eyebrow. "Too bad. They say I can't eat if I don't help around here, so I'm gonna help get you out of that bed."

Earl glared at Jo. "I can . . . w-walk . . . on . . . my own. No n-need that kid—"

"Whatever, dude." Cheyenne shoved off the door-jamb, walked across the room, and tugged the sheet off Earl's legs. "Grump all you want but you're getting in that wheelchair. Sooner we do this, the sooner we can eat."

"Come on, Earl," Jo said, joining Cheyenne and easing his legs, one at a time, over the side of the bed. "You may think you're able to walk but I don't want to risk you taking a fall. We'll have a better idea of what the therapist thinks is appropriate exercise for you after his visit this afternoon, but for now, we're going to play it safe. Now let's get you in that wheelchair, down the hall, and to the kitchen table."

Earl didn't like that. He grunted, glared at Jo, then settled his gaze on Cheyenne. His eyes narrowed and his scowl deepened. "Y-you . . . just . . . hold chair."

Cheyenne made a face as though the task was beneath her but did as Earl directed. She walked over to the wheelchair, stood behind it, and placed her hands on the handgrips.

"All right," Jo said, sliding her arm around Earl's back and waiting as Frankie did the same on his opposite side. "On three."

They both heaved on three, and with a little patience and a lot of effort, they managed to lift Earl from his bed and settle him in the wheelchair. To her credit, Cheyenne didn't complain about helping. As a matter of fact, she helped shift Earl's weight in the wheelchair to a more comfortable position once he was seated, then took it upon herself to wheel him down the hallway and into the kitchen.

"Here's your napkin," Cheyenne said, dropping a napkin in Earl's lap after she positioned his wheelchair at the head of the table. "Jo likes good manners around the table."

"Get way . . . kid!" Earl sagged back against the wheelchair, closed his eyes, and waved a hand weakly in the air. "Go. . . . on. Get!"

Cheyenne frowned. "Whatever, dude. It ain't like you could just say thank you or something."

Jo quickly stepped between them. "Cheyenne."

She and Earl continued exchanging glares. It was amazing, really, finding someone as stubborn and hard-headed as Earl who gave as good as she got.

"Cheyenne," Jo repeated, prompting the girl to drag her attention away from Earl. "Let's go outside and work on sprucing up the training track while Earl eats lunch with Frankie."

"Training track?" Cheyenne asked as Jo hustled her outside. "What's that for? The horses?"

"Yep." Jo shielded her eyes from the glare of the afternoon sun as they stepped out onto the front porch. "Another Round, in particular. He's a racehorse and needs regular workouts to keep his . . ."

A familiar truck rumbled up the driveway and drowned out her words. Hauling a flatbed trailer loaded down with various sizes of lumber and toolboxes, it slowed as it reached the main house and drew to a stop.

The door opened and Brooks hopped out of the cab and strode over to the porch, grinning wide. "Afternoon, ladies."

Jo smiled back, trying not to allow her gaze to linger on his flirtatious grin. His broad chest and lean hips were encased in a casual long-sleeved shirt and faded jeans as though he were prepared for manual outdoor labor. "This is a surprise. Especially, seeing as how I haven't called or beckoned."

He grinned wider as he climbed the porch steps. "Well, I figured I'd beat you to it." He looked at Cheyenne. "Hello, Cheyenne. How's it going so far?"

She looked away, crossed her arms over her chest, and shrugged.

Brooks glanced at Jo and raised on eyebrow. "No profanity-laden outburst? I suppose I'll take that as a good sign."

Jo gestured toward the trailer that was hitched to the back of Brooks's truck. "What's up with the lumber?"

He motioned toward the front steps he'd just ascended. "I got to thinking, it'll probably be a while before Earl will be able to walk up and down these steps without trouble, so I figured I'd help him out by building a ramp and a small deck. That way he can use his wheelchair to get outside on his own if he'd like and have a place to sit in the sun."

His words stirred a tender sensation in Jo's chest. "That's . . . very kind of you." She staved off that inconvenient sensation by kneading the center of her chest as she glanced around the porch. "I don't know that this is the best place for the deck, though. Maybe at the back of the house instead? Where the paddocks are? There's a set of steps leading off the back door of the house and there'd be a much better view of the horses from that vantage point." An ache spread through her as she glanced at the open window of the kitchen. "Earl always enjoyed having a cup of coffee out there in the afternoons while watching the horses graze."

Brooks nodded. "Then that's where we'll build it."

Cheyenne shot him a glare. "We?"

"Yep." Brooks's grin widened. "We'll unload everything now and get started early tomorrow morning. And by 'we,'" he said, looking at Cheyenne, "I mean you."

Cheyenne flung her head back, closed her eyes, and groaned with disgust.

CHAPTER 7

Brooks had never had so much fun performing manual labor. He supposed it could be a result of not having engaged in such physical activity in years, or it could be the invigorating feel of warm sun and cool air mixing on his sweat-slicked skin that made the work such a joy. But he suspected the true reason was the fact that building the deck allowed him to spend more time with Jo.

After delivering the lumber and tools yesterday afternoon, he'd returned to Lone Oaks Crossing early this morning and found Jo and Cheyenne waiting for him on the porch of the main house. Cheyenne, Jo had informed him, had already dressed, eaten breakfast, mucked the stalls, and had taken a breather to prepare for the day's physically taxing project. Cheyenne, a bitter but resigned look on her face, didn't seem as enthusiastic as Jo suggested, but that was okay with Brooks.

Today he was doing something good for Earl, Lone Oaks Crossing, and Jo. The investment of time, back-breaking labor, and waves of sweat rolling over his skin was well worth the smiles Jo flashed in his direction.

"Okay," Jo said, "the frame is in place and looks sturdy." Standing beside the wood frame they'd spent the past couple hours measuring, leveling, and securing, she looked over at him. "Do you think we can lay the boards now?"

Brooks smiled, admiring the rosy flush on her tan cheeks and the excited gleam in her beautiful blue eyes. "You're anxious to get this decking down, aren't you?"

Jo dropped the hammer she held onto the ground and dragged her forearm across her sweaty brow. "I'm anxious for Earl to be able to join us out here and enjoy the sun." She tilted her head back and eyed the sky, her gaze scanning the expanse of blue above them as the crisp fall breeze ruffled the hair she'd pulled back in a ponytail. "It's a beautiful day," she added. "It's a shame for him not to be out here watching the horses and enjoying the weather right now, before the real cold begins to set in."

Brooks glanced over his shoulder toward the paddocks in the distance. It was a beautiful day, all right, and the horses—including Another Round—were enjoying their tranquil surroundings by strolling lazily across the fields and grazing at their leisure.

When he'd first arrived, Jo and Cheyenne had already led the horses out to the pastures, allowing them to roam freely during the warm afternoon hours and soak up the sun. They were all brushed, their carefully cleaned and groomed hides gleaming under the bright sun, each gust of cool fall air rustling their lush tails and manes. The bluegrass along the rolling hills of the farm lent an emerald hue to land that stretched out for acres and extended beyond the oak trees that lined his neighboring property.

Lone Oaks Crossing was naturally beautiful. There

was no doubt about it. And no amount of man-made manipulation like his distillery, state-of-the-art stables, or aesthetically pleasing gift store could enhance its natural beauty.

Lone Oaks Crossing—despite financial difficulties and years of weathering—was, as Earl had once described Brooks's estate, a dream.

"By this time tomorrow," Brooks said, "Earl will be sitting where you're standing, enjoying the sun and admiring his land." He glanced over to his left, where a stack of lumber sat waiting, "We'll go ahead and tackle the decking, and when we finish, we'll test it out then take a break."

"A break?" Cheyenne, squatting several feet away with a drill in hand, shot to her feet, her eyes wide with relief. "It's time for a break?"

Brooks laughed. "Soon, Cheyenne." He glanced at his watch. "It's barely one in the afternoon. We can knock out the decking before we break for lunch."

But he had to give the kid credit. She'd worked her tail off. Sure, she'd complained, but she'd followed all his and Jo's directions to the letter and had worked as hard as either of them.

Cheyenne groaned, dragged a hand through her sweaty hair, then fanned her T-shirt away from her middle. "I'm sweating like a pig. Can we at least go inside for a little while?"

Jo walked over to the pile of lumber and started searching for the right boards to complete the deck. "You're welcome to go inside and take a short break if you'd like. But sometimes, when you're this close to ending a phase of a project, it's better to push through and just get it done. Then when you take your lunch break, you can sit back and admire your handiwork."

"And once you've rested, you can tackle the next phase of the project," Brooks said, chuckling.

Cheyenne stomped her foot. "Whatever! Let's just get this deck over with."

They jumped back to work, laying boards for the deck, drilling them in place, and finally, testing each plank out for sturdiness and secure footing.

"Looks great." Brooks smiled at Cheyenne. "You did a fantastic job. You're a fast learner."

Cheyenne, who was walking across the other end of the deck, testing boards, ducked her head and shrugged. "I didn't know I could build something like this," she said. "I've never had anyone to show me before." She glanced at Brooks, the guarded look in her gaze slipping just a little. "Who taught you how to do this kind of thing?"

Brooks, kneeling by the supporting posts of the deck, stood and joined Cheyenne on the deck, walking across its expanse and focusing on each step he took, testing his weight against the platform. "My father taught me. Quite a long time ago."

"Where's he now?" Cheyenne asked.

Brooks hesitated, his skin tingling where he could feel Jo's scrutiny settle on him. She was walking the length of the deck as well, checking their handiwork. "He passed away years ago."

Cheyenne stopped walking and stood still on the deck, staring out at the horses grazing in the pasture before them. "And your mom?"

Brooks stepped onto another section of the deck and bounced, testing its stability. "I lost her not long after I lost my father." He grimaced. "Broken heart syndrome, they told me."

Cheyenne frowned at him. "She died from a broken heart?"

"Stress," he said dully. "An overwhelming amount of grief and pain that was too much for her heart to bear apparently. It became so weak it just gave out." He shook his head. "That type of thing was new to me, too, at the time."

"How old were you?" Cheyenne asked.

"Cheyenne," Jo said softly. "I don't think—"

"It's okay." Brooks faced Jo then, meeting her concerned gaze, the empathy in her eyes bringing heat to his cheeks. He faced Cheyenne instead. "I was around your age, Cheyenne. Fifteen at the time, actually."

Cheyenne resumed staring at the horses. "You have any brothers or sisters?"

"No," Brooks said. "It's just me."

"Then who took care of you?" Cheyenne asked.

"Ms. Agnes." Brooks smiled as Cheyenne looked at him, her eyes surprised. "The same Ms. Agnes that was taking care of you."

Her eyes widened. "You lived in Dream House?"

He nodded. "For three years, until I aged out and could make it on my own."

Cheyenne gaped at him, and he could almost see the wheels turning in her mind as she surveyed him once more, reevaluating and reassessing the man she thought he was. "So, you're alone, too? You got no family at all?"

"No," he said softly. "But I have neighbors." He looked at Jo, the affectionate gleam in her eyes as she returned his gaze filling him with pleasure. "Great neighbors, actually." He returned his attention to Cheyenne. "And I've enjoyed spending time with you today, working on this deck and, hopefully, the wheelchair ramp after lunch if you decide to stick around and continue helping? Either way, you've been a huge help already."

Cheyenne blushed—the kid actually blushed! His comment clearly pleased her.

Seemingly uncomfortable with the praise, she spun away again and walked farther across the deck to stare at the horses again. "Jo said your horse is a racehorse."

Brooks glanced at Jo and smiled. "That's right. His name is Another Round and he's a fierce competitor. He's friendly but won't let anyone walk all over him."

Much like Cheyenne, he mused. Ms. Agnes had been right. The kid's anger, stubbornness, and distrust of others reminded him of himself at that age . . . much more than he cared to remember, in fact.

A slow smile lifted Cheyenne's lips. "He's gorgeous, you know."

"That he is," Brooks said.

"Jo said he needs regular workouts."

"That he will, especially now that the Derby is approaching."

Cheyenne spun back to face him again. "The Derby? At Churchill Downs?"

Brooks laughed. "That'd be the one, kid."

Cheyenne beamed, her eyes skittering over to Jo. "Can I ride him? Will you show me how? Brooks said I'm a fast learner. I could learn so f—"

"Whoa, there," Jo said, holding up a hand. "If you want to get anywhere near that thoroughbred, you need to learn the basics first."

Cheyenne smirked. "What basics? Throw on a saddle and hop on?"

"The basics that involve Another Round's daily care," Jo said patiently. "As in checking for potential health issues, bathing and brushing him, learning his likes and dislikes, his personality and—"

"His personality?" Cheyenne tilted her head. "You talk like he's a person."

Jo's brows rose. "Not at all. Horses are better than people in my opinion. They have their own standards and expectations, which don't change depending on who's around them, and they're always honest about how they feel."

Cheyenne turned her head and gazed at Another Round, a new, curious light in her eyes.

"The position of groom is a great place to start," Brooks said, glancing at Jo. "From what I've been told, Jo's not only a fantastic trainer but she was the best groom on the backside, too."

"The backside?" Cheyenne asked.

"Behind the racetrack and out of the limelight," Brooks said. "Where the hardest work is done by people whose top priority is to protect and care for horses. A groom dons many hats when caring for a horse—parent, vet, protector—and a good one is the first to know if a horse is not feeling well, has an injury, or is having a bad day."

"I can do that," Cheyenne said. "I can take care of him. Will you show me how, Jo?"

Jo returned Cheyenne's eager stare, her eyes studying the teen's expression, an almost excited light appearing in her own eyes.

Brooks grinned. Perhaps Jo hadn't put teaching behind her as completely as she'd thought. "What do you say, Jo? You willing to give her a shot? I'm game to help. Another Round needs a groom and while Cheyenne's learning the ins and outs, I can have that exercise track of yours cleaned up and leveled for workouts. Then maybe, if Cheyenne performs her duties well, she might graduate to exercise jockey at some point."

"Let's not get ahead of ourselves," Jo said, laughing. But she seemed to consider the idea, the tip of her tongue touching one corner of her mouth endearingly as she thought it over. "Cheyenne's a smart girl," she said gently, eyeing the teen. "I think she could handle the duties of a groom if she's willing to be patient and follow directions."

Cheyenne practically jumped up and down with excitement. "Fantastic! When can I start?"

Jo raised her hand again. "Easy," she said. "I'm not promising anything. I'm just saying we can give it a try. How does tomorrow morning sound? The sooner we get a routine in place for Another Round, the better."

Cheyenne contained her excitement—just a tad. "That'll work," she said. "First thing?"

"Not exactly the very first thing," Jo said, smiling. "But after we muck the stalls, yes."

Cheyenne rolled her eyes at the mention of mucking stalls but seemed satisfied with that response. Her gaze sought out Another Round again, an eager but somber expression appearing.

"It's time y'all had a break." The back door of the main house opened and Frankie bustled out onto the newly built deck, carrying a large tray stacked with bacon, lettuce, and tomato sandwiches, several bags of potato chips, and three large bottles of spring water. "Oh, my." She glanced around at their handiwork, admiring what they had done. "This is better than I imagined it would be. Earl is going to love it."

"How's he doing?" Jo asked, striding across the deck to relieve Frankie of the tray.

"He's doing very well." A laugh burst from Frankie's lips. "Though he's giving his physical therapist a fit. He's having Earl start with small exercises and take things slow, and Earl's champing at the bit to jump out of that wheelchair and hit the ground running."

"It's good the therapist is making him take things slow," Brooks said. "The more time he takes to build his muscles up, the sooner he'll be able to walk out here on his own without the wheelchair."

Frankie nodded. "I better get back. I don't like leaving Earl alone with that physical therapist for too long. He's a great therapist and we don't want to scare the guy away right off the bat." She spun on her heel and headed for the door, calling out over her shoulder, "Y'all eat up. There's plenty more if you're still hungry afterward."

"Break time?" Cheyenne asked, eyeing the sandwiches on the tray Jo held.

"Break time," Brooks confirmed.

They dug into the BLT sandwiches with gusto, relishing every mouthful as they sat on the edge of the deck and dangled their legs off the side. Cheyenne sat between Brooks and Jo, and the three of them gazed at the horses as they milled about in the pasture.

"How much more do we have to do?" Cheyenne asked between bites of her sandwich.

Brooks shielded his eyes and glanced up. The sun had dipped lower toward the horizon but there was plenty of daylight left. Enough so that they might be able to finish the ramp by dark.

"Oh, we've gotten the worst part of it out of the way," he said. "If we get started as soon as we finish eating, we should be able to knock out the rest by dark." He glanced over at Jo, who drank deeply from a bottle of water. "This time tomorrow, Earl will be sitting out here, watching the horses, and feeling the sun on his face."

Jo set the bottle of water on the deck, leaned back on her hands, and smiled, meeting his eyes. "Thank you so much for this, Brooks."

Brooks held her gaze and smiled back. His hand, resting on the deck behind him only a couple feet from hers, itched to reach out and glide along her soft cheek. But he refrained, choosing instead to admire her smile and savor the warmth in her voice.

"You're welcome," he whispered.

They sat there for almost an hour, admiring the view, soaking up the warm sun and the cool fall breeze, and watching the horses amble about the pasture.

Then Cheyenne, still gazing at the horses, whispered, "I kinda like this."

Brooks glanced at her somber expression. "You like what?"

Cheyenne looked down at the empty sandwich wrapper and bottle in her hand, then sneaked a shy glance at him and Jo. "The horses, food, drink, and work. Being here with y'all." She peered ahead, her gaze fixed on the dancing leaves of the oak trees that bordered his property in the distance. "I like not being alone."

"Yeah." Brooks studied her, then Jo, seated by his side. Watched the way they studied the peaceful view before them in the comforting stillness. "So do I."

It was amazing how one thoroughbred could change everything.

Jo stood in the pasture behind the main house at Lone Oaks Crossing and smiled at the chestnut colt standing in front of her. "Whatcha think, baby boy? You feel up to meeting someone new today?"

Another Round dipped his head and nudged her shoulder. His nose worked overtime, sifting through the unfamiliar scents floating on the fall air of his new home.

"You all right over there, Cheyenne?" Jo asked, eyeing the teen as she slowly walked across the grass to join them.

"Yeah." Cheyenne's eyes remained fixed on Another Round. "Will he . . . um, bite?"

Jo shrugged. "I can't tell you with one hundred percent certainty what he will or won't do. Horses have a mind of their own. Likes and dislikes. Preferences. If one of us were to do something he didn't like, he might very well nip. But if you're respectful of his space and comfort level, you won't have anything to worry about."

Cheyenne listened intently to her words, but the eager excitement she'd displayed yesterday afternoon about becoming Another Round's groom had faded overnight—or at least, once she had come face-to-face with the thoroughbred.

Jo didn't blame her. Horses could be intimidating to a lot of people, especially if they hadn't had prior experience with them. But despite her obvious worries, Cheyenne had seemed more than willing to embark on the new adventure of learning to groom the thoroughbred.

After they'd finished building the wheelchair ramp yesterday evening, Brooks had said his goodbyes and returned home, leaving Jo and Cheyenne to join Frankie and Earl for dinner, then retire for the night. Jo had been anxious to show the new deck and wheelchair ramp to Earl, but his eyes had grown heavy at the kitchen table during dinner, and it had become obvious that he would not stay awake for much longer. Instead, Jo and Frankie had helped Earl to bed early while Cheyenne had washed the dishes. Jo had thanked Cheyenne once more for her help that day and reminded her to set an alarm, be up, dressed, and down at the stables by the time the first light began to trickle over the horizon the next morning.

Cheyenne had done exactly as instructed. Earlier, she'd been waiting by Another Round's stall when Jo had arrived, and they'd led the other horses out to a pasture, while Another Round enjoyed a separate pasture of his own; then they'd mucked the stalls. Now, here they stood, under full morning sunlight, a stack of grooming tools nearby and Another Round waiting patiently for attention.

"So, what do I do first?" Cheyenne asked, eyeing Another Round.

"He's going to need extra attention compared to the other horses," Jo said. "To be a great groom and for a racehorse, you need to do certain things in a certain order every day," she stressed. "But first, you need to let him get to know and trust you."

Jo moved closer to Another Round's side, stroked his neck gently, and whispered in a low voice to him. After a moment, she glanced over her shoulder at Cheyenne. "Do you hear the way I'm speaking to him? Slowly, calmly, and with reassurance?"

Cheyenne nodded.

"This is how you should always approach him," Jo said. "You need to be consistent with your demeanor, touch, voice, and interactions. Once you get to know him better, you can relax a little, share more of yourself, and he'll share more with you. But for now, you need to play it by the book." She held out one hand toward Cheyenne. "Come closer."

Cheyenne walked over slowly, placed her hand in Jo's, and allowed her to lift and settle her palm against Another Round's neck.

"There," Jo said softly. "Talk to him. Touch him gently and allow him some time to get to know your voice and touch."

Jo stepped back but remained close enough to be on hand if needed. But, after a few minutes of Cheyenne speaking softly to Another Round, it was evident that the thoroughbred had taken to the girl almost as quickly as she had taken to him. His strong muscles relaxed, and his head nudged her palm, seeking her touch.

"Looks like he enjoys your attention." Jo smiled. "Horses pick up on things, you know? They can sense your mood and emotions. Seems like he's at ease with you. Maybe he senses the two of you have quite a bit in common."

Cheyenne glanced up, a shy smile appearing. "You think so?"

Jo nodded. "It looks that way. Though for the next few days, at least, I'd like you to continue following my lead, learning the routine, and getting to know Another Round better before you take over, okay?"

Cheyenne nodded eagerly. "So, what's the routine?"

Jo walked over to the stack of grooming tools, grabbed a brush, and returned to join Cheyenne and Another Round. "Do you remember what we did in the stables before we brought Another Round out to the pasture?"

"We checked his feet," Cheyenne said.

"We did," Jo affirmed. "We checked his hooves to make sure they were clean and healthy. Seemingly little things like a crack or ridge on the outer wall can tip you off to a potential injury or significant change in health. Checking his shoes—racing plates—every day is essen-

tial. I also checked his legs for injury or any signs of in-
fection. It may sound redundant to do it every day, but if
you want to be the best groom—"

"I do," Cheyenne piped in excitedly.

Jo grinned. "Then you must be very thorough every
day on every level. As a groom, you are Another Round's
caretaker. The person who will know him the best and
look out for him."

"Like a guardian angel?" Cheyenne asked, gazing up
at Another Round.

Jo studied the eagerness in Cheyenne's eyes. The desperate longing in the girl's voice reminded her of Cheyenne's misfortunes in life. Cheyenne was tough on the
outside, but it was very possible that beneath that gritty
exterior, a frightened, lonely little girl still desperately
sought affection. Affection that was much easier to trust
and accept when it came from a horse.

I like not being alone.

Jo blinked back the sting of tears as she recalled Cheyenne's words the afternoon before. For some reason, her
comment had struck a chord in Jo and Brooks, too, judging by the tone in his voice when he'd responded.

So do I.

All three of them, in fact, had remained seated on the
newly constructed deck after Cheyenne had shared the sentiment, staring out at the horses in the pasture and the line
of oak trees in the distance, remaining silent but somehow
connected on a deeper level.

Jo had to admit, it had been nice having someone by
her side yesterday afternoon—two someones, really—
who were working alongside her, with her rather than
against her. And the fact that Brooks had initiated the
venture with his act of goodwill had made the moment
even sweeter.

What was it he'd said in the stables the other day?

We'd make a good team.

Yep. After completing the deck and wheelchair ramp with him yesterday, she had to admit they did make a good team and probably would do so in other arenas. Maybe even racing? Or something more?

"There's something about horses," Jo said quietly, meeting Cheyenne's eyes. "Something about being with them, outside under the sun, the grass beneath your feet and blue sky overhead. It's nothing like being stuffed inside the concrete walls of a school or foster home." She studied Cheyenne's expression. "You can be yourself here and the relationship you develop with Another Round can bring a deeper level of meaning to your life, if you're willing to open up and allow it."

A solemn look entered Cheyenne's expression as she stroked Another Round's neck gently. "I like what you said yesterday. About horses being better than people." She looked at Jo, her own eyes glistening beneath the morning sunlight. "You said they are always honest. That they don't play games with you like people do, right?"

Jo nodded. "Right."

Cheyenne returned her attention to Another Round and whispered something into the thoroughbred's ear.

"First up," Jo said, "we clean his mane and tail." She walked toward the back of Another Round. "It's dangerous to stand behind a horse who's not familiar with you, so I'll take care of his tail today and once you've formed a bond of trust with him, you'll take over this task, too. For now, come stand to the side and watch how I do it."

Jo took her time, carefully brushing the horse's tail, dislodging bits of shavings from the stall, dirt, and specks of dust. Once that was finished, she led Cheyenne toward Another Round's head, stroked his neck, and spoke gently to him for a few moments, then flipped his mane over and began brushing through it.

"It helps to flip his mane over first," Jo said as she worked. "Doing that helps get the dirt from underneath so you can clean it more effectively. When you finish brushing in this direction, you flip it back to its natural side and brush through it some more. Just move carefully and gently."

Once they finished that step, Jo led Cheyenne through wetting the brush and combing down the mane and tail until they shined. Next, Jo retrieved a spongelike brush with no bristles and began brushing down Another Round's head and body.

"Use this tool to brush the rest of him. It feels like a cat's tongue to him and is more comfortable." Jo brushed gently underneath Another Round's belly. "It's important to brush every part of his body, especially the parts you don't normally see. Some grooms skip that step, but if you want to be the best and if you want to have a race-horse in great health, you'll do this thoroughly every day."

Cheyenne watched raptly as Jo worked her way through the process.

After Jo finished brushing Another Round's face and body, she set the scrubber down, picked up a clean towel from the stack of supplies, and held it out to Cheyenne. "Here. This is the next-to-last step. Take the towel and wipe him down everywhere I brushed. That removes whatever dust might remain on his coat to leave him shiny and eye-catching."

Smiling, Cheyenne began gently smoothing the towel over Another Round's back. "I think he's already eye-catching. What's the last step after this?"

"Oh, that'd be the quarter marks," a deep voice drawled behind them.

A tall man, decked out in a tailored business suit and expensive boots strolled across the backyard to the pasture, leaned on the white fence, and lifted his chin at Cheyenne. "You put quarter marks on to emphasize his muscles and give him some glamor." He gestured toward Another Round. "I take it that's Brooks Moore's thoroughbred?" He looked at Jo, a charming, but somewhat sly grin lifting his lips. "That would make you Jo Beth Ellis, I presume?"

Frowning, Jo surveyed the man. He appeared to be several years older than Brooks but had an equally impressive physique, blond hair, and green eyes. It was the latter that bothered Jo. His gaze, though direct, lacked warmth and sincerity even though he exhibited a pleasant façade.

"You presume quite a bit," Jo said, "considering you took it upon yourself to wander onto a stranger's property uninvited and ask questions about their horse."

Laughing, the man leaned his elbows on the fencing. "My apologies. I forgot we haven't been formally introduced." He held out his tan hand, his nails clean and immaculately manicured. "I'm Spencer Harris. I live up the road a few miles. Maybe you've heard of me?"

Cheyenne had stopped wiping Another Round with the towel. She stared at Spencer, a look of dismay on her face. "Why would she have heard of you?"

He grinned wider. "Because I breed the best thoroughbreds in the nation, sweetheart. Ones that would outshine even"—he pointed at Another Round—"this one, here."

Cheyenne scowled. "So what? That's supposed to make you tough shi—?"

"Cheyenne," Jo said. "Please finish wiping down Another Round. It'll make Earl happy to see his coat shining under the sun in the pasture when he's able to come out and sit on the deck this afternoon." She walked over to the fence, ducked between the rails, and joined Spencer on the other side. "Wait here," she said to Cheyenne, "while I have a word with our guest."

She glanced at Spencer, noting the slight dimming of his smile as she led him away from the pasture and across the backyard before facing him again.

He followed her lead, stopping when she did, and casually slid his hands into the pants pockets of his suit. "I didn't mean to interrupt."

Oh, he had. That much she could tell right off the bat. She couldn't put her finger on it, but something about him was too slick. Too sly.

"What can I help you with, Mr. Harris?" she asked.

"Spencer, please." His grin returned. "I doubt you're quite as formal with Brooks."

Jo narrowed her eyes. "You're on my property, Mr. Harris, and you're taking up my time. Either you get to the heart of why you're here or you stroll those shiny boots back across my yard and go back to where you came from."

He smiled wider. The crisp fall wind picked up, sweeping across the ground and shoving his blond hair over his brow. He pushed it back with one hand, his gaze roving over her from head to toe. "I didn't expect you to be so direct, Jo."

"It's Ms. Ellis," she said. "And get to it before I toss you out."

He held her gaze and his smile lost its forced charm, becoming only an emotionless baring of teeth. "I thought

I'd let you know you have competition up the road, Ms. Ellis."

Jo tilted her head. "What competition might that be?"

"The finest thoroughbred ever to hit the track." He gestured toward Another Round, still being wiped down in the pasture. "Better than that one, even. You're getting in over your head with Brooks." His gaze moved over her again, slowly, insultingly. "I just thought I'd let you know. Be a good neighbor and all."

Jo stiffened. "It's nice of you to offer your neighborly advice, Mr. Harris, but I assure you I'm not in need of it."

He lifted his chin, his tongue sweeping across his lower lip. "You're not training that thoroughbred then?"

Jo raised one brow. "That's none of your business, Mr. Harris."

He returned her stare for a few moments, then glanced around, his eyes scanning the grounds. "This is a nice place," he said softly. "But I understand you're having a bit of trouble lately." He looked at her again, a mocking expression of sympathy crossing his face. "My best wishes to your grandfather, Earl. I understand he's had some health problems of late."

Jo remained silent.

When she didn't respond, he withdrew his hands from his pockets and placed them on his lean hips, shifting from one shiny boot to the other. "Look," he said, his tone softer . . . more cajoling. "I know you think Brooks can help you, but he can't." He leaned closer, his broad chest encroaching a bit too much for Jo's comfort, but she resisted the urge to step back. "I know he sank a lot of money into this place, and I know he brought that thoroughbred around here for you to train. I know he's telling you he can solve your problems if you team up with him, but what he's not telling you is that his intentions aren't honorable."

Jo laughed. "You're telling me yours are?"

"He wants your help to get back at me," he said softly. "That's what Brooks wants—to get revenge—that's all. Join my team instead, Ms. Ellis, and you'll work with the most prized thoroughbreds in the business. I'll pay off your debt—including what you owe for breach of contract and your broken lease in Stone Hill. I'll make sure Lone Oaks Crossing stays in your family and I'll leave you with a nice tidy sum of cash in hand to take care of your grandfather's medical needs."

Inwardly, Jo cringed. This man—this stranger—knew way too much about her life. "I don't know you, Mr. Harris, but I can tell you this isn't a neighborly way to approach someone. Whatever you're offering, I'm not interested."

He eased away from her, a stony expression appearing. "You're a talented woman, Jo. You'd be a treasure to any stable owner . . . any man, even." The slick tone of his voice sent a shudder through her. "You want to train again? See another winner across the finish line at Churchill Downs? Just say the word and I'll make it happen."

"And if I don't?" she asked.

He grinned again, a sinister twist of his mouth. "If a horse you've trained steps on that track," he said, "you're either on Brooks's team or mine. That's your only option. Brooks may have money now but he's no better than he was years ago. No better than that weak, gambling addict of a father of his who took his own life when he couldn't face his losses."

Jo bit her lip, an overwhelming mix of anger, disgust, and pain swelling within her.

"He's alone," he added softly. "Brooks is a nobody who's got no one. That's why he's trying to sucker you into training that horse of his. You partner up with him and you'll get nothing but bad luck. I'd hate to see some-one of your talent—and charms—lose what little you have left."

"Leave." She pointed at the driveway. "Now."

Spencer stood there a moment more, surveying the grounds, then glanced once more over his shoulder at Another Round. "The kid's right. That horse is eye-catching," he drawled, strolling past Jo toward the driveway. "Eye-catching as can be."

Jo stood there, frozen in place, watching as he saun-tered off, then disappeared around the front of the house, his scornful words resounding in her head with each painful beat of her heart.

Brooks is a nobody who's got no one.

CHAPTER 8

B rooks leaned back in his office chair and scanned the papers spread out across his desk. Each page he'd printed detailed the specifics of one of the races leading up to the Kentucky Derby. It had been almost two weeks since Rhett had quit, and although Another Round had been exercised by other riders in his stable, the thoroughbred had not been worked out, to Brooks's knowledge, since he'd delivered him to Jo at Lone Oaks Crossing.

For Another Round to have a fighting chance on the track, Brooks had to put together a training program fast and schedule the races Another Round would run in as soon as possible. The schedule would be tight, considering the time needed to prepare Another Round for competition and ensure he had enough opportunities to earn the winning points required to qualify for the Derby.

Sighing, Brooks propped his elbows on his desk and pored over the papers again, sifting through the details of each race, eyeing the locations and dates.

The Breeders' Cup Juvenile in November would more

than likely be the first race that Another Round would be ready for if the thoroughbred began regular workouts immediately. Then, possibly the Gun Runner Stakes in New Orleans in December. There were a few other races in February that he could consider as well as the Rebel Stakes in Arkansas in late February.

But first, he had to find a new trainer.

Brooks shoved the papers away and sagged back into his chair, dragging his hand over his face. The problem was that he didn't want another trainer. He wanted Jo.

If he could only let Jo go, the idea of having her as a partner, and simply choose another trainer—anyone at this point—he'd have a better shot at racing Another Round. By continuing in limbo like this, waiting for Jo to change her mind, he was endangering any opportunity he might have to enter Another Round into any race, much less train him to be competitive enough to win enough races to qualify for the Derby in May.

Brooks closed his eyes and squeezed the bridge of his nose. Everything would be so simple if he could just move on and choose another trainer.

His cell phone, resting on the edge of his desk, vibrated. He answered the call.

"Mr. Moore," the voice on the other end of the line said. "You asked me to notify you if Ms. Ellis returned."

It was his security guard.

"Yes, Vince," Brooks said. "When did she arrive?"

"Just now, sir. I let her in immediately as you requested. She's on her way to the main house now."

Heartbeat racing, Brooks stood and headed for the door of his office. "Thank you, Vince."

Slipping his phone in his pocket, he walked down the hallway, crossed the foyer, and went outside. Moments later, a truck he recognized as belonging to Earl drove up

and parked. The driver's side door opened, and Jo exited
the truck, rounded the front of it, and stood several feet
away, looking up at him.

He smiled, just the sight of her setting his tense muscles at ease. "This is a pleasant surprise. How's Earl
today? Has he had a chance to test out the deck?"

It was a cool September afternoon, and she'd dressed
for the occasion. The faded jeans she wore clung to her
curves, and her long wavy hair spilled over the collar of
her denim jacket, shining in the afternoon sun. His hands
flexed at his sides, yearning to sift through the shiny
strands and feel their soft texture between his fingertips.

"Who is Spencer Harris?" she asked. "And why does
he have it out for you?"

Brooks froze at the sound of the other man's name, his
hands curling into fists by his sides. "It's the other way
around actually," he said quietly. "Why are you asking
me about Spencer Harris?"

She stared up at him, her big blue eyes searching his
expression as always, seeking answers he wasn't quite
ready to give. "I just bumped into him," she said. "Or
rather, he bumped into me. He left Lone Oaks Crossing a
little while ago."

Brooks frowned. "Why was he at L—?"

"He stopped by to introduce himself," she continued.
"To let me know who he is and, I suspect, to see exactly
who I am. He knew about you wanting me to train Another Round."

Brooks bit his lip and looked away, his eyes scanning
the green acres of his estate, staring blindly at the groups
of guests strolling from stables to distillery.

"He knew about Lone Oaks Crossing being in financial trouble," she said. "He knew about me owing money
for breaking my teaching contract and my apartment

lease. And . . . he knows Earl is having health trouble and accumulating a pile of medical bills."

Brooks's attention snapped back to her, the flash of fear in her eyes matching the fleeting tremble in her voice as she spoke Earl's name. His fists tightened. "Did he threaten you? What did he say to you?"

"Enough to let me know there's bad blood between the two of you and that if I don't want to lose Lone Oaks Crossing, I should either join his team or stay away from the racetrack and from you."

Brooks clenched his jaw so tightly he thought his teeth would shatter, but he forced himself to remain silent, rather than risk losing his temper in front of Jo.

She took a hesitant step toward him, then stopped, her blue eyes seeking his. "Brooks? What did he do to you?"

Brooks held her gaze and slowly unfurled his fists. "I told you I had a family once and that I lost my father and mother years ago. What I didn't tell you was that my father was a gambling addict. That he lost everything—our home, his money, and self-respect. Most people knew he had a gambling addiction, but they also knew he had a family. My father wasn't careful with his money. He lost everything to Spencer Harris and his father. They took advantage of his addiction and when he lost it all—including our farm—they put us out on the street. My father was so ashamed, he took his own life, and my mother passed not long after. Losing him was too much for her to bear."

Jo remained silent as he spoke, tears coating her lower lashes.

"Don't feel sorry for me, Jo," he rasped. "Don't pity me."

"I don't," she whispered. "I just want you to know you're not alone."

Her soft words drove through him, threatening to weaken

his resolve. To dissolve his steely intent to do what was right—to claim the vengeance his father should have had.

"Spencer Harris took everything from my family," he forced out through stiff lips. "I only aim to take back what's mine."

Jo's brow creased and she glanced around her, eyeing his estate. "What more could you possibly need?"

"My family's honor. My father's name. My self-respect. Every damn thing you can't buy and that can almost never be recovered once lost."

She blinked up at him then slowly walked over, stopping mere inches from him, close enough that he could feel the warmth radiating from her skin and smell the sweet fragrance of her hair.

"Spencer Harris has none of those things," she whispered. "And there's more honor in you than any man I've ever known. You're not the man I thought you were when we first met. You're better . . . the best kind of man. And you're worth more than a million Spencer Harrises of this world."

Her hands lifted, her warm palms cupping his jaw, her fingers sliding into the hair at his nape. She lifted to her toes and parted his lips with hers, her kiss soft, slow, and tender, conjuring up a swirl of emotions within him that he'd never felt before. Emotions so strong that he had to wrap his arms around her, pull her close, and hold on, just to stay steady, just to keep his feet solid and on the ground.

When she pulled away, cool air rushed in and the intoxicating taste of her on his lips and tongue faded with each passing second, provoking a surge of fear that he'd never felt before. The urge to cover her mouth with his again, to pull her close, hold her tight, and never let go was strong, but he forced himself to remain still, save for keeping his hands snug at her waist, where the feel of her warm flesh beneath his palms was a small comfort.

"Is revenge the only reason you're doing this?" she whispered, her hands smoothing over his chest, leaving a trail of fire in their wake. "Is it the only reason you want to race Another Round?"

He leaned into the slight pressure of her palms and lowered his head, touching his forehead to hers. "At first, but now . . ."

"Now?" She smoothed her hands up his chest and cradled his jaw, tipping up his face, and bringing his eyes to hers. "Will this feud with Spencer end with the Derby? Win or lose, will it end there?"

He wished it would. He wished he could give her a definitive answer, tell her that a win at the Derby would restore his sense of pride and self-respect. That a win over Spencer would banish the anger, pain, and resentment he still carried, but he couldn't.

"I don't know, Jo."

She stared up at him for a few moments longer, then closed her eyes and stepped back, her hands slowly—reluctantly, it seemed—trailing away from him. "In Spencer Harris's eyes, we're already in this together. Any loss you suffer, Earl and Lone Oaks Crossing will suffer as well if Spencer Harris has his way. You've helped me, so now it's time for me to help you."

She turned away and walked back to the truck.

"Jo—"

"You're not alone, Brooks. You've got yourself a trainer." She faced him again, brushing her hair back from her cheeks, her fingertips lingering briefly on her lips as she looked up at him, studying his mouth. "We're

a team now. So, we had better start planning. I'll break
the news to Earl and Frankie. We'll need their help—and
Cheyenne's—and the sooner we get started, the better."

"You're not obligated to do this, Jo."

"I know," she said. "But I'm your neighbor . . . and
friend. And friends don't turn their backs on each other.
Swing by the farm in the morning—same time as usual—
and we'll get started."

Brooks stood there, overcome with so many conflict-
ing emotions he couldn't define them. He watched as Jo
climbed back into the cab of Earl's truck, cranked the engine, and drove away, waiting until the truck disappeared
over a hill in the distance. Then he pulled out a cell
phone, dialed the number he'd memorized years ago, and
waited for the other person to answer.

"Brooks," a male voice drawled on the other end of the
line. "I figured I'd hear from you, just not quite so soon."

There was gleeful menace in Spencer Harris's tone. It
had always grated on Brooks's nerves.

"I understand you've been to Lone Oaks Crossing,"
Brooks said quietly, his eyes fixing on the line of oak
trees that separated his property from Earl's.

"I may have stopped by," Spencer said. "To introduce
myself and pay a neighborly visit."

"What's between us," Brooks said, "remains between
us. You're reaching too far this time."

"Who says I'm reaching? When you're in the game,
Brooks, you're in the game."

"As of now, I consider Lone Oaks Crossing an extension of my property. You're to keep your distance."

Spencer's low chuckle crossed the line. There was a
hint of menace in his tone this time. "You've always been
territorial, Brooks. First, Rose Farm. Now, Lone Oaks
Crossing. Do you consider Jo your property, too?"

Brooks clenched his teeth. "As I said, what's between us, stays between us. Keep your distance—especially from Jo."

"Oh, but now that you consider Lone Oaks Crossing your property," Spencer drawled, "that makes the land and whoever inhabits it yours, which means they're fair game." Silence fell across the line for a moment, then Spencer continued. "All you have to do—all you've ever had to do—was give me a call, like you've done today, and let go of that grudge you've been holding against me for decades. Neither I, nor my father, is the monster you try to make us out to be."

Brooks continued staring at the oak trees, watching the leaves on their branches flutter in the cool breeze, some falling to the ground. "You're not monsters, Spencer. You're opportunists. You take whatever you want, without concern for others." He tilted his head, listening to the breeze. "I'm just setting things right. Taking my turn at the table, so to speak. Growing my wealth and business as you sought to grow your own over the years. Only, I've chosen to do it the fair way." His muscles tightened. The image of Jo's tender expression as she stared up at him minutes earlier exposed a vulnerability within him he hadn't known he possessed. "Until now. Stay away from Jo, her family, and Lone Oaks Crossing, or I may see fit to change my strategy."

Brooks disconnected the call and shoved the cell phone back into his pocket. He stood there for a while, scanning his extensive estate, thriving business, and the guests milling about his property. Then his attention returned to the line of trees separating his property from Earl's. A sense of fear he hadn't experienced since his time spent in Dream House, when he'd grieved his parents and wondered about his future, resurfaced. Until now, his losses had been his own. His risks only affected his business, his home, and his land. But things had changed.

Jo, an innocent party—a woman he found himself falling for—had just been placed right in the middle of his conflict with Spencer.

Jo drove up the driveway of Lone Oaks Crossing and parked the truck, cut the engine, and slumped over the steering will, resting her forehead against her hands.

What had she done? What had she just gotten herself into?

Lifting her head, she looked at the main house, then glanced at the stable and rolling hills of her family farm. She had no choice but to defend her home and her family. Spencer Harris might not have come right out and said he would steal Lone Oaks Crossing from under Earl, but the threat—however unspoken—remained all the same.

It had only taken moments for Jo to sense Harris's real nature and ill intentions. During her time training horses years ago, she'd learned to sense the true nature of each horse she encountered. And as a teacher, she'd learned to spot ill intent in the students she worked with as well as assess their needs and limitations.

Spencer Harris was a different breed of man from those she'd encountered in her lifetime. He was, she admitted ruefully, the exact opposite of Brooks.

Her hand rose absently, her fingertips trailing across her lips, which still tingled from the feel of Brooks's mouth against her own. Even now, after leaving his presence, driving the short distance between their homes, and achieving distance from his magnetic appeal, she could still feel his presence, sense the pressure of his palms and strong fingers cradling her waist as he'd deepened their kiss.

Brooks had been tender and gentle in all of her interactions with him.

Spencer, however, was ruthless and aggressive. The disgusting man's words had conveyed more meaning than he'd probably suspected. The man had it in for Brooks, made no secret of it, and appeared more than willing—almost eager—to bring down anyone who got in his way of inflicting damage. Jo turned her head, her eyes seeking the familiar line of oaks at the edge of Lone Oaks Crossing. The trees weren't the only dividing line between herself and Brooks. A massive amount of wealth, possessions, and power lay at her neighbor's disposal. But Brooks didn't wield those things in the same way that Spencer did. Brooks used his resources for good purposes, graciously loaning her money to stave off foreclosure of Earl's farm, going above and beyond to bring her new boarders, and providing a helping hand to children in need like Cheyenne, who had, in the short time since she'd arrived at Lone Oaks Crossing, sensed the peaceful serenity and security the farm provided.

I kinda like . . . not being alone.

Jo closed her eyes at the memory of Cheyenne's words, picturing Brooks as a young teenager, around Cheyenne's age, alone at Dream House, grieving the loss of his parents and family home alone, unsure of what the next day might hold for him and who would be there to help him through it. Wet heat burned her eyes and she blinked hard, staving off a fresh surge of tears.

Brooks, from what little he'd shared with her about his

conflict with Spencer and the damage the other man had inflicted upon Brooks's family, had every reason to be angry, vengeful, and to despise Spencer.

But that wasn't Brooks's true nature from what she'd seen.

Brooks was a far better man than Spencer could ever dream of becoming. And she knew, for a fact, that Brooks was a kind man. More than that. Brooks was the best of men.

Jo pressed her hand to her chest, where a strong surge of emotion throbbed. She, of all people, knew how much could transpire in the two minutes or less that comprised the Derby. Lives were made or broken on the racetrack in the flash of a millisecond. But she'd never anticipated her heart opening so quickly to a man she barely knew . . . but whom her heart insisted she'd known forever.

Jo wiped her eyes and exited the truck, trying not to focus on the layers of obstacles today's events had introduced. Instead, she strode purposefully toward the back of the main house and focused on what needed to be done now.

To beat Spencer on the track—and hopefully in whatever other way Brooks sought to achieve—they needed to form a team, formulate a plan, and put both to action as soon as possible. And she needed to get Another Round into the best shape of his life, prepare him for the competition that lay ahead, and foster his passion for running to enable him to cross the finish line first.

It had been years since she'd trained. She just hoped she still had it in her.

"There she is." Frankie, seated on the newly built deck attached to the back of the main house, smiled and waved as Jo walked up the ramp toward her. "We've been wondering where you were." She looked at Earl, who sat in his wheelchair beside her, a small smile on his face and his head tilted toward the sun. "Earl had a hefty breakfast and felt pretty good today, so we decided to give this deck of y'all's a try. I think he's taken a liking to it."

Earl looked up at Jo and raised his hand toward her. "Beautiful."

The tears she'd fought earlier returned, and Jo blinked hard as she pulled a lawn chair over and sat in it beside Earl. "I'm glad you like it," she said, covering his hand with hers on the wheelchair's armrest. "It was Brooks's idea. He wanted you to be able to feel the sun on your face and have a nice view of the horses."

Earl, his eyes brightening, nodded and lifted his hand again, pointing at Cheyenne, who stood in the pasture in front of them, leaning against the rail, watching Another Round graze. "Beautiful," he repeated.

"That kid's giving me whiplash with her moods," Frankie mused, a small grin flickering across her mouth. "She's like a completely different kid now that you've introduced her to Another Round. Earl has had a hard time taking his eyes off that thoroughbred ever since Cheyenne finished up his grooming session an hour ago."

Jo studied Cheyenne, noting her relaxed stance and the peaceful expression on her face as her eyes followed Another Round, admiring his every movement . . . and possibly her handiwork.

"Cheyenne is proud of herself," Jo said, smiling. "As well she should be. She was very attentive this morning. She listened closely and followed my directions well. I think she could be an excellent groom and stable hand if she decides to be. She seems to love thoroughbreds."

Frankie laughed. "Too bad her online classes don't deal with them. Matter of fact, if they had horses at that school she was attending, she probably wouldn't be in the predicament she's in now. And she certainly wouldn't have had time to get herself into the trouble that obligated her to serve community service hours."

Jo shook her head. "No. Cheyenne probably would have taken a completely different path had something sparked her interest the way Another Round has. Some kids aren't meant for four walls and stifling, standardized restrictions. Sometimes open space, fresh air, and autonomy are more effective than any academic lesson in a classroom."

"Seems that way," Frankie said. "It's a good sign for your new plans, isn't it? I mean, if Cheyenne can find healing here, anyone can, right?"

Jo bit her lip, glancing at Frankie and then Earl. "Speaking of plans, that's what I wanted to talk to you both about. I just came from Brooks's place."

"Oh, yeah?" Frankie asked. "I thought that might be where you'd gotten off to. Does he have any other surprises for us?" She grinned. "Hopefully, not another foster child yet. I think our hands will be full with Cheyenne for a while."

Jo shook her head. "Actually, I had a surprise for him. I've agreed to train Another Round."

Earl, who'd watched her silently, returned his attention to Another Round, then glanced up at her, his eyes widening with surprise and what she suspected was excitement. "T-train?"

"You've agreed?" Frankie slid to the edge of her chair, a mixture of surprise and confusion in her expression. "But . . . you were adamant that it wasn't something you wanted to do." A hard glint flashed in her eyes. "Is Brooks holding something over your head? I know he's been very helpful to us, but it's not worth accepting his help if it means—"

"No," Jo said. "Brooks had very little to do with it. Did Cheyenne mention to you that we had a visitor this morning?"

Frankie nodded, her lips twisting. "She said some rich-looking dude stopped in and was asking about Another Round. Someone looking to buy him?"

Jo looked down, her hands fidgeting in her lap, wondering exactly how much to share in front of Earl. "Our visitor was Spencer Harris. And he wasn't interested in Another Round so much as he was interested in my association with Brooks."

A look of dismay crossed Frankie's features, and Earl, staring at her silently, frowned, too.

"The bottom line is this," Jo said. "Spencer has caused a lot of trouble for Brooks over the years and there's bad blood between them. The man seems determined to make life difficult for Brooks and, I assume, the intention is mutual for Brooks." She looked at Earl, her tone hesitant. "I could walk away from that—from a disagreement between two men, I mean. But Spencer mentioned Lone Oaks Crossing's financial troubles this morning. And from the impression I got of him, he would have no qualms about taking this farm away from us if it meant hurting Brooks."

Earl's hands clenched the arms of his wheelchair and a muscle in his jaw ticked.

"He threatened in a veiled way to make things difficult for us if I didn't walk away from Brooks and his thoroughbred." She looked at Earl then, her eyes appealing to his. "I know the last thing we need is risk right now, but Brooks has done a lot for us. And," she whispered, looking down, "he's a good man that I've grown to admire. I think it's time we returned the favor."

Earl's expression changed. He leaned closer, a fierce

light in his eyes and a proud smile stretching across his face. "Get Lee. You . . . train him."

Jo reached out and cupped Earl's cheek in her palm, her voice firm and encouraging. "No," she said softly. "I'll find Lee, and then *we'll* train him. Together, like the winning team we used to be."

CHAPTER 9

The next morning, five minutes after the sun rose, Brooks drove up the long driveway of Lone Oaks Crossing and parked his truck in front of the main house. Before he could exit the cab, Jo had already opened the passenger door, hopped in, shut the door, and pointed back to the driveway.

"Let's go," Jo said.

Brooks glanced over at her from the driver seat and frowned. "Go where?"

"To Anderson Stables," she said. "To pick up your jockey."

"My jockey? I wasn't aware I had one."

"And that's exactly why we're going," she said. "You can't race a thoroughbred without a rider. And I've found the perfect one."

"Without me meeting him first?"

Jo raised one eyebrow. "What makes you think it's a him?"

Brooks's lean cheeks flushed, and he shrugged his shoulders. "Okay, then. Who is she?"

Jo settled back in the passenger seat and buckled her seat belt. "You were right the first time. Our new jockey is a he."

And it had taken hours to track him down.

Yesterday afternoon, after breaking the news of their new venture to Frankie and Earl, Jo had dug through the old belongings in her room at the main house, searching through drawers, old albums, and address books from ten years ago. After hours of hunting, she had managed to find the number of the man she'd been looking for.

Lee Simmons. One of the best—if not the best—jockeys Jo had ever known. An integral part of the team Lone Oaks Crossing once had in residence with Earl at the helm.

Jo hadn't seen or heard from Lee in years, but she remembered how impressed she'd been with his passion for the sport and the horses he rode. He'd started interning early—just as she had, waking up at the crack of dawn, following a rigorous training routine that involved stringent workouts, healthy eating, and strict attention to the pounds on the scale. Despite the challenging regimen, she couldn't remember him ever complaining—not even once.

Even early in his career, Lee had possessed an innate gift for quickly determining a thoroughbred's strengths and weaknesses and would tailor his approach to match each horse's unique abilities. And Lee had been fearless—almost to a fault. He'd remained calm in the face of overwhelming challenges on the track, maintaining his focus and encouraging the thoroughbreds he worked with to do the same.

She and Earl had been blessed to have Lee on their

team ten years ago and she doubted, wholeheartedly, that they would have achieved what they had if Lee had not been part of their team.

Jo hoped—and prayed—Lee would bring the same energy, discipline, and talent to Brooks's thoroughbred and guide Another Round to a Derby win despite the misfortune they'd suffered ten years ago. A misfortune that had proven to be not only her downfall but Lee's as well. The loss of Sweet Dash had been too much for Lee to bear, and from what she'd been told by Lee's current employer, he had abandoned racing not long after, just as she had, and ventured out on his own in search of a fresh start.

Only, she suspected things hadn't quite turned out as well as Lee had perhaps hoped. But there was no need to share that bit of information with Brooks just now. And besides, once Brooks met Lee, he'd recognize the rare qualities Lee possessed that made him the perfect jockey for Another Round.

"So," Brooks asked. "Who is this fantastic new jockey you've found?"

"Lee Simmons," she said. "He's the first and only jockey that came to my mind yesterday."

Brooks put the truck in drive and headed down the driveway. "You've worked with him before?"

"Yeah." Jo looked out the passenger window, staring at the highway. "I worked with him years ago."

Brooks reached the end of the driveway and stopped the truck. "Years ago? As in the year you won the Derby?"

"That would be the one." She gestured toward the road in front of them. "Take a left here. The stable he's working at is about an hour and forty-five minutes away. I know a couple back roads that might get us there faster though."

The truck remained parked as Brooks stared at her, his

brow creasing. "This Lee you're talking about . . . he rode Sweet Dash, right?"

Jo looked down and picked at one of her thumbnails. "Yeah."

"Did he ride Sweet Dash in the Preakness Stakes, too?"

Jo bit her lip. "Yeah."

Brooks sighed. "And this is the jockey you think would be a good rider for Another Round?"

Jo looked up and spoke firmly. "Lee is a great rider. What happened to Sweet Dash wasn't his fault. A horse could have the best rider in the world and still stumble. Lee had no control over what happened."

Brooks studied her face. "What other horses has he raced?"

Jo held his gaze. "None. Sweet Dash was the first."

"And he hasn't ridden in competition at all since then?"

"No," she confirmed quietly. "He started interning young—around thirteen, I think—with his uncle. Then at sixteen, he started homeschooling like me and took jockeying up pretty much full-time, training on a regular schedule. He had an innate talent for riding that you just can't teach someone. Everyone noticed it. I haven't seen or heard from him in years though. The old cell number I had for him didn't work, so I called a few more of my connections to track him down. From what I've been told, he took what happened to Sweet Dash pretty hard. He walked away from racing like I did and has been traveling and taking up odd jobs since then."

Brooks leaned his head back against his headrest and rolled his eyes toward the ceiling of the truck. "And you really think he will give us the best shot at winning the Derby? Someone who hasn't raced or trained in years?"

"I'm telling you he's the best. He had an awful experience—just like I did—and it devastated him. But he's a natural rider who truly cares about his horses, and he deserves another shot at his dream." Jo reached over, placed her hand on his knee, and squeezed. "I wouldn't steer you wrong, Brooks. When I say he's the best, I mean it. I don't know what shape he's in so, yeah, it may take some extra effort to get him back in shape and acquainted with Another Round, but I believe he's the right choice."

Raising his head upright again, he looked down at her hand on his knee and covered it with his own, squeezing gently. "Okay. I trust you."

"And I trust him," Jo said softly. "Trust is the most important thing between a trainer, a jockey, and a horse. Lee knows what he's doing, and despite what happened to Sweet Dash, I trust Another Round with him."

Sighing, Brooks removed his hand from hers and cupped her cheek. "I trust your judgment, Jo. But Lee has already had a bad ride with Sweet Dash. What makes you think things will turn out any better with Another Round?"

"Nothing," she said. "Except hope and the fact that I'm willing to take a chance on him. Lee's a great rider and deserves another opportunity to make his dream come true. That's all any of us can do when it comes to racing—take a chance, right?"

Brooks was silent for a moment, then nodded. "All right. But if we're taking back roads to this place, you'll need to give me directions along the way."

Brooks took a left and they drove on. The journey to Anderson Stables, the farm where Lee was currently working, took almost as long as Jo had estimated, their travel time clocking in around one hour and thirty minutes. Because it was early on a weekday morning, traffic was light, but once they drove up the long winding entrance to Anderson Stables, it was clear everyone at the working farm had woken early and hit the ground running.

"This is a nice spread," Brooks said as he drove along the dirt road toward the main stable. "Do they breed or board?"

"Board," Jo said, craning her neck for a better view as they approached the main stable.

It was, as Brooks had put it, a nice spread. The large, main stable was white with stonework and housed multiple stalls. Two other stables and one barn were stationed on opposite sides of the grounds along with several paddocks and pastures enclosed with black fencing.

"Max Anderson, the owner, told me on the phone that they do a pretty good business even though they're a small operation compared to the larger farms in this area," Jo said. "He says he's short on help though, which is why he hired Lee."

She bit her tongue as soon as the last comment left her lips, wishing she'd thought better of it before speaking aloud.

"So, the only reason the owner of this stable hired Lee," Brooks repeated slowly, "is because he's short on help? Is that what you're telling me?"

Jo winced. "Um . . . yeah. That's the way he put it."

Brooks glanced at her as he parked the truck near the main stable and cut the engine. "And what else did he say about this Lee of yours?"

Jo shrugged, ducking her head and evading his dark, probing gaze. "Not much."

Just that Lee was on the verge of being fired. Apparently, Lee liked to sleep late, drink copious amounts of alcohol, and chase women. All of which had become an impediment to his job performance at Anderson Stables . . .

and the dozens of other jobs he'd lost as a stable hand over the past few years.

Jo forced a bright smile, opened her door, and hopped out. "Come on. Let's see if we can find him, shall we?"

Finding Lee turned out to be a bit harder than Jo had imagined. After leaving the truck, she and Brooks walked to the stables, introduced themselves to a tall stable hand named Zeb who, despite being shorthanded and obviously overworked, took the time to stop mucking a stall, set aside his shovel, and smile widely while introducing himself. His smile, however, vanished as soon as Jo asked about Lee.

"That sumbitch?" Zeb spat on the ground. "What you want with him?"

Brooks shot a look at Jo, the uneasy expression on his face intensifying.

"He's an old friend of mine," Jo said, shifting nervously from one boot to the other. "I'd just like to see him. Maybe catch up with him a bit. Max told me he was working here and said I could stop by and talk with him."

Zeb laughed. "Well, good luck with that. We've been looking for that loser all morning and still haven't set eyes on him yet. If you do manage to find him, tell him I'm looking for him and that if he doesn't show at his post, drunk or not, within the next ten minutes, I've a good mind to tell Max he ain't cutting it and give him the heave-ho. Matter of fact, I might just put my boot in his ass and kick him to the curb without even telling the boss. Considering the scant amount of work that boy's done, no one would miss him around here anyway."

With that, Zeb walked away and joined the other hands who were already busy mucking the stalls.

"Great," Brooks said, dragging a hand through his

hair. "Just great. This jockey of yours can't even manage to show up for a stable hand position sober and from Zeb's reaction, seems to be more trouble than he's worth." He scowled. "Not to mention the fact that they can't even find him. So, what do you propose we do now?"

Jo put on a brave face despite her misgivings. "We take a look around."

And they did. They must've walked at least two miles across Max Anderson's land, moving from paddock to paddock, pasture to pasture, and stable to stable, searching for Lee. He was nowhere to be found in the places they'd looked, so they returned to the main stable near the front of the property an hour later.

Stomach sinking, Jo stopped by the stable and thanked Zeb for taking the time to speak with them earlier. It wasn't until she joined Brooks walking back toward the truck that she heard a low moan emerge from behind two large bales of hay stacked beside the stable. She walked over to the bales, Brooks following close behind, and peered around them.

And there he was. Lee Simmons, in all his glory, with the bleary-eyed, slack-jawed expression of a hangover, lying on his back amid a bed of hay where, she guessed from his appearance, he'd spent the previous night.

"Lee?" she asked. "It is you, isn't it?"

He looked up at her from his sprawled position on the bed of hay and narrowed his eyes. "Jo?" His drunken slur was so thick she barely recognized her own name. "Jo Beef Ellis?"

Brooks, standing beside her, snorted.

Jo elbowed him and grimaced. "Beth," she stressed, staring down at Lee. "It's Jo Beth." She shook her head, taking in his disheveled appearance. His T-shirt, dirty and stained, was rolled up almost to his chin, exposing his potbelly. "Did you spend the night out here? What happened to you?"

Lee swiveled his head, straining to focus his gaze on his surroundings. "Don't know. Last thing I remembered I had a beer in each hand and a woman on each arm." He looked back up at her and grinned, a goofy expression on his face. "But I don't remember you being one of them. If you were, I would remember. 'Cuz you're the kinda gal a man wouldn't forget spending the night with."

"Hey, watch that." Brooks shook his head and stared down at Lee with disgust before narrowing his eyes at Jo. "There's no way I'm letting him get on Another Round."

Jo touched his arm. "But Brooks—"

"Nope." Brooks held up a hand. "Forget it. I'm not letting this rude, inebriated kid anywhere near you or my thoroughbred. How old is he anyway?"

"Around my age." Jo rubbed her temples. "He's older than he looks."

"Twenty-eight." Lee glared up at Brooks, his eyes not quite focusing on his face. "I'm twenty-eight and I bet you I can ride any horse you put in front of me. Gimme ten minutes," he slurred, "and I could ride a donkey across the finish line at the Derby and put him in first place." He grinned, gazing up at the sky as though an angel hovered above him, patting his head. "That's right. I'd ride that donkey right into first place."

Brooks raised one eyebrow, an exasperated tone entering his voice. "You plan on doing that with a beer in each hand, too?"

"Any horse would be proud for me to ride it"—he patted his belly—"beer gut and all. I'm the best rider there is." He hiccupped, then made a face, his confident expression drooping. "I mean . . . I used to be the best." He looked at Jo, his hazel eyes filling with tears. "Wasn't I, Jo Beef? Wasn't I the best back in the day?"

Oh, gracious. Despite his slovenly appearance, inebriated state, and slurred ramblings, there was still a hint of the old Lee in the pained expression on his face. The same young boy she'd known as a girl, both of them working hard to find their place in the sport, exerting themselves beyond expectations for a chance at winning. And when the win at the Derby had finally arrived, despite all the odds being stacked against them, she remembered the sheer joy that had enveloped Lee, the broad smile on his face as he'd entered the Winner's Circle, beaming with pride at the realization that all his hard work had finally paid off. And then . . . the crushing sorrow and desperation after his fall from Sweet Dash at the Preakness Stakes. The sheer anguish in his eyes at the news that the injuries the thoroughbred had sustained were dire enough to necessitate putting him down.

Lee had changed in an instant that day, morphing from the laser-focused, dedicated athlete he'd been to a broken man full of remorse. And, judging from the regretful shadows haunting his eyes, it seemed as though the years hadn't brought him any relief from the pain of that day. Resignation was embedded in every inch of the slack frame that lay sprawled in the dirt before her.

A pang of sympathy squeezed Jo's chest at how far he'd fallen. She was all too familiar with feeling like a failure.

"Oh, Lee." She sank to her haunches beside him and reached out, brushing a strand of hair out of his eyes. "You were the best rider in Lone Oaks—the nation, even—no question. Not only that, but you could be again if you'd be willing to come back to Lone Oaks Crossing and work hard."

He stared up at her, remaining silent.

"What would you say," she asked, "if I told you that you had another chance? If I told you that Brooks, here, has a winning horse that needs a rider?"

Lee's expression crumpled. "But Sweet Dash," he said, his voice wavering. "I'm the one that—"

"No," Jo said. "Don't ever say that. You did everything right that day. You were a good rider, Lee. A great one. That's why I'm here." She glanced up at Brooks, who looked slightly less irritated than he had before. Lee's expression, contorted with pain, seemed to have tugged at his innate sense of empathy and goodwill. "That's why *we're* here," she continued, looking back at Lee. "Brooks, too. We're here to give you another chance, if you want it."

He continued staring up at them, his gaze moving from Jo to Brooks, then back.

At a loss, Jo struggled for words, recalling the words Brooks had used that had finally prompted her to accept Cheyenne as a stable hand at Lone Oaks Crossing. "What do you have to lose, Lee?"

Lee blinked, his mouth growing even slacker as he struggled to think it over. "Nothing," he finally said. "I ain't got a damn thing."

Jo tilted her head, feeling the odd urge to laugh and cry at the same time as she held out her hand. "So, we got a deal then? We'll offer you great pay, free room and board, as well as meals for your expert riding skills."

His brow creased. "Do I still get two days off a week?"

"Yes," Jo said.

"And I can still drink?"

Jo frowned. "No. You have to stick to a strict training regimen and get yourself back in shape."

"But—"

"I'm offering you a chance," Jo said firmly. "But I can't take it for you. You have to reach out and take it. Wholeheartedly and with complete dedication. The kind you used to have for the sport. This moment, right now, is your opportunity to turn your life around. Otherwise, you stay right where you are." She narrowed her eyes and added for good measure, "Sprawled on your back, in the dirt, hoping you'll be able to scrounge up another job in another town after you get fired from this one."

He swiveled his head around, gazing slack-jawed at the dusty hay and hard earth, then nodded. Lifting his hand, he attempted to grab her outstretched fingers and haul himself up, but a bit of hay fell from the sleeve of his raised arm onto his nose, and he sneezed, his palm jerking with his body, so he missed her hand by a mile.

Grimacing, Jo shoved herself off the ground, rose to her feet, and summoned an encouraging smile for Brooks, who scowled back at her. "You mind helping me get him in the truck?"

Though Brooks crafted the best bourbon in Kentucky and was known to frequently indulge responsibly himself, he was not accustomed to transporting drunks in his truck—especially so early in the afternoon.

He sat outside the Dixie Mart, a convenience store located halfway between Max Anderson's stables and Lone Oaks Crossing, and stared at Jo, who stood outside, waiting beside the closed door of the men's restroom. This was the third pit stop of their trip back to Lone Oaks Crossing.

Lee, whom Brooks had grudgingly picked up off the

dirt of Max Anderson's stable yard, lugged in his arms to his truck, and settled into the back seat of the extended cab, had complained of a headache and feeling carsick several times during the journey back. His most recent complaint, however, had been accompanied by dry heaves, which had led Brooks to swerve off the highway and into the parking lot of the gas station. The hungover, overly flirtatious, and out-of-shape jockey had been inside the men's restroom now for almost twenty minutes.

Brooks rolled down the window and stuck his head out, shouting across the parking lot to Jo, "He still alive in there?"

Jo waved away his concern. "He's fine. Just give him another minute."

Growling, Brooks slumped back against the driver's seat and closed his eyes. They'd already been parked on this cracked tarmac for what seemed like forever, wasting time rather than working with Another Round.

"Oh, Lord," Brooks groaned, rubbing his forehead. That was another worry altogether.

After Jo had shared that Lee had been the jockey who had ridden Sweet Dash at the Preakness Stakes, he'd wanted to shut down Jo's idea of hiring him right then. No way did he want to take a chance on a jockey who'd been part of such a disaster—despite a one-off Derby win—especially when he'd worked so hard for so long to put himself and one of his thoroughbreds in a position to possibly win the Derby this year.

Another Round wasn't just any thoroughbred. Another Round was born with a natural instinct and love of competing as well as a spirited personality—three of the most cherished traits of a winning racehorse.

And now, with everything on the line—including Earl's

home and Jo's future business venture for Lone Oaks—
here they were, risking everything for a drunk who probably didn't yet understand that he'd agreed to ride as a
jockey again, much less realize the pain he'd encounter
transforming himself from an inebriated slob back into a
physically fit, disciplined athlete.

. . . I trust him.

Oh, man. That's what Jo had said and yes, he believed
she did trust Lee. But she'd said herself that she hadn't
seen or spoken to the guy in years. Lee could have become a completely different person from the one she'd
known years ago, and judging from first impressions,
Brooks would bet his last dime that Lee had completely
changed—in the worst of ways. Not only that, but Jo had
seemed as shocked by Lee's miserable appearance as he
had been.

But . . . there was another reason he needed to bite his
tongue, agree to Jo's request that he give Lee a chance.

Brooks touched his fingertips to the seam of his mouth
as he thought of Jo's kiss, missing her touch and taste
as much as he had every moment since she'd first kissed
him yesterday. She'd stated she was his neighbor . . . and
friend, but he wanted more than that, and he trusted her
judgment.

So, agreeing to give this drunkard a chance hadn't
been up for debate after he'd realized how dead-set Jo
was on bringing Lee onto their team. In that moment,
standing on Max Anderson's land, looking down at Jo's
earnest—almost pleading—expression as she'd asked
him to carry Lee to the truck, Brooks had discovered that
he'd have trouble denying her anything.

The realization had both pleased and scared him simultaneously.

He knew his feelings for Jo had deepened. That had become evident to him when his heart kicked his ribs every time he got his first sight of her for the day; when at night, he found himself seeing her face even after he'd closed his eyes.

He was, he suspected, falling in love. The intense sensation was new to him—the strong stirring of emotion in his chest an unfamiliar one—but one he enjoyed as much as he feared. This longing he'd developed for Jo was wild, unpredictable, and all-consuming. And, as he'd quickly discovered earlier today, the intense attachment left him at her mercy . . . as well as her beck and call.

The door of the men's restroom banged open, clanging against the brick wall as Lee stumbled out.

Jo immediately rushed over to him, slung her arm around his back, and braced his weight against hers. The guy was less than five feet tall, his head just reaching Jo's shoulders. He had a slight build—the perfect kind for a professional jockey—except for one thing.

Brooks frowned. That beer belly he sported.

Not that he would've noticed it, much less minded, had Lee been embarking upon any occupation other than one that involved him straddling the back of Brooks's prized thoroughbred. Lord knows, Brooks enjoyed savoring his own bourbon from time to time. There was no better end to a cold winter's day than sipping a prized bourbon by a warm fire and pairing it with a quality cigar.

But Lee's circumstances were different. To ride skillfully and competitively, Lee had to be stone-cold sober, physically fit, clear-eyed, and meet a specified weight requirement. The more weight he slung over Another Round's back, the slower the thoroughbred would run. And if Lee's current state were any indication, the man would have a heck of a time weaning himself off the booze, cleaning himself up, and strengthening his lungs. It would take hours of exercise, intense self-discipline, and the utmost commitment to turn his physical, mental, and emotional health around and, quite frankly, Brooks wasn't sure the guy had it in him.

The passenger side door opened, and Jo helped Lee inside, shoving him with both hands into the back seat of the cab. After Lee was settled upright, she climbed into the passenger seat and shut the door.

She flashed a smile at Brooks, one far too bright to be sincere. "I think things went really well in there. Lee managed to take an aspirin, eat a few bites of a hot dog, drink half a bottle of a sports drink, and wash his face, so he should feel more hydrated and awake now." She glanced in the rearview mirror. "Don't you feel better now with something in your stomach to soak up all that alcohol, Lee?" Receiving no response, she prompted, "Are the sports drink and aspirin helping to ease your headache?"

A muffled groan emerged from the back of the extended cab.

Brooks glanced in the rearview mirror just in time to see Lee double over, lower his head toward the floor mat, and issue the most stomach-churning sounds and smells he'd ever had the misfortune of witnessing.

"God help me," Brooks whispered, struggling not to gag or think of his recently cleaned floorboards. "Please tell me those are more dry heaves."

Jo, a dismayed look on her face, swiveled in her seat, glanced at the back floorboard, then swiftly faced forward again, clutching her mouth and nose with both hands. "No," she said softly, her throat moving on a hard swallow. "They're definitely not dry."

Brooks cranked the engine, rolled down the windows, and pumped the gas pedal, violently revving the engine for good measure. "Jo . . . I adore you. But the second I stop in front of your grandfather's house, I want his ass out of my truck."

CHAPTER 10

Two days later, Lee was sober, clear-eyed, and miserable.

"I've run that track once already and it ain't even eight o'clock in the morning yet." Lee, standing in the backyard of the main house at Lone Oaks Crossing, bent, braced his hands on his knees, and coughed uncontrollably. His chest heaved as he struggled to draw in a breath. "This is inhumane!"

"Mercy me." Frankie, standing beside Jo on the deck, made a face as she stared down at Lee. "You think he's gonna vomit again?"

Wincing, Jo shook her head. "No. He barfed up everything but his lungs the night he got here."

Which, she reflected with a deep sense of gratitude, Brooks had not stayed to witness.

Two days ago, after Brooks had driven up the driveway of Lone Oaks Crossing and parked in front of the main house, Jo had dragged Lee out of the back seat of

Brooks's truck as quickly as possible while trying not to focus on the deepening glare on its owner's face.

She didn't blame him for being angry. Lee was a mess. An absolute hungover, slovenly, sick mess that had, more than likely, left a permanent stain in the back floorboard of the truck. Though, she had to admit, the bout of nausea had seemed to do Lee a bit of good as he'd been able to walk into the house under his own steam.

Jo had remained outside a moment longer, standing by the driver's side window as she'd smiled up at Brooks and apologized for Lee's drunken state. To his credit, Brooks had refrained from bad-mouthing Lee again or repeating how much of a mistake he thought it was to bring the man into their racing venture. Instead, he'd nodded in silent acknowledgment of her apology, then glanced at her and said two things.

I'll be back in two days. He'd better show improvement.

"Come on, Lee," Jo shouted down at him from the deck. "Once more. That track's only half a mile long and you still have three rounds of squats, burpees, and bear crawls left to do."

And goodness knows, Brooks might form a better second impression of Lee if he were in actual motion rather than bent double, gasping for breath as though he were about to keel over at any moment.

"What time is Brooks coming?" Frankie asked, sipping coffee from the mug she held. Steam curled above the rim, mingling with the cool morning air.

Jo glanced over her shoulder and tilted her head, listening for any sounds of a truck engine. "I'm not sure. He just said he was coming back in two days to check on Lee's progress."

Laughter burst out on the opposite end of the deck.

Cheyenne, seated in a lawn chair beside Earl, who was seated in his wheelchair, laughed again as she stared down at Lee. "I bet you Brooks is gonna toss that dude out on his ear."

Jo frowned. "That's not a very kind sentiment, Cheyenne."

Though, she reluctantly acknowledged, it was a distinct possibility.

"You know it's true," Cheyenne said. Her grin fell as she looked beyond Lee's bent form and focused on Another Round, who grazed in the neighboring pasture. "Brooks loves Another Round and isn't gonna let that dude anywhere near him. Only the best horseman should ride him."

"Lee is the best," Jo said. "He just needs some time to get back in shape." She walked across the deck, stopped by Cheyenne's side, and squeezed the teen's shoulder, saying quietly, "And he can probably hear every word you're saying, so please keep your voice down."

Cheyenne looked up at her and narrowed her eyes. "I don't want him riding Another Round either. He's not . . ." She shrugged. "Oh, I don't know. He's just not good enough."

"Give him time." Jo glanced at Earl. "He's the best, isn't he, Earl?"

Earl, who'd been studying Lee, looked up at Jo and nodded. "Could be . . . if he works . . . more." He faced Cheyenne, raised one hand and pointed at her. "Same as you. If you . . . keep g-grooming."

Cheyenne's disapproving scowl eased as she met Earl's eyes. "Yeah," she said quietly. "I guess."

Jo smiled. For the past two days, ever since Earl had first managed to roll his wheelchair out onto the newly built deck, her grandfather had risen early, eaten breakfast, and joined Frankie on the deck to watch Jo lead Cheyenne through the steps to groom Another Round. And when their routine had to be adjusted to make time for Jo to drag Lee out of bed and push him through his workouts in the backyard, Cheyenne had taken to joining Earl and Frankie on the deck to watch Another Round graze in the pasture.

Cheyenne had begun asking questions about Another Round and thoroughbreds overall—some of which Frankie didn't have the answers to—and gradually, Earl had taken over, explaining with focused effort. At first, he'd struggled to speak for any period of time, but after two days' worth of morning and afternoon visits on the deck with Cheyenne, his stamina had improved slightly and it had become obvious that their new racing venture had sparked Earl's interest, giving him extra motivation to work hard at physical therapy, leave the house, and make his way out to the deck every day to watch Another Round and witness Lee's progress.

It was amazing, really, how fast Earl and Cheyenne, two stubborn souls, had begun to bond during those daily conversations about horses. Earl enjoyed sharing his knowledge and expertise and Cheyenne reveled in his rapt attention.

"Lee is on our team now," Jo reminded Cheyenne. "And as Another Round's caretaker, you should be the first and foremost teammate to welcome Lee and help him improve. After all," she said, looking down at Cheyenne, "your most important responsibility is to ensure Another Round is taken care of, and helping Lee be the best he can be means Another Round will have a better rider."

Oh, boy, that was a stretch. But she needed Cheyenne's help—everyone's really, if they were going to pull off a win at the Derby. Or any racetrack, for that matter.

It'd be all too easy to find another jockey and start training right away. But Jo didn't want a decent shot for Brooks or Another Round—she wanted the best shot for them both—and that meant pushing Lee to give it his all, to succeed in recapturing the phenomenal skills he'd displayed years ago on the track. It might be a long shot, but they were already making progress. Lee hadn't consumed a drop of alcohol in forty-eight hours and had managed to drag his fatigued body around the course she'd marked out for him.

"Whatever," Cheyenne said. "I guess I could help him out."

Jo glanced at Frankie and sighed. Good grief, it took a lot to impress the kid and motivate her to action.

Cheyenne shoved to her feet and rubbed her hands together. "What do you want him to do?"

"He needs to run that half-mile track that I plotted out for him around the pasture again," Jo said. "Then he needs to complete three rounds of ten sets of squats, burpees, and bear crawls before he can take a short break."

Cheyenne nodded in what seemed to be nonchalant agreement, but the mischievous gleam in her eyes was disturbing as she began walking down the ramp toward the backyard. "No problem."

"Cheyenne?" Jo called.

She kept walking. "Yeah?"

"Just . . . go easy on him," Jo said. "All he really needs is a pep talk, you know?"

Cheyenne waved a careless hand over her head and kept walking, joining Lee, who had sat down on the grass, in the backyard.

"Mercy," Frankie repeated, sitting in the chair Cheyenne had vacated and sipping her coffee. "This should be entertaining."

Just then, the growl of an engine rumbled in the distance.

"Great," Jo whispered, glancing over her shoulder. "Just great."

Brooks was here. Just in time to witness Cheyenne dragging Lee through his workout.

"Oh, boy." Frankie chuckled, pointing down at Cheyenne, who'd joined Lee in the backyard and had begun tugging at his arms, trying to pull him to his feet. "Look at 'em. They're like two moody kids tussling out there."

Jo groaned and rubbed her temples.

"Morning, everyone."

Jo looked at the bottom of the wheelchair ramp at the sound of Brooks's deep, soothing voice and forced a bright smile to her face. "Morning, Brooks."

He strolled up the ramp toward her, Frankie, and Earl, then turned and focused on the two figures arguing in the backyard. Cheyenne had Lee by one wrist, pulling as he yanked back from his seated position, grinning up at her.

"This kid of yours is rude!" Lee shouted. "And weak! Ain't you, kid?" He laughed, clearly enjoying Cheyenne's stubborn struggle.

Despite the situation, the delighted sound was a welcome relief to Jo's ears as it echoed across the grounds. She smiled. It seemed Lee still had some life left in him yet.

"You ain't getting me on my feet no matter how hard you pull," Lee shouted at Cheyenne.

"What's going on down there?" Brooks asked.

Frankie laughed. "Two of your employees are fighting

it out, that's what." She glanced at Earl. "Whatcha say, babe? I bet you two bucks Cheyenne will have Lee on his feet within the next ninety seconds."

Earl chuckled and stuck out his hand, shaking Frankie's hand on the bet. "Thirty seconds."

Jo shook her head. "Okay, let's not encourage them." She cupped her hands around her mouth and called out, "Cheyenne! I asked you to give Lee a pep talk and gentle nudge, not drag him over the ground."

"Get up!" Cheyenne shouted, heaving once more at Lee's arms.

Sure enough, that last pull did it. Cheyenne managed to jerk Lee to his feet and shove him forward a few steps.

"Aha!" Earl, smiling ear to ear, stuck out his hand, palm up, and wriggled his fingers. "Pay . . . up."

Frankie grumbled but smiled back, dug two dollar bills from the pocket of her jeans and shoved them in Earl's open hand. "There. Don't spend it all in one place."

Brooks frowned, watching as Lee jogged a couple steps, then deliberately stopped, waited for Cheyenne to shove him in the back, then laughed and jogged a couple more steps, starting the pattern over again.

"You call that getting in shape?" Brooks asked as he looked on in disapproval.

"I call it a start," Jo said, walking over to his side and joining him at the edge of the deck. "He's already completed one jog around the makeshift track I marked out, and once he finishes this second round, he'll start his first set of workouts, then take a break and do it all over again." She looked up at him, noting the tight clench of his jaw. "You have to admit it's progress of some sort, Brooks. I mean"—she waved a hand toward Lee, who jogged around the side of the pasture with Cheyenne close behind—"he's moving, isn't he? Getting fresh air, strengthening his lungs, and he hasn't had a sip of alcohol since you dropped him off here two days ago."

Brooks dragged his attention away from the two figures jogging around the pasture and looked down at her, a small grin twitching his sensual mouth. "You call being chased in the backyard by a teenager progress?"

"Well . . ." Jo shrugged, smiling. "At least he's not throwing up." She closed one eye and peeked up at him. "Did you have your truck cleaned?"

Brooks's grin fell. "Yes. But I would've been better off buying a new one. My memory of that truck has been tarnished by Lee forever."

Jo laughed. "Cut him some slack, please?" She stopped laughing, her eyes following Lee as he fell into a rhythm and started jogging with purpose, leaving Cheyenne behind and undertaking a second lap around the track she'd laid out for him. "He's had his misfortunes in life—like everyone else—and at least he's showing a hint of drive now, as though he might actually follow through."

Brooks continued staring at the younger man as he ran around the pasture, the tense set of his broad shoulders easing slightly. "Do you think he has it in him to pull this off?"

"I know he does," she said. "He just needs a fair shot and plenty of support." She hesitated, looking up at Brooks, weaving her arm around his muscular bicep and tugging his gaze back to hers. "Lee lost his uncle years ago and he's been on his own for a long time. He had everything going for him back in the day when he'd started out in this sport, but life dealt him a tough hand and he's had trouble recovering." She studied Brooks's face, encouraged by the empathy in his expression. "Here he'll have the support he needs to make something of his life again and, hopefully, help us in the process. He was the best part of our team years ago and, with support and encouragement, he will be again." She snuggled closer to his side, her belly fluttering at the feel of his muscular frame against hers. "Besides, you said you trusted me. And . . . adored me. And that you were at my beck and call. So, you can sit back, relax, and know that I have this under control."

A slow smile rose to Brooks's lips as he looked down at her, his eyes darkening to midnight pools. "Are you trying to bat those beautiful lashes of yours and manipulate me into giving in to your wishes without question?"

She grinned and tilted her mouth up closer to his, a heady sense of pleasure moving through her at the thought of feeling his warm mouth again. "Maybe . . ."

"You've succeeded," he murmured, lowering his head and touching his lips to h—

"Hey." Earl's growly tone cut across the deck. "P-pay attention," he said, jabbing one finger toward the two figures running around the pasture as he frowned up at Brooks. "Business . . . first."

Brooks cleared his throat, his cheeks burning brightly as he straightened. "Yes, sir."

Late October had arrived at Lone Oaks Crossing, bringing with it a burst of color that splashed the trees surrounding the rolling green acres with patches of orange, red, brown, and yellow, lighting up the landscape with vibrant energy.

Jo, leaning against the white fence of the pasture in the backyard, smiled as she watched Another Round gallop past her, his glossy mane and tail rippling in the crisp autumn wind. The thoroughbred had taken to the change in temperature and season immediately, seemingly falling in love with the feel of the cold autumn air sweeping over his hide and the mix of autumn scents lingering on the air.

"He loves a good run first thing in the morning." Brooks, standing beside her, his forearms propped on the top rail of the fence, tilted the screen of his cell phone toward her. "And it's showing." He tapped the screen with one blunt fingertip. "Check it out. He's shaved even more off his time. Last I averaged, he's clocking upward of thirty miles an hour. That gives him a good shot at winning the Derby."

"I wouldn't say it's a good shot. But it's definitely a decent one." Jo glanced at the digital stopwatch ticking away on the phone, then looked to the opposite side of the pasture where Another Round and Lee shot around the curve and over the hill in the distance, out of sight. "And you have to admit, Lee's surprised us all."

Brooks nodded, his brows rising. "He's certainly surprised me. But you?"

Jo grinned. "Yes. Most definitely."

Over the past month since Lee had arrived at Lone Oaks Crossing, he'd shown remarkable dedication despite getting off to a rocky start.

After Lee had detoxed and abstained from alcohol for a substantial amount of time, his strength had seemed to return slowly but steadily. Each day, he'd roused himself at dawn, sauntered down to the stables to spend a few minutes introducing himself to Another Round before Cheyenne began her grooming routine for the day, then walked across the grounds to the backyard, where he and Jo had put together a workout routine.

First, Lee would run the half-mile trail Jo had marked out for him across the grounds, the distance gradually increasing each week until Lee could run three miles with ease first thing in the morning. Next, he'd cool down on the deck and drink some water, then jump into circuit training in the backyard, running through various sets of repetitious lunges, squats, and bear crawls as well as burpees, which he hated with a passion.

Lee had always been a hard worker, but even Jo had experienced doubts during the first week when he'd struggled to jog the half-mile trail and dragged during the exercise circuits. He'd seemed pale, weak, and unsteady on his feet. Clearly, he'd been living hard over the past ten years and had neglected his health.

But after the initial two weeks, his complexion had brightened, his muscles had grown stronger, and his steps had become firm and confident. Enough so that after the third week, he'd dropped almost ten pounds and felt good about taking his first ride.

Slow and steady had been the approach. Jo, along with keen-eyed Cheyenne, had supervised every moment of the process, making adjustments as Lee and the thoroughbred worked, calling out directions, recording times, and carefully checking the weather and ground conditions every morning prior to commencing any of Another Round's workouts for the day. Lee had been equally as careful and attentive, developing a fondness for Another Round that Jo had hoped for and nurturing a special bond of trust with the thoroughbred so that they felt at ease in each other's company.

"I knew Lee was a great rider," Jo said. "And I knew he'd find a way to connect with Another Round. But I hadn't anticipated him bouncing back into shape as quickly as he has." She glanced at Brooks, noting the approving look in his eyes as he watched Lee ride. "If I had to guess, I'd say he's impressed you as well."

Brooks's dark eyes met hers, warming with affection

as they roved her face. "He has. I'd say trusting your judgment is the only way to go."

Her cheeks heated at the teasing tone in his voice. "Remember that on the days I frustrate you."

He smiled, transferring his cell phone to one hand and sliding his free one around her waist. "I'd say I'm frustrated now."

Oh, gracious. She grinned. He was turning on the charm . . . the scoundrel. "In what way?"

"In the way that I haven't had any time alone with you in the past month." He dipped his head, his soft lips warm against her cool temple. "I'd kill to have you to myself for an hour. You in my arms, a glass of bourbon, and a nice view . . ."

"Oh, given those conditions . . ." She closed her eyes and leaned in, her grin growing. "I think we'd need much more than an hour."

He moved closer, his strong chest pressing against her arm and his thick thigh brushing hers.

"But," she said, leaning away and brushing her hand through his hair, "business needs to come first, right now."

A low groan left his lips as he kissed the top of her head, then stepped back, allowing the crisp autumn wind to whip between them. "Forgive me. Your grandfather's orders slipped my mind momentarily."

Jo laughed, recalling Earl's stern tone a month ago when they'd stood on the deck watching Lee undertake his first morning workout.

"He just wants us to have the best possible shot at winning," she said.

Brooks sighed. "I know. And he's right. Business should come first . . . for now."

She propped a hand on her hip. "I'm judging from your tone that you think that'll change at some point?"

"After the Derby." He looked down at her, a confident gleam in his eyes. "Once we win at Churchill Downs, we'll have all the time in the world together."

Jo stilled as he returned his attention to the grounds, his dark eyes seeking Another Round and Lee as they ascended a hill and emerged back into view.

She didn't doubt that Brooks was attracted to her. That he had more than a neighborly or friendly interest in her. But she'd be lying if she didn't admit—at least to herself—that she'd noticed a change in him with each passing day since Lee had shown such improvement and devotion to his new charge.

With each of Lee and Another Round's new accomplishments, Brooks's energy grew more excited, eager and, in a sense . . . ruthless. It was clear he was delighting in the prospect of beating Spencer at his own game, gaining the upper hand and stealing the glory.

"Will we?" Jo asked quietly.

Facing her, Brooks tilted his head, confused. "What?"

"After the Derby, I mean. You said, win or lose, the Derby would end this rivalry you have with Spencer."

He held her gaze silently for a few moments then said, "I'd rather win, Jo. I know win or lose were my words at the time, but if you want me to be completely honest—"

"I do."

He nodded. "Then, I'd rather win."

She bit her lip. "You mean, it would take a win to end it."

He looked away, his eyes avoiding hers. "Let's just focus on winning first, hmm? That's what's important right now."

The back door of the main house opened. Frankie walked out and held the door as Earl rolled his wheelchair out onto the deck.

Brooks smiled, glancing down at her and squeezing her arm before walking away. "Let's go show Earl Another Round's new stats, shall we?"

Jo stood there, her earlier excitement waning as she watched Brooks stride across the grass and onto the deck, every step taking him farther away from her. And that's where her worries truly resided, she supposed. In the fear that Brooks's attention would remain on his feud with Spencer rather than her. That after the Derby—win or lose—he'd focus on inflicting pain on Spencer rather than pursuing a relationship with her.

She dragged in a ragged breath as she strolled after him toward the deck. That was a bitter pill to swallow. The thought that Brooks might not feel as deeply for her as she already did for him. Because somewhere during the past month and a half since she'd met him, he'd secured a place in her heart with his kind disposition, caring generosity, and protective strength. He was unlike any man she'd ever known and she wanted to know him better. She wanted to be more than his friend. But she wasn't sure how much more he wanted from her . . . or if his feelings for her were stronger than his animosity for Spencer and his determination to right the injustice he'd inflicted on Brooks's family.

Jo tilted her head back as she walked, her eyes smarting as the cold wind hit them. She blinked her vision clear of the cold moisture, reminding herself to focus on the task at hand and take one step at a time. As Brooks had said, they'd have time after the Derby win to explore what existed between them.

And that, she thought, smiling, was what she really looked forward to.

". . . think we should try for the Breeders' Cup Juvenile," Brooks was saying as she approached. "It's scheduled for the first week in November at Keeneland and—"

"No." Jo walked up the ramp and joined Brooks, Frankie, and Earl on the center of the deck where they were gathered around a small table laden with papers. "We're not ready yet."

Brooks spread his hands. "What do you mean?" He gestured toward Lee, who'd finished his workout with Another Round and was dismounting in the pasture to hand the reins to Cheyenne for Another Round's cooldown. "You just saw how fast his time has gotten and how much progress he's made over the past month. Any speed higher than thirty miles per hour makes for a good Derby contender."

"A decent contender," Jo corrected. "Look, I'm not negating the fact that Another Round and Lee have made enormous strides over the past few weeks. What I'm saying is that we should take small steps and stay upright rather than run right off the bat and fall flat on our faces. They need more time to prepare, and their first race needs to be one that has lower stakes."

"How low do you want to go, Jo?" Brooks studied her face. "I mean, we need to win at least forty points to even have a shot at qualifying for the Derby, and if we don't start racking them up now, we won't have time to collect enough."

"I know, but . . ." She looked down at the papers on the table, studying each before she found the page she was looking for and held it up. "Look. This one—the Gun Runner in New Orleans. It's a lower stakes race and it's not until Christmas. That'll give us almost two more months to train and, more importantly, for Lee and Another Round to learn each other's strengths and weaknesses. I think we should start there."

Brooks took the paper from her and studied the details printed on it, then nodded. "Okay, let's say we go to the Gun Runner as the first race. What next? Even if we place first, we'd still need upward of thirty points by April."

"Next . . ." She rifled through more of the printouts, picked up two more pages, and handed them to Brooks. "The Rebel in Arkansas. That one's at the end of February and has a great point payoff for first place. Concentrating on training between the Gun Runner and that race would give us two more months to take what we learn from our performance in the Gun Runner and rectify any mistakes we make as well as strategize better based on Another Round's behavior on the track. We'd walk into the Rebel with a new, better game plan."

Brooks held up one of the papers she'd given him. "And the Jeff Ruby? I assume that one's our last saving grace?"

Jo nodded. "Not necessarily. There are a few more races in April with stakes as high as the Jeff Ruby, so even if we only place second in the Jeff Ruby, we'd still have a decent shot at getting into the Derby. Either way, placing third or higher in all three of those races would give us the shot you're hoping for to qualify for the Derby."

Brooks reviewed each of the three pages in his hand for a few minutes, then looked at Earl. "What do you think, Earl?"

Earl, seated in his wheelchair with a big smile on his face, pumped his fist in the air and said, "So long as you take me to every one of 'em . . . let's go kick some butt!"

Frankie laughed. "That therapy's paying off, huh, Earl? He'll be running the show 'round here in no time."

Brooks smiled at Jo. "That's approval enough for me."

CHAPTER 11

Spending Christmas in New Orleans was an exciting prospect for a tourist. There were decorations galore: lights strung along wrought-iron fences and live oak trees, decorated streetcars, steamboats, and carriages. There were bonfires on the levee, caroling in Jackson Square, and lavish feasts packing tables in every restaurant on every corner. The city throbbed with joy, celebration, and festivity.

But Jo, Brooks, Frankie, Earl, Cheyenne, Lee, and Nancy (a groom from Brooks's stables) had traveled to New Orleans for a different reason. After being packed into trucks and transporting Another Round along the interstate for a total of eleven hours, they were eager to let Another Round stretch his legs and settle in at the Fair Grounds Race Course as well as unpack their bags and get a good night's sleep. Nervous tension combined with a packed schedule of race preparation had left them with little time or inclination to sightsee. Instead, they spent every spare moment they had (and a few they didn't have) seeing to all of Another Round's needs, getting acquainted with the racetrack, and praying for a safe race.

Finally, the day after Christmas, one hour and twenty minutes from the start of the Gun Runner race, Jo and Nancy escorted Another Round across the racecourse grounds to the receiving barn. The winter sun hung low in the late-afternoon sky as they fell in line with the other horses, trainers, and jockeys, all preparing for the race.

"What do you think?" Nancy asked Jo, eyeing the sweat glistening along Another Round's bare neck. "He looks like he's starting to wash out."

Jo glanced at Another Round and noted the stressed look in his eyes as he took in the other horses and the unfamiliar surroundings. "He's nervous. That's to be expected."

But she had to admit that Another Round's high level of nervous tension was cause for concern.

Over the past two months, she'd put Another Round through a safe but vigorous training routine to enhance his strength and stamina. The colt had performed well, growing stronger and more confident every day. Their hopes had been high during the drive down to New Orleans. Another Round's times were great, his love of running had intensified during his training, and his personality remained upbeat and friendly through it all. There had been nothing to indicate that Another Round would react negatively heading into a formal race.

But in racing, nothing was certain and very little before or during the race could be controlled.

"It's the other horses," Nancy said, glancing around as they entered the receiving barn. "They're putting him on edge."

Inside the receiving barn, other colts walked around, some grinding their teeth and others kicking, most of them eyeing each other suspiciously.

Jo nodded. "Another Round's a born competitor, and he knows he has competition. Let's just hope he puts that nervous energy to good use."

"At least the weather's perfect," Nancy said. "We couldn't ask for a better track."

That was true. The December air was cool, but the climate was similar to that of Kentucky this time of year—weather Another Round was used to training and running in—and the dirt track was dry and welcoming. Conditions for the night's race were pretty much the best they could possibly be—save for Another Round's emotional response to his surroundings.

"Should we pull him?" Nancy asked, eyeing Another Round again, this time with intense concern.

Jo shook her head. "Not yet. If nothing else, he needs the experience. We may have practiced with starting gates in the pasture, but he needs to enter a gate beside competitors and get a feel for what it looks and sounds like." She patted Another Round's neck and murmured soothing words. "Let's give him a chance," she said quietly. "If he doesn't want to run, he'll let us know."

Nancy laughed and rubbed Another Round's forehead. "Yeah. Lee told me he learned that the hard way a couple weeks ago. He said he's never met anyone more stubborn than Another Round and Cheyenne."

Jo smiled, recalling the incident. It had been a normal day—perfect for training—like today, but Another Round had planted his feet the moment he'd hit the exercise track at Lone Oaks Crossing and refused to run. Lee had tried to coax him into participating for quite some time, but Another Round was stubborn (possibly more so than

Cheyenne) and had refused to train that one and only time.

"Cheyenne's probably going nuts in that hotel room right about now," Jo said. "She's probably asking Earl and Frankie a million questions and angry about not being able to be here with Another Round."

Cheyenne had done a great job of taking care of Another Round over the past two months and had developed a close relationship with the colt, but the Fair Grounds Race Course housed a casino and, unfortunately, due to age restrictions, she'd had to sit this race out.

"I'm sure she's having a fit and probably giving them a fit, too. Lee said the kid sure gave him one his first week back at Lone Oaks Crossing." Nancy laughed. "Boy, I hope Another Round does well. Cheyenne will think I didn't do my job if he doesn't."

Moments later, the horse identifier came their way to verify Another Round as well as Jo and Nancy. Soon after that, they moved to the paddock, where Jo saddled Another Round.

When she finished saddling the colt, Jo stood beside him, stroked his neck, and whispered soothingly in his ear. "You're a winner, sweetheart, no matter what. When it's time, take off and enjoy every moment. Then come back to us, safe and sound."

She kissed his neck, then stepped away so Nancy could lead him to the walking ring, where spectators and potential bettors might view him.

Brooks joined Jo inside the walking ring and watched as Another Round slowly made the circuit. The sun had dipped below the horizon since they'd left the receiving barn and the floodlights were on, casting garish light across the track and grounds.

"How's he looking?" Brooks asked, standing beside Jo.

She wove her fingers together and squeezed. "I don't know. He seems nervous, and we can tell the tension's getting to him."

Brooks reached out and took her hands in his, the calm strength of his touch melting away the anxiety she hadn't been aware she'd been harboring. "He'll be fine. Win or lose, he'll have an opportunity to compete. That's what's important, right?"

She nodded. "Just think good thoughts in the stands, okay?"

He kissed her forehead, then smiled down at her, his familiar features a welcome sight. "He's going to be great. I can feel it."

Moments later, Lee joined them in the walking ring, dressed in black-and-white quartered silks and a black cap with ORIGINAL SIN printed in white lettering on the back.

"Well, don't you look smart," Jo said. "You spiffy up well."

Lee laughed. "Doesn't take much when your boss gets you the finest stuff."

Brooks smiled. "You've earned every penny and then some, Lee. You've worked your backside off the past two months." He held out his hand. "Good luck out there."

Lee shook his hand. "Thank you."

Casting one more glance at Another Round, Brooks wished Jo luck as well, then left to return to his box seat.

"How're you feeling?" Jo asked, though she already knew the answer. He was nervous. She could see it in the way he opened and closed his hands by his sides, his eyes flicking over the crowd and horses.

"I'm good." He grew quiet, his expression turning somber. "No matter how this all turns out, Jo, I want to thank you for the opportunity to ride again."

The earnest gratitude in his tone made Jo's breath catch. "I should be thanking you for agreeing to join our team. You've worked wonders with Another Round and picked up right where you left off years ago. I really hope we win a few—for all our sakes."

Lee nodded. "Let's hope things turn out well."

Ten minutes before starting time, Lee was allowed to mount. Jo gave him a leg up and once he was settled, he and Another Round headed to the track, accompanied by a pony horse and rider.

Jo hoped the track pony would help calm Another Round down as he passed the crowd in the stands and made his way to the starting gate. She watched as Lee warmed Another Round up, cantering him around a bit, and hopefully settling their nerves.

Soon, the horses were loaded, one at a time, into their starting gates. Jo bit her nails, watching and waiting, her heart beating erratically until finally, the seven gates swung open and the colts took off, bolting down the dirt track at high speeds, each vying for a position in front.

To Jo's relief, Another Round didn't freeze or plant his feet. Instead, he ran with the others, though his gait seemed restrained, as though he were holding back, or perhaps hesitant to go full throttle in such unfamiliar territory.

"Come on, boy," she whispered, the shouts of the crowd echoing in her ears, almost drowning out her thoughts. "Pick up the pace."

Lee rode well, urging Another Round on, keeping his seat with confident purpose.

"Crowd Pleaser takes the lead along the clubhouse turn," an announcer blared over the stadium speakers. "They're heading to the back of the track now and Mighty Soldier is taking over, stealing the lead from Crowd Pleaser. And we have Another Round surging from the back now, overtaking Outside Margin and Perfect Day . . ."

Jo rose to her tiptoes, straining for a glimpse of Another Round, seeking a flash of Lee's black-and-white silks. "Come on, come on, come on . . ."

"They're rounding the far turn now and coming to the top of the stretch," the announcer continued. "Crowd Pleaser resumes the lead at the quarter pole but Mighty Soldier is powering on and—oh, Another Round has lost steam, sliding behind Outside Margin . . . now Perfect Day."

Jo caught sight of him, her eyes fixed on Another Round's face as he ran, chasing the horses that surged ahead of him. "You can do it, boy. Just shift gears."

"Mighty Soldier is charging up on the outside," the announcer blared, "but it's Crowd Pleaser that takes the win, followed by Mighty Soldier, Outside Margin, and Royal Flush."

Jo exhaled, her shoulders sagging with her spirits as Another Round dashed across the finish line in last position.

The eleven-hour drive back to Lone Oaks Crossing was more excruciating than the initial trip to New Orleans had been.

"If I had been there, he would've done better." Cheyenne, seated in the back seat of the extended cab, crossed her arms over her chest and slumped back against her seat. "There's no way Another Round would have come in last in that race had I been with him."

Jo, seated in the passenger seat, shook her head and sighed. "Cheyenne, we've talked about this. At length, I might add. Because of your age, you weren't allowed into the racecourse and Nancy did a fine job of standing in for you."

"Not as good a job as I would have done," Cheyenne said, her eyes meeting Jo's in the rearview mirror. "Another Round knows me. He wouldn't have been as nervous or scared if I had been there with him."

Brooks removed one hand from the steering wheel and adjusted the rearview mirror as he sought out Cheyenne's gaze. "Another Round would have been nervous no matter what. Even if you had been able to go inside the racecourse with him, you still wouldn't have been allowed on the track. You wouldn't have been at the starting gate with him, and you wouldn't have been able to run the race with him. There's only so much we can do, Cheyenne. Another Round has to play his part, too."

Cheyenne frowned, appearing to think this over as she stared out the window at the dark countryside passing with each mile Brooks drove. "Then what will it take to get him to do his part?"

Brooks stared ahead at the highway before them. "I don't know. But what I do know is that Jo, Lee, and you have done an excellent job preparing Another Round for this race."

Jo sneaked a glance at his profile, noting the tight clench of his jaw and the firm set of his mouth. Brooks hid it well, but he was just as disappointed in Another Round's performance as Cheyenne.

After the race had ended, Jo had waited patiently as Lee and a hot walker cooled Another Round down, took him to be drug tested with the other horses, then returned him to his stall to be bathed. Brooks had joined her, a disappointed expression on his face despite the smile he'd forced as he exchanged idle pleasantries with her while they watched the winning horse and his connections revel in their achievement in the Winner's Circle.

Though Brooks hadn't come out and said it, Jo knew he was inwardly devastated at the prospect of having backed a losing horse.

"One bad run doesn't mean you've backed a bad horse," she said softly. Reaching across the console, she placed her hand on his knee in a comforting gesture. "Another Round may have come in last, but he did really well fighting through his nervous tension. A lot of other horses, feeling the fear he did, would have balked at leaving the gate, but he didn't. He faced down his fears and joined the other horses in the race. At one point, he even came close to the front of the pack."

"'Close' doesn't cut it," Brooks whispered back. "We're betting everything we have on earning enough qualifying points to win a place in the starting gate at the Derby. If he doesn't start performing, we don't stand a chance of securing a spot."

The finality in his tone intensified Jo's own fears. She sat back in her seat, turned her head, and looked in the side mirror at the set of headlights following close behind Brooks's truck. Earl, Frankie, Lee, and Nancy traveled in the truck behind them, and Jo wondered briefly if they were having the same conversation.

Lee was probably thinking the same thoughts as Brooks. He'd left the track disappointed in himself and Another Round. And worst of all, he'd had a difficult time looking Jo in the eye as they'd loaded Another Round into the trailer for the return trip to Lone Oaks Crossing.

It broke her heart to think that he felt his hard work had been for nothing or that he no longer measured up in her eyes. Lee had worked hard for two months, exercising every day, putting Another Round through his paces, and working patiently with her and Cheyenne to provide the best care and attention to Another Round. Nothing he had done—or hadn't done—contributed to Another Round's loss in the Gun Runner.

She'd told him as much, just as she'd tried to console Cheyenne and Brooks. But none of them had listened. They were all too consumed with disappointment.

The air in the truck's cab grew thick and still. Jo lowered the passenger side window and leaned her cheek against it, inhaling the cold night air as it rushed into the cab. Thankfully, the familiar landmarks of Lone Oaks appeared, and soon Brooks had turned onto the driveway of Lone Oaks Crossing and brought the truck to a halt in front of the main house.

Brooks cut the engine, then glanced in the rearview mirror, eyeing the truck that drove up behind them and parked as well. "I'll stay for a while and help Lee unload Another Round and get him settled for the night."

"But that's my job," Cheyenne piped from the back seat. "I should be the one to wash him off and settle him down."

Brooks smiled indulgently. "I know. But we've all had a long ride home and I imagine Frankie and Jo could use some help getting Earl inside and settled, too, don't you think?"

Cheyenne sighed, the sound an equal mixture of frustration, anger, and resignation. "I guess."

They all exited the truck, and for the next half hour, the sounds of truck doors opening and closing, trailers being unhitched, and hooves stepping across metal echoed over the grounds. The night air was cold, and Jo shivered as she helped Frankie and Cheyenne get Earl inside the house and to the kitchen table in his wheelchair.

Earl was cold, too. He sat in his wheelchair, clutching his gray sweater around his shoulders, shivering.

"Let me get you some coffee, Earl," Jo said, crossing the kitchen to where the coffeemaker sat on the counter. "I bet you're freezing after that walk outside and probably starving from the long drive."

Though they'd split the hours of the drive back to Lone Oaks over two days, they'd had to take several breaks along the way and had gotten a late start that morning, causing them to arrive home later than expected. They'd last stopped for lunch around noon, and it was after seven in the evening now.

"I expect he's going to need more than coffee." Frankie, standing by the kitchen window, staring out at the others as they unloaded Another Round from the trailer and walked him to the stable, faced Jo, an expectant expression on her face. "Do you know what day it is?"

Jo sifted through a basket on the kitchen counter, looking for a pod of Earl's favorite coffee to put in the single-serve coffee maker. "Yep. It's Wednesday."

"Yes, it's Wednesday," Frankie repeated. "But what's the date?"

"It's the twenty-eighth of December," Jo said.

"Exactly." Frankie propped her hands on her hips. "We've spent the last week so focused on that darn race that we missed the most important part of the week."

Jo's hand stilled around the coffeepot, her gaze rising to meet Frankie's. "Christmas," she whispered. "We've completely missed Christmas."

"Yeah." Cheyenne plopped in a chair beside Earl at the kitchen table and rested her chin in her palms. "We missed presents, cards, decorations, ham, pecan pie—"

"I have a ham in the fridge," Frankie said, thrusting one finger in the air. "And a pecan pie in the freezer." A second finger joined the first, then a third. "And I think there are some green beans in that freezer, too."

Jo smiled. "Either way, that sounds like enough food to feed the lot of us and give us a reason to enjoy each other's company without any stress for the first time this week."

Frankie nodded. "Sounds like a winning plan to me."

One hour later, Jo, Frankie, and Cheyenne had managed to round up enough food to create a small feast for Lone Oaks's racing team. While Brooks, Lee, and Nancy settled Another Round in the stable for the night, Jo, Frankie, and Cheyenne worked feverishly in the kitchen to rustle up an impressive, though belated Christmas dinner comprised of ham, green beans flavored with the ham bone, creamed corn, some dinner rolls Frankie had bought prior to their trip, and a recently warmed pecan pie for dessert.

Cheyenne, having caught the Christmas spirit at some point during the process, had even found a white lace tablecloth on a shelf in the pantry and spread it out on the kitchen table along with enough place settings, silverware, and glasses of ice for everyone.

Frankie, who'd frequently glanced out of the kitchen window as they'd cooked, checked it one more time, then waved Cheyenne over toward the front door. "Cheyenne, run on out there and ask those three to come on in, please. They look about done out there and the food's ready."

Cheyenne complied eagerly, her hunger the driving force if the rumbles from her stomach were any indication.

Jo and Frankie had just finished filling each glass of ice with sweet tea when the front door opened, and Cheyenne returned with Brooks, Lee, and Nancy following close behind.

"Oh, my word," Nancy said, "what's that wonderful smell?" She walked into the kitchen behind Brooks and Lee, then stopped in her tracks as she spotted the food-laden table. "That looks delicious. I'm starving!"

"Well," Frankie said, "we figured y'all were starving just like us and we got to thinking that we all missed a decent Christmas dinner together, seeing as how we were so focused on the race and all."

Jo waved a hand toward the table. "Please, have a seat, everyone. We'll say the blessing and dig in."

It was a tight fit, but they managed it.

After everyone was settled, Jo looked at Cheyenne. "Would you like to say the blessing, Cheyenne?"

Cheyenne, seated opposite Jo, held her gaze for a moment, then looked around the table and shrugged. "Sure." After everyone bowed their heads, she began. "Dear Lord, thank you for letting there be a ham in Frankie and Earl's fridge. And the pecan pie in the freezer. I love pecan pie. The green beans I could've done without, but I suppose the pie will make up for it."

A strangled cough emerged from the end of the table and Jo cracked open one eye, catching sight of a grin on Lee's face.

"Thanks for letting Another Round race, too," Cheyenne continued. "Except for him losing. You could've gave him that one. I mean, you know how hard we've worked and—"

"Cheyenne." Jo met her eyes across the table. "Let's keep it humble and grateful, please."

She rolled her eyes. "Anyway, I'm going to wrap this up because I'm hungry, but I do want to thank you for sending me here." Her tone had softened, lowering almost to a whisper. "Thank you for letting me stay here. Thank you for letting me work with Another Round. And thank you for everyone at this table. Thank you for letting me not be alone this Christmas. Because even though we didn't win the race, I still had fun on the ride there and in the hotel. And the best part . . . the best part that I want to thank you for is that I got to come back to Lone Oaks Crossing. Coming back here tonight, felt . . . like, well, like coming home. Amen."

Jo's vision blurred and she blinked hard as she raised her head and looked around the table. Everyone was silent. Frankie was wiping her eyes, Lee and Brooks had a contemplative look on their faces, Nancy smiled at Cheyenne, and Earl had wrapped his arm around Cheyenne's shoulders and hugged her close, tears rolling down his cheeks.

"Well . . ." Jo cleared her throat, realizing that the loss on the racetrack was nothing compared to the heartfelt gratitude in Cheyenne's voice as she'd prayed. As far as Jo was concerned, despite their huge loss in New Orleans, Cheyenne had just given them the best win. "Amen."

CHAPTER 12

"He's gorgeous, isn't he?"

Brooks glanced at Cheyenne, who stood beside him on the back deck of Lone Oaks Crossing's main house. Her eyes, wide and fascinated, were fixed on Another Round, whom Lee was breezing along the track around the pasture.

Another Round was a sight to behold, for sure, as he galloped across the dirt, his lush mane and tail rippling behind him as he surged ahead. The crisp air of winter had given way to spring at Lone Oaks Crossing, and every inch of the rolling acres was a healthy green, the oak trees bordering the property full of broad leaves that danced in a gentle breeze. And it seemed the soothing late-March air filled Another Round's lungs and spirit with a hefty dose of enthusiasm.

The colt picked up even more speed, stretching his legs, galloping freely and powerfully across the serene landscape without any additional encouragement from

Lee who, judging from the smile on his face, was clearly enjoying the ride.

"I've never seen a horse as perfect or happy as he is." Smiling, Cheyenne looked up at him. "Don't you think he's happy?"

Brooks stared down at her, the joy in her bright eyes bringing a smile to his own lips. "Yeah. I'd say he's happy."

Although he couldn't say Another Round was perfect.

Brooks watched his thoroughbred gallop along the track, a relaxed ease in the horse's muscular movements that Brooks only saw here, never on the racetrack.

After placing a disappointing last in the Gun Runner Stakes in December, Another Round had delivered an equally disappointing performance at the Rebel Stakes in February and another at the Tampa Bay Derby two weeks ago. Though his times had improved, he'd finished last in both races. Each time, he'd taken off from the starting gate with his competitors, but there had been a visible tension in his gait and a hesitant air about him that eventually led to his holding back, then surging forward, only to quickly fall back again to place dead last.

Brooks didn't expect perfection, but he'd been so sure that Another Round would deliver. He'd thought from the moment Another Round was born that the thoroughbred was different, special even. His hopes for Another Round had been high. So high that the thoroughbred's disappointing performances hurt all the more.

But Another Round had delivered in a different way. Cheyenne, for one, seemed to have found her calling in life, having developed a strong bond with the thoroughbred. In the months since the Gun Runner race, Cheyenne had bounced back from her disappointment at Another Round's loss. She'd jumped back into her duties as the colt's groom with enthusiasm, complimenting the thoroughbred despite his shortcomings and eagerly consoling him upon his return after each race, stroking his neck, kissing his shoulder, and hugging him close, all the while assuring him that she couldn't be more proud of his performance on the track.

That had surprised Brooks. Cheyenne had been so disappointed with Another Round's performance in his first race that he'd thought she'd become increasingly downtrodden with each of his subsequent losses. Instead, she seemed to have shaken off the disappointment of not winning and embraced the joy of spending time with Another Round.

"Jo said this is his last workout for today," Cheyenne said. "She said after I help cool him down and get him settled back in his stall, she'll let me help her strategize for the Jeff Ruby." She tilted her head, a confused expression appearing. "I looked it up online. Why do they call it the Jeff Ruby Steaks rather than stakes?"

Brooks grinned. "It's a homophone. The sponsor of the race owns restaurants with the same name so it's a play on words and a nod to the sponsor. I'm glad Jo is including you in the preparation process for the race, but I can't help wondering if you're keeping up with your classes, too?"

"Of course." Cheyenne made a face as though offended. "Jo won't let me near Another Round if my grades drop. I've got an A in everything right now and even made the distinguished honor roll." She lifted her chin, a self-satisfied gleam in her eye. "What do you think of that?"

Brooks chuckled and ruffled her hair with his hand. "I think you'll do, kid."

He couldn't help but smile wider at the beaming look

of pride on Cheyenne's face. The kid had worked hard in every area of her life over the past six months. She'd grown in patience, maturity, and dedication, eagerly adhering to all of Jo's, Frankie's, and Earl's instructions in regard to caring for Another Round as well as completing her studies. Clearly, Cheyenne was happy at Lone Oaks Crossing, though Brooks hadn't anticipated anything different.

He recalled her prayer at their makeshift Christmas dinner three months ago. For that brief moment of time, her tough façade had been set aside in exchange for raw honesty and gratitude. He'd known Jo and Lone Oaks Crossing had a lot to offer Cheyenne, but he hadn't anticipated what it would mean to her to have others around who cared about her, pushed her to be a better version of herself, and praised her for following through with her commitments.

What was it she had said about their trip back from New Orleans?

Coming back . . . felt like coming home.

Brooks had to admit he'd felt the same. His gaze wandered farther out, seeking Jo's familiar form in the distance. She stood with Frankie at the white fence of the pasture, watching as Lee and Another Round galloped past. Shielding her eyes against the sharp rays of the morning sun, she smiled, her soft mouth moving as she called something out to Lee, then laughed with Frankie.

A sensation Brooks had grown accustomed to over the past few months flooded him yet again. A pleasurable mixture of desire, need, and admiration. He longed to stride across the grounds, tug her close, and hold her tight forever, safe and protected in his arms.

He'd fallen in love.

The realization, though welcome, still disconcerted

him. It had become increasingly difficult over the past
weeks to focus on Another Round and his own plans to
qualify for the Derby rather than his urgent desire to redirect his time to Jo. Lately, he'd found himself longing to
simply sit on the back deck of the main house with
Cheyenne, much as he did now, and enjoy the serene
sights and sounds of Lone Oaks Crossing.

The truth was, he'd fallen in love with the farm as
well. Lone Oaks Crossing had begun to feel like home.

"You like her, don't you?"

Brooks started and tore his gaze away from Jo, his
eyes meeting Cheyenne's curious—and slightly giddy—
expression. "What?"

"Jo." She smiled up at him. "You really like her."

It wasn't a question so much as it was a statement
of fact.

"Cheyenne—"

"Don't even try to deny it," she said. "I've seen the
way you look at her."

Despite the uncomfortable heat snaking up his neck,
Brooks grinned. "And what way is that?"

"You know." Shrugging, Cheyenne jerked her chin toward Jo in the pasture below. "All moony-like." A mischievous expression appeared on her face as she adopted
a teasing tone. "Like your heart is melting. Like a fire is
raging inside you. Like you can't stand the thought of living another moment without—"

"All right, kid," Brooks said, laughing. "I can do without your sarcasm this morning. We've got a race coming
up in a few days. A very important one, I might add, that
deserves all of my attention."

Cheyenne smirked. "You're trying to change the
subject."

"Heck, yes, I am. No way am I having that conversation with you."

Cheyenne rolled her eyes. "I don't know why. It's not like it's a secret or anything." She stared out at Jo again, then said softly, "It'd be nice, you know."

Brooks studied her face again, noting the bashful but yearning light in her eyes. "What would?"

"You two getting together. You and her being here every day . . ." She looked up at him, meeting his eyes. "With me, Frankie, and Earl. It'd be like . . . you know, a family."

Brooks fell silent, surprised by a deep-seated yearning of his own that unfurled deep within him, filling him with pleasure at the prospect. The thought was enticing, mesmerizing even. But guilt rushed in soon after, flooding him with a sense of regret and remorse at having forgotten, however briefly, the family he used to have before Spencer had ripped it all away.

"I suppose it might," Brooks said quietly.

Cheyenne brightened, searching his eyes. "So, you agree? That it really would feel like a family?"

Brooks hesitated, then reached out and gently ruffled her hair again. "I'm saying it's okay to dream, Cheyenne. It's okay to imagine a different life from what you have, to pursue an ideal of what you hope your life will be."

The hopeful light in her eyes vanished as she stared up at him, a wounded expression on her face. "So, it's okay for me to dream just as long as I don't expect it to come true?"

Brooks turned away, unable to face the pain lacing her words and unable to answer.

* * *

"He's looking at you again."

Jo, standing by the white fence of the pasture, looked away as Another Round galloped past and glanced at Frankie, who stood beside her. "Who? Another Round?"

Laughing, Frankie elbowed her gently, then motioned toward the back deck of the main house. "Our benefactor."

Jo glanced over at the main house, her eyes searching for and finding Brooks, who stared back at her. Noticing her eyes on him, he lifted a hand and waved, smiling wide.

She smiled and waved back, enjoying the delicious tingles she always felt when looking at him.

"He's having trouble keeping his eyes on his horse instead of you." Frankie leaned onto the fence and tossed a teasing glance in Jo's direction. "Why do you think that is?"

Oh, Lord. Here we go.

Jo ducked her head and rubbed her hands over her warm cheeks. Early on, Cheyenne, Frankie, and Earl had picked up on the undercurrent of tension between her and Brooks. Frankie had noticed it first, teasing her every now and then about Brooks's admiring glances and frequent compliments. Then, Cheyenne had joined in, making silly kissy faces behind Brooks's back whenever he and Jo were talking.

Eventually, even Earl had commented on Brooks's lack of focus.

Two weeks ago, on the warmest day so far in March, Brooks had insisted on joining Jo in the pasture to observe Another Round's workout. Despite his stated intention of getting a closer look at Another Round's progress, he'd spent most of his time leaning into Jo as they stood by the fence, murmuring softly in her ear, and sneaking a kiss on her cheek and neck every now and then.

Earl, who'd ventured out onto the back deck, walking slowly and carefully as he'd practiced in PT, had shouted down that Brooks should keep his hands and eyes off Jo and on his horse instead.

At the time, Jo could've died from the mortification of being chastised by her grandfather as though she and Brooks were teenagers stealing a passionate moment under a parent's watchful gaze. But at the same time, she delighted in the moment, realizing that Brooks had seemingly developed the same attraction to her as she felt for him.

Her fears of three months ago had eased just a bit, leading her to hope that he might be willing to redirect his focus from revenge on Spencer to loving her instead.

"I think he's paying me a lot as his trainer," Jo said. "So I'm guessing he's keeping an eye on me to make sure I'm getting the job done."

"Uh-huh," Frankie said, chuckling. "You keep telling yourself that if you want, but it hasn't escaped anyone's notice around here that you two have taken a liking to one another."

"I never said we haven't. But Brooks is of the same mind as Earl," Jo continued. "He agrees that business should come first, and his focus is on Another Round qualifying for the Derby."

Though that prospect seemed to grow farther out of reach with each of Another Round's losses. Since the Gun Runner race in New Orleans, Another Round had continued to place last in every race, dashing Brooks's hopes of possessing a winning thoroughbred.

Jo glanced over her shoulder as Another Round galloped along the track without encouragement from Lee. But Another Round *was* a winning thoroughbred and displayed his natural talents every day when training at Lone Oaks Crossing. He just couldn't seem to transfer that performance to a formal racetrack.

Apparently, the colt suffered from stage fright. It was a shame that the thoroughbred had been unable to overcome his fears of the track to perform at his best. Here at Lone Oaks Crossing, he ran fast and free without any tension or prompting.

"I'm afraid Brooks may be in for a disappointment," Jo said softly. "We're about a month away from the Derby, and at the moment, Another Round has zero wins to his name. And zero winning points, I might add."

Frankie frowned. "And how many points are on the line with this Jeff Ruby race coming up?"

"More than enough to qualify a thoroughbred for the Derby," Jo said. "The first-place finisher is awarded one hundred points, second gets forty, third gets thirty, then twenty and ten respectively. Another Round needs to finish in at least second position to have even a remote shot at qualifying for the Derby. In addition to that, he'd need to place in at least one more race in April as well. Pairing an additional win with a second-place finish at the Jeff Ruby would be our next best shot at qualifying for the Derby."

"And what would be our best shot?" Frankie asked.

Jo closed her eyes, visualizing what could only be called a dream at this point, considering Another Round's prior performances on the track. "A first-place finish in the Jeff Ruby would be ideal. One hundred points would pretty much guarantee us a spot on the track at Churchill Downs."

Frankie sighed and looked at Brooks again. "And if Another Round comes in last again? What would be Brooks's game plan after that?"

Jo shook her head, eyeing Brooks, who stood on the deck, his eyes following Another Round now as he galloped around the track. "I don't know. But I imagine his plan would change drastically."

The question that bothered Jo was whether Brooks's new plan would include her.

One week later, the stakes at the Jeff Ruby race could not have been higher. Jo stood beside Brooks in the walking ring, just prior to starting time, and watched as Another Round circled in front of the crowd.

"How's he looking today?" Brooks asked quietly. "Is he showing any improvement over the last race?"

Jo hesitated, knowing how much today's performance on the track meant to Brooks. "I'd say he looks the same." She glanced up at Brooks, noting the way the lines of tension bracketing his mouth deepened. "But things could change, you know? Anything can happen once he leaves the starting gate."

The words were true, but Jo still had trouble believing them herself.

Almost every day since Brooks had watched Another Round's workout with Lee from the deck, Another Round had delivered similar performances on the track at the farm. Each time his feet hit the dirt, he'd taken off with purpose and passion. Another Round had been in his element, racing like the born winner Brooks had once suspected he would be.

But considering the colt's disappointing finishes in the

past, Jo had little hope that the thoroughbred would overcome his stage fright and run freely on the synthetic track of Turfway Park, which hosted the day's race.

"I don't believe you," Brooks said. He glanced about at the crowd surrounding the walking ring, then ducked his head and whispered in her ear, "You say the words but they hold no conviction. I know you well enough to know when you're holding back on me."

Jo leaned toward him just a bit as she eyed Another Round circling the ring. "Then you know there's more I'd like to say that you'd probably rather not hear."

His head turned slightly, just enough that his nose brushed her cheek. "And that would be . . . ?"

"Would it be so bad?" She glanced up, holding his gaze. "Putting this behind you? Taking Another Round home and letting him continue to run for enjoyment rather than money and prestige?"

Brooks stared back at her, his eyes roving over her face, a flash of something akin to longing showing in his expression, disappearing almost as soon as it had appeared. "That's not part of my plan." He straightened, the emotion fading from his expression as he fixed his gaze on Another Round again. "There are other races besides this one. Win or lose today, we could still make it happen."

Jo nodded. "There are always other races. And I suspect there'll always be opportunities for disagreements, wins and losses, and more feuds. What I'm asking is whether you've ever considered putting all of that aside and embracing a new plan."

He remained silent and issued a tight smile toward the crowd surveying Another Round with admiration.

"If Another Round had a choice," she asked softly, "what do you think he would choose?"

Brooks glanced back at her, answering immediately. "He'd choose to run."

"But where?" She gestured toward the walking ring, the crowd, and the track in the distance behind them. "You think he'd prefer to be here or at Lone Oaks Crossing?" She bit her lip, unsure of how much more to say. "I know what I'd prefer. I'd prefer to be back at Lone Oaks Crossing, enjoying a nice view in good company. Having the choice to spend my time the way I wanted each day." She stared at Another Round, watching his muscular form stride across the walking ring. "I guess what I'm asking is, if this feud between you and Spencer no longer existed, where would you rather be? At tracks like this or back at Lone Oaks, enjoying your estate?"

A muscle clenched in his strong jaw, but he didn't answer.

Moments later, the jockeys were introduced, and Lee entered the walking ring in his pristine silks and cap, smiling broadly as he joined Jo and Brooks.

"I'd say it's a beautiful day in the neighborhood," Lee drawled, glancing around them at the sun-drenched spring day.

Jo laughed. "What makes you so peppy this afternoon? You know something we don't?"

Lee lifted his chin, a proud look on his face. "Not really. Just looking forward to the ride." He motioned toward Another Round. "Let's just hope he brings the same energy to the track that he's had at Lone Oaks Crossing for the past week."

"If he'd just run here like he runs back there, he'd take it all," Brooks said.

Lee sighed. "Yeah. I know. That's the problem, isn't it?"

"We were just discussing that," Jo said. "I was asking

Brooks where he thought Another Round preferred to spend his time?"

"I think that's obvious." Lee's smile dimmed just a little as he continued studying Another Round. "He loves to run, only not on the track."

"And you?" Jo asked. "Do you enjoy racing as much as you used to?"

Lee thought it over, his gaze remaining on Another Round, then shifting to Brooks. "I enjoy racing, but my favorite days are training days." He shrugged. "I appreciate your letting me work with Jo again, Brooks. I've learned a lot from her over the past few months." He looked at Jo. "Matter of fact, been thinking about training myself at some point."

Jo smiled, sneaking a glance at Brooks, who continued to watch Another Round silently. "That sounds like a plan," she said. "If I manage to get Lone Oaks Crossing back into good financial standing and the new business I hope to open on its feet, I'd love to have you back on our team on a permanent basis. I know Earl would love having you around."

Lee smiled even wider. "I'd like that."

Jo waited, hoping that Brooks would join the conversation again and possibly commit to working with Jo and Lone Oaks Crossing on a permanent basis rather than a temporary one. That maybe, just maybe, he'd consider a different path that didn't include racing.

But the moment was gone, the walk was over, and Another Round rejoined them, ready to undergo final preparations for the start of the race.

Brooks wished Lee good luck, patted Another Round's neck, then walked away.

"Be careful out there," Jo said, giving Lee a leg up onto Another Round. After Lee was settled in the saddle, she leaned close to Another Round, stroking his neck. "I know you're nervous," she whispered to the horse. "But don't pay any mind to the fanfare or the end result. Just run, handsome. Run your heart out and have fun."

Lee nodded at Jo, then guided Another Round off to join the pony horse and rider that would escort them to the track.

Jo watched them leave, then rubbed her hands together and began walking toward her viewing position by the track, stopping when a deep voice called her name. She glanced over her shoulder to find Brooks had stopped several feet away, his eyes holding hers, a somber look on his face.

"I enjoy being here," he said, "because you're here." His smile returned, brightening his expression. "Good luck out there. I'll be watching."

Jo smiled back, that pleasurable tingle returning, raising goose bumps on her skin. "You better be."

Later, Jo stood near the track, watching as the jockeys warmed up their horses near the starting gate. Another Round moved the same as always when he neared the starting gate, his movements showing signs of tension and hesitation. Lee continued warming him up though and Jo could see him leaning close to Another Round's ear as though giving him a pep talk.

All too soon, the horses were led one by one to their positions at the starting gate. Soon after, the gates were swept open and a bell rang, signaling the race had commenced.

Jo's hands clenched into fists by her sides as she watched the thoroughbreds race along the track. The afternoon sun was strong, glinting off the stands and the lenses of spectators' sunglasses. The crowd was on its feet, cheering the horses on, adding to the tension in the air.

Jo searched the racing horses until she managed to catch a glimpse of Another Round and Lee. They were struggling at the back of the pack, keeping pace but behind all the other horses as usual. The announcer blared overhead, calling out the names of horses who'd taken the lead, detailing each thoroughbred's move.

There was excitement in the spring air, lending an even more urgent feel to the competition. Jo watched with increasing dismay as the pack rounded another bend of the track, Another Round still lagging at the back.

"And there's about a quarter to go here, and Royal Jade still leads the pack." The announcer's voice continued to drone over the stadium speakers. "Mercy Angel is holding on to a close second and Praying Marksman third."

Jo closed her eyes, a familiar sinking feeling settling in her gut as she envisioned the finish line drawing closer and closer and Another Round lagging farther and farther behind.

Brooks would be disappointed with yet another loss; his confidence in Another Round might very well be shattered after this. He'd scour the listings again as soon as the race ended, begin strategizing new opportunities to race over the next month, planning to enter races with the highest points, spending every spare moment he had stressing over a new approach, which might very well include replacing Another Round with a different, more dependable—if not faster—horse that could—

"And out of nowhere, there goes Another Round, blasting up the outside, weaving his way in and out of the pack!"

Jo's eyes sprang open at the announcer's voice, shocked and electrified, blaring overhead.

"Another Round's kicking it into high gear now, picking the others off, one by one. He's past Praying Marksman, now Mercy Angel, and now Royal Jade! He's overtaken Royal Jade and he's not stopping! He's not stopping, folks!"

"Go, boy!" Jo sprang up and down, throwing her arms in the air and cheering as Another Round passed the pack and tore down the track, leaving the other horses behind, and thundering past the finish line.

"He's done it!" the announcer shouted. "Another Round has just bagged the Jeff Ruby with a time of one forty-four and three!"

Screaming with joy, Jo took off, weaving her way through the crowd, making her way toward the Winner's Circle and craning her neck for any sign of Brooks headed in that direction as well. But before she could get very far, a pair of strong arms wrapped around her from behind, spinning her around and lifting her up against a hard, broad chest.

"He did it, Jo! He did it!" Brooks's deep voice vibrated against her chest as he shouted above the crowd, hugging her tight. "We're in!"

Jo stumbled back as he released her, but he shot out a hand, steadying her on her feet, then grabbed her hand and tugged her toward the Winner's Circle, weaving in and out of the milling crowd.

Their time in the Winner's Circle flew by, the flashes of cameras, shouts of onlookers, and enthusiastic hand-shakes from well-wishers rolling over Jo in a harried frenzy. She stood there by Brooks's side as he introduced her and, after Lee had joined them with Another Round, praised Lee for his riding and praised Another Round as well. They were presented with the trophy, then posed for more pictures, engulfed in compliments, optimistic predictions for future wins, and admiration for Another Round— the surprising underdog who'd bolted out of nowhere and overtaken all his competitors in a flash at the last moment.

"It's what I've suspected all along," Brooks said happily to a reporter. "Another Round is a closer. He's the winner I hoped he was. He just needed the right training and a great rider." He motioned toward Jo and Lee, beaming proudly. "This is the winning team that made Another Round's win today possible. They're all winners." He reached out and tugged Jo close, tucking her into his side and wrapping his arm tight around her as he lifted his chin proudly toward the onlookers. "We hope to see you at the Derby, folks."

Brooks's praise and joy at the prospect of Another Round having the opportunity to race at Churchill Downs should have lifted Jo's spirits even higher. Instead, she found herself sagging against him, her mood plummeting into a downward spiral at the thought of undertaking yet another race, of yet again leaving Lone Oaks Crossing behind.

CHAPTER 13

A little more than one month later, on the first Saturday in May, over one hundred and fifty thousand spectators filled the grounds of Churchill Downs in Louisville, Kentucky. The stands were packed with the crowd, bright colorful hats of every style peppering the stands surrounding the racetrack. Mint juleps—a mixture of bourbon, sugar, mint, and water poured over crushed ice—were passed around, moving from hand to hand, then sipped under the warm spring sun.

The spectacular grounds of Churchill Downs displayed lush green grass and miles of white fencing. Everyone was dressed to the nines and looking their best, including the twenty thoroughbreds waiting to hit the track.

For the past two weeks, ever since Another Round had arrived at Churchill Downs, he'd been treated like royalty despite the fact that he still remained the underdog with eighty to one odds. Another Round's daily schedule didn't vary much from the one he enjoyed at Lone Oaks Crossing, though the stable at Churchill Downs was much more luxurious and prestigious.

Several times over the past few days, Another Round had been escorted to the starting gate on the track and had practiced standing in his place at the starting gate. All twenty thoroughbreds followed the same routine, which allowed them to become familiar with and better accustomed to the starting gate as well as waiting in their positions for all the other contenders to take their places. Jo hoped this would help dispel some of Another Round's performance anxiety.

The colt had continued training while staying at the track, preparing for the big race, and after each workout, he was cooled down and bathed with aromatic soap that left him clean, polished, and looking spectacular.

Another Round, however, wasn't the only one looking spectacular on race day.

Jo, standing outside the backstretch barns, glanced over at Cheyenne, who stood with Another Round, gazing up at him adoringly. "You look beautiful, Cheyenne."

Cheyenne glanced over at her and smiled, sweeping her arm toward her long white skirt, then tapping her fancy pink hat. "I hate wearing dresses," she said. "But I like this outfit."

As well she should, Jo thought, smiling.

After Another Round's win at the Jeff Ruby stakes over a month ago, she, Brooks, and Lee had joined Cheyenne, Frankie, and Earl to celebrate their win. Nancy, too, had become a part of the team, having taken a liking to Another Round and offering to help Cheyenne with the thoroughbred's daily grooming. Brooks and Jo had accepted her offer eagerly as they needed all the help they could get preparing for the Derby.

The one hundred points Another Round had won with

his first-place position in the Jeff Ruby Stakes had secured his place as one of the twenty thoroughbreds that would compete in the Kentucky Derby. After learning this, Cheyenne had been over the moon and eager to begin planning their trip to Churchill Downs. Brooks had been just as ecstatic, explaining to Cheyenne the ins and outs of the race as well as the festivities—some of which lasted an entire month leading up to the race—that Cheyenne could look forward to enjoying.

The first priority on the agenda had been finding a dress and a hat worthy of such a fancy occasion.

Jo and Frankie had taken Cheyenne shopping. At first, Cheyenne hadn't seemed too excited about the idea, but once she had visited a couple of boutiques and had seen the vast array of choices at her disposal, she'd found a hat she'd fallen in love with on the spot and a skirt to match. Since then, the attire she'd chosen for the race had been prominently displayed in her closet in eager anticipation of the big day.

"Have you seen Nancy's hat?" Cheyenne asked, grinning. "It's baby blue and gorgeous."

Jo laughed. "I think you might be fonder of formal attire than you imagined. And yes, I've seen Nancy's hat. It's adorable."

As a matter of fact, Jo had noticed everyone was looking their very best. She ran a hand through her long hair, tidying her curls as she studied the members of the group surrounding Another Round. The walkover, a tradition at the Kentucky Derby, was about to begin, and all of Another Round's connections, which included caretakers, friends, family, and guests, were allowed into Churchill Downs to escort Another Round from the backstretch barn to the paddock tunnel.

Frankie and Earl, both dressed impressively for the occasion, stood with Cheyenne near Another Round, admiring the thoroughbred as well. Frankie looked beautiful in a mint-green dress and hat and Earl had donned his best suit for race day and had worked especially hard with his physical therapist over the past month to build up enough strength and stamina to make the quarter-mile walk from the backstretch barn to the paddock tunnel. He seemed to stand just a bit taller today, his chest puffed out with pride and an excited gleam in his eye.

Jo walked over and looped her arm through his. "Does any of this feel familiar?" she asked, a sense of nostalgia enveloping her as she recalled their Derby win ten years ago.

Earl, smiling, looked down at her and practically beamed. "Just like yesterday," he whispered. He tapped her chin with one finger, then kissed her cheek. "You work miracles."

Jo rose to her toes and kissed his cheek, too. "You mean, *we* do. It took all of our hard work to get here today."

"Truer words were never spoken." Brooks, dressed the sharpest she'd ever seen him, strode over in a tailored suit that made him look all the more dashing. His eyes were warm and his smile affectionate. "You look absolutely gorgeous."

Jo's cheeks heated as she glanced down at her pink dress and shoes. "Thank you. But check me out again in about an hour and I'll probably have more dirt on me than couture."

Brooks laughed, tucking a strand of hair behind her ear. "It's a beautiful day for a race."

Lee, standing with Cheyenne and patting Another Round's neck, agreed. "God couldn't have given us a more perfect day."

Jo had to admit, he was right. She looked around, noting a few other horses and their connections mingling in the area. At the moment, things were calm before the storm. Most of the horses were quiet and reserved and their connections were reflective as well, absorbing the atmosphere and basking in the glory of the rare moment.

"What happens next?" Cheyenne asked, her eyes scanning their surroundings with excitement.

"We do the walkover," Jo said. "All twenty horses and their best friends and employees will gather up in one group and walk over to the paddock tunnel past the crowds." She tapped Cheyenne's nose affectionately. "Enjoy the quiet moments while we have them. Soon, you won't be able to hear yourself think."

The time came much sooner than Jo expected.

The call was made, and everyone was directed to begin the walkover. The calm silence that had lingered earlier dissipated and excited murmurings, the sounds of hooves, enthusiastic laughter, and nervous talk rippled through the group of horses and the hundreds of people accompanying them.

The group strolled from the backstretch barns across the grounds to the paddock tunnel, walking in front of the massive crowd of almost one hundred thousand screaming fans seated in the stands that rose above them. Jo walked beside Brooks, her hand brushing his occasionally, his strong fingers curling around hers every now and then, squeezing her hand as his eyes met hers, silently celebrating their achievement and the rare moment they were savoring together.

The horses who would be competing walked to the right of them and the throng of people shouting and cheering rose above them on the left. The energy in the air was electric, raising the hairs on the back of Jo's neck, sending thrills over her skin, and kicking her heartbeat into high gear. She glanced at Another Round, who was being led by Cheyenne on one side of him and Nancy on the other. Though he seemed a bit taken aback by the crowd and noise, he remained calm and focused. His gaze darted around a bit, taking in the scene, much as they were.

When they reached the end of the walkover, the group was allowed to linger for a short time to give their last well wishes to the thoroughbreds and each other, cherishing the final few minutes of exhilarating anticipation before the start of the race.

"You're going to be wonderful," Cheyenne said, stroking Another Round's neck. She glanced over her shoulder at Jo, a sheen of moisture in her eyes. "He's perfect, isn't he? Whether he wins or not, he's the best in the crowd."

Nodding, Jo walked over and hugged Cheyenne briefly before patting Another Round too. "That he is." She rested her forehead against his neck and patted him once more, whispering soothing words in his ear as she always did before a race. "You hear that, boy? You're perfect, just as you are."

"Every owner's horse is perfect in his eyes," a deep voice drawled behind them. "But just because you believe it, doesn't make it true."

Frowning, Jo turned around and found Spencer Harris standing a couple feet away, his eyes narrowed on Another Round. Seeing him there was not a surprise as she and Brooks had noticed him arrive the day after they had brought Another Round to Churchill Downs. Spencer's thoroughbred, Mad Warrior, had qualified for the Derby as well and had a much better standing than Another Round.

"That goes both ways." Brooks walked over to Jo's side. Spencer smiled. "I heard Another Round ended up with the gate farthest from the rail. It's a shame he's starting off in the worst position."

Brooks held his gaze. "Doesn't matter. Anything can happen on race day, and any one of the twenty horses could finish first despite where they start."

Spencer chuckled, his laughter holding little humor. "That it can. I have to say I'm rather surprised you're here at all. But then again, any horse can get lucky once." He dragged his teeth over his lower lip, his eyes sliding over Jo, leaving an uncomfortable shiver on her skin. "It's nice to see you again, Jo. I hope you enjoy the show."

Feeling Brooks tense beside her, Jo slid her hand in his and squeezed. "Good luck, Mr. Harris." She glanced up at Brooks as she tugged at his hand. "Let's go find our places, shall we?"

Spencer dipped his head, spun on his heel, and walked away, disappearing into the throng of people milling about the track.

"Don't let him ruin this," Jo said softly to Brooks. "Win or lose, it's an honor just to be here. Remember that when the race is over, okay?"

Brooks looked down at her, the firm set of his mouth softening slightly. "I'll do my best." He glanced over his shoulder and motioned toward the rest of their group. "Let's head to the sidelines, y'all. Things are about to crank up."

A few minutes later the group who'd participated in the walkover had dispersed and returned to their viewing positions near the track. The competitors lined up and the pony horses escorted each horse to the starting gate.

Jo, Brooks, Cheyenne, Nancy, Frankie, and Earl all stood on the sidelines, their attention fixed on Another

Round and Lee as they warmed up near the starting gate. The crowds behind and above them continued chatting, shouting, and cheering for their favorite horses, adding to the nervous anticipation that gradually grew thicker with each second that passed.

Jo glanced around her, observing the other owners, trainers, grooms, and their respective friends and family who were gathered in groups along the sidelines of the track, eagerly anticipating the start of the race.

She had the same thought as the one that had struck years ago when she'd stood near the very same spot prior to Sweet Dash placing first.

"We're a very small fish in a very, very big pond." She looked up at Brooks. "Most of these teams have dozens of people working with their thoroughbreds."

Brooks smiled, lowered his head, and kissed her temple. "But we have you. That makes all the difference in the world."

Jo groaned and pressed her face against his chest, mumbling, "Oh, I can't take this. Just let me know when it's over."

"You'll know when it's over from the deafening sounds behind you." Brooks laughed, the sound rumbling through his chest beneath her cheek. "But I'll let you know when it starts." His blunt finger tapped her chin, then nudged it upright and turned her face toward the starting gate. "And that's right about now."

All the competitors had taken their places at the starting gate, the gates swung open, and a bell rang, signaling the competition had begun.

Twenty thoroughbreds barreled out of the gates and galloped along the track, each vying for an advantageous position.

"Go, boy!" Cheyenne shouted. "Go!"

The crowd roared louder than ever before, screams and wails punctuating the shouts behind and above them. Jo craned her neck, straining to find Another Round in the pack. There he was, trailing at the back as usual.

"Give him time," Brooks shouted beside her. His gaze fixed on Another Round as the pack rounded a turn and headed toward the backstretch. "Just give him a little more time. He's a closer. He'll kick it into gear."

Frankie and Earl stood on the other side of Brooks, clutching each other's arms and cheering Another Round on, their shouts lost among the collective yell of the crowd.

"And here they come," the announcer shouted over the stadium speakers. "Around the bend and down the home-stretch. It's Surfer Girl, followed by Mad Warrior and Gemini Cry."

"Come on, come on . . ." Brooks chanted as the pack surged along the track. "There he goes! Look! There he—"

"And it's Another Round!" the announcer shouted. "He's blazing from the back, dashing through the pack and finding his way to the front. We saw him do this before, folks. He pulled this trick at the Jeff Ruby and I think he's gonna pull it again today."

The crowd erupted, feet stomping on the stands, shrieks and bellows punctuating the spring air as the horses thundered down the final leg of the race.

"Mad Warrior is putting up a fight," the announcer shouted. "Now it's Another Round and Gemini Cry. No! It's Mad Warrior—oh, Another Round just took over! He's taken it, folks! He's taking it—he took it! There you have it, folks! Another Round just rose to the top of the pack and has won the Kentucky Derby!"

The crowd burst into riotous applause, shouts, and raucous cheers.

"He did it!" Cheyenne shouted, pumping her fists in the air. "He won!"

"I can't believe it," Frankie yelled, leaning over Cheyenne to smile at Jo. "He did it again!"

Jo, her heart thundering in her chest, blinked back tears at the pride shining in Earl's eyes as he looked at her.

"My girl," he said, raising his fist in the air like Cheyenne.

The air left Jo's lungs as Brooks dragged her close, wrapped her in a bear hug, and squeezed. Her heart melted at the throb of affection in his tone on his next whispered words. "We did it, baby! We did it!"

After Another Round won the Derby, the next few hours flew by so fast Brooks barely had time to take it all in.

He remembered the winning moment clearly, the exhilaration he felt as Another Round shot to the front of the pack and crossed the finish line, the shout of joy that had erupted from his chest as his colt was announced as the official winner and, most vividly, the feel of Jo in his arms, her cheek pressed against his chest and her head tucked under his chin, celebrating the moment with him.

He couldn't have asked for a better day at the Derby.

Once Another Round had cooled down a bit, a garland of roses had been draped over his neck and Lee had escorted him to the Winner's Circle to meet up with the rest of the team. It had been a surreal moment, standing there before a cheering crowd with his winning colt nearby and the woman he loved by his side.

The moment had been too magnificent to pass up and Earl, along with the rest of them, had wanted to savor every second of it. He'd been so overcome with emotion that tears coursed down his cheeks during the award ceremony. But he'd remained standing through it all, refusing to take a seat even when his legs began to tremble. Even Cheyenne had cried, smiling as she wiped her tears and peppered kisses all over Another Round's neck.

The day had been a great one, and no one wanted it to end.

As a continuation of the celebration, they'd all walked Another Round from the Winner's Circle back to the barn. Another Round had earned a pampering cooldown and a peaceful rest in his stall. Everyone pitched in. Cheyenne and Nancy took the lead, hosing the colt down, soaping him up and massaging his tight muscles, helping him relax after the feverish race.

Jo and Brooks helped as well while Earl and Frankie stood nearby, taking turns patting his neck and rubbing his forehead, whispering praise.

A small crowd had gathered near them, watching the routine quietly so as not to startle Another Round. They admired him from afar, taking pictures and selfies, whispering to one another the qualities they admired most about him.

"You've got some new fans, boy," Cheyenne said, kissing his forehead. "They can't get enough of you."

"And that's how it should be," Brooks said, rubbing Another Round's back. "We all knew he was a winner at heart and now so does everyone else." He looked at Jo, his eyes warm and adoring. "I'd say he earned this win. We all did."

"I think we should celebrate." Frankie, her arm looped through Earl's, supporting him as they stood watching, smiled. "I can check with our hotel," she said, "and see if the private room is available for a late-evening dinner. We could all be together like we were at Christmas to celebrate our win."

Jo paused in the act of brushing Another Round's mane and nodded eagerly. "I think that'd be a perfect way to spend the evening."

Brooks agreed. There was nothing he wanted more at the moment than to spend time with Jo and the rest of the team who'd helped Another Round cross the finish line first. It was Jo and Earl's second Derby win but more than likely, the last one for all of them . . . at least for a while. After all their hard work, it was time to celebrate, kick back, and simply enjoy each other's company.

Three hours later, after Another Round had been returned to his stall for a healthy meal and a well-deserved rest, Brooks had returned to his hotel and now, he stepped out of his own hot shower, toweled off, and dressed in nice jeans and a dress shirt, taking care to comb his hair and adjust his collar neatly to look presentable for dinner despite the fact that all he wanted to do was slip down the hall, knock on Jo's hotel room door, and sweep her into his arms.

He had, as Earl had suggested, put business first for months now. It was past time he put pleasure first for a change.

Apart from Frankie and Earl, Brooks was the first to arrive downstairs at the hotel restaurant. The staff, excited over Another Round's recent win, had set aside a private room for them, free of charge, with a complimentary dinner to celebrate. Brooks entered the private room where a large oak table with high-back chairs sat center stage and a wide picture window presented a view of the moonlit grounds outside the restaurant.

"Come take a seat, Brooks," Frankie said, standing. She'd exchanged her fancy Derby outfit for a more relaxed but equally nice pants suit. She waved her hand toward a seat at the head of the table next to where she and Earl were sitting. "As the boss of this operation, I think you should take the head of the table."

Brooks smiled, crossed the room, and hugged Frankie. "That's kind of you, Frankie. But we all know I'm not the boss around here."

Earl, seated next to Frankie, chuckled, then held up a hand, beckoning Brooks closer. "You know a winner when you see one. You were the first to see it in Another Round. Thank you for bringing us along on this journey."

Brooks bent and hugged the older man, patting his back. Earl had made remarkable strides of his own over the past few months, working hard to regain his strength and improve his speech.

Brooks, basking in Earl's rare approval, took a chance, and whispered in his ear, "Now that we've gotten the business end of things out of the way, I guess I have your permission to spend a little time with Jo?"

Earl pulled back, his eyes narrowing at Brooks. "For the right reasons?"

Brooks nodded. "Yes, sir. When it comes to Jo, I have nothing but honorable intentions."

Earl smiled wide and patted his arm. "Then I'd say you've earned some free time. You have my permission to set business aside for a while and celebrate instead."

Brooks straightened and glanced around. "When's Jo coming down?"

Frankie looked up, her gaze moving toward the entrance to the private room as she nodded. "Right about now, it looks like."

And sure enough, there she was. Jo stood on the threshold of the private dining room, flanked by Cheyenne, Nancy, and Lee who walked across the room, all smiles, and took seats at the table. Brooks barely noticed though. His eyes were on Jo. The peach dress she wore clung to her shapely curves, her long curls flowed freely over her shoulders, and she wore minimal makeup, her naturally lovely complexion glowing.

Man, she was beautiful.

Jo remained standing on the threshold, a small smile curving her mouth as he walked slowly across the room to join her. "You cleaned up rather nicely," she said, lifting one hand and smoothing her fingertips across his clean-shaven jaw. "And you look as though you have the world at your feet. You're quite a sight to behold, Mr. Moore."

He smiled and dipped his head, his mouth tingling as it brushed the soft shell of her ear. "You almost got it right, Ms. Ellis. Tonight, I'm at your feet."

Her head turned, her warm cheek briefly brushing his as she whispered teasingly, "You mean, you're still at my beck and call?"

Unable to resist, he tilted his head and pressed his lips against her temple, kissing her softly and lingering a moment longer, breathing in her sweet scent and savoring the feel of her smooth skin against his lips. "Always. In every way." Reluctantly, he eased back and bent his arm in her direction. "Shall we join the celebration?"

Her gaze, soft and warm, lingered on his mouth as she answered, "I'd love to."

Over the next two hours, everyone ate, drank, and laughed to their heart's content, relishing their win and basking in each other's relaxed company. It was a nice

Chuckling, he covered her hands with his and lowered his head, skimming a kiss across her forehead. "You could say that."

She closed her eyes at the feel of his mouth against her skin, then looked up at him again, a hopeful light in her eyes. "So, things have changed?"

He stared down at her, taking time to admire the play of moonlight in her hair, on her pink lips and flushed cheeks. "What do you mean?"

She blinked up at him, expectation in her gaze. "Another Round has won the Derby and our business is done, so I'm hoping we can focus on other things now." Her palms drifted over his chest, making warm circles that radiated pleasurably over his skin beneath his dress shirt. "Things like each other."

Need and want flared in his gut. He leaned forward, nudging his leg between hers, cupping her delicate jaw and smoothing his thumbs over her tempting mouth. His blood pounded in his veins, roaring in his ears, raising a heady sense of longing within him to touch, to taste . . .

"Things like going home," she whispered. "Returning to Lone Oaks Crossing, putting all of this behind us, and starting fresh. Building something new."

His thumbs stilled against her lips, her warm breath tickling his skin as he blinked, trying to focus on her words. "Put what behind us?"

"This." She lifted one finger from his chest, gesturing toward the hotel and parking lot in the distance. "The traveling. The competition. The need for retribution." Her brows rose as she stared up at him. "You've won, Brooks. Your plan worked, and Another Round walked away from the Derby a winner. You can relax now.

You've got all the power and prestige you could want in the racing world. Every door is open to you professionally. You can let the past go now and start over. And I'm hoping you'll choose to do that"—her fingers stroked the base of his neck—"with me."

Gut clenching, Brooks closed his eyes, gathered her hands between his, and stepped back. "There's nothing I want more than to be with you, Jo, but—"

"But what?" Her gaze, wounded, held his. "You said a win at the Derby might change things. That you might be able to let this feud with Spencer go and turn your attention elsewhere."

He shook his head. "I can't do that, Jo." A helpless breath left his lips. "The Derby win means Another Round has a shot at the Triple Crown. All he needs to do is win the Preakness Stakes in two weeks and then the Belmont two weeks after that. As long as we keep his workout routine the same as before and prepare him well, he's in prime position to take both."

"And if he doesn't?"

"He will."

"There's no guarantee that once he hits the track, he'll leave it safely." She removed her hands from his and stepped back as well. The spring breeze rushed in, rustling her peach dress against her slender form, highlighting the distance between them. "That's where we lost Sweet Dash, and I'm not willing to risk Another Round's safety again. Are you? Are you willing to risk his well-being just to prove a point? You've earned your place among the elite, and your family name will be well-known now for a positive reason. Why not end it now while you're ahead? Take Another Round home, let him rest, and give him a new, peaceful retirement to run at ease where he's happy. You wanted the Derby, and you've won it. What more do you need?"

"I want to go all the way, Jo."

"Why?" Her arms moved restlessly at her sides. "If you had a deep love for the sport, I could understand. But I don't think you do. I don't think you take to it like others have. I don't think you even actually enjoy participating in these races." She moved closer, her expression one of appeal. "You told me you liked being at the racecourse because I was there. But what if I wasn't? What if it were just you and Another Round? Would you still want to be there? And if so, for what reason? Just to get back at Spencer Harris? Beat every thoroughbred he puts on the track? What would that get you? How would that take away any of the pain you still carry from losing your family and your home?"

"I'm not going back, Jo." He firmed his tone. "I'm seeing this through. There's no reason to turn back now."

"No reason?" she asked softly. "Even if I weren't here? I agreed to train Another Round to help you and to earn enough money to keep Lone Oaks Crossing safe from Spencer. We've both done what we came to do, and I don't want to do this anymore. I don't want to spend my time on the road, traveling from one place to another, competition after competition. I want to take Earl home so he can rest and continue healing, and I want Cheyenne to get back to a normal routine."

"Jo . . ."

She eased past him, walking back toward the hotel.

"Jo." He stood there, his heart kicking his ribs and his hands hanging heavily by his sides as she stopped and turned to face him once more. "Please stay and continue training Another Round. Two more races. That's all I'm asking."

Her mouth twisted. "And more races after those?"

"Please," he said. "Just think it over before you make a decision."

She closed her eyes and pressed her lips together, remaining silent for a moment. "All right. I'll sleep on it and give you an answer in the morning."

CHAPTER 14

Morning arrived sooner than Jo expected . . . and much earlier than she wanted.

Last night, after she'd left Brooks on the hotel grounds and returned to her hotel room, she'd stood just inside the threshold and closed her eyes, trying to process the enormity of what he was asking of her.

Cheyenne was snuggled under the covers in her double bed, sleeping deeply and snoring lightly.

The sight of her had brought a smile to Jo's lips despite the dilemma she faced. Cheyenne, her long hair mussed about the pillow and expression relaxed in deep, peaceful sleep, had become almost unrecognizable from the girl she'd been. There was no trace of the anger and pain she'd exhibited when she'd first arrived at Lone Oaks Crossing.

She'd grown so much over the past six months. Clearly, the predictable routine of caring for horses outdoors in the fresh air and sunshine had helped Cheyenne shake off some of the cynicism and disgust that had festered inside her when Jo had first met her at Dream House.

Dream House. The name alone inspired so many hopes but had delivered so very few for Cheyenne—or Brooks—during the time they'd spent there.

Now, Jo, sitting on the edge of her double bed in the hotel room, stared at the thin curtain covering the window, watching the morning sunlight begin to peek through the white material, her thoughts turning again to Brooks's painful losses.

Her eyes burned. She knew he'd suffered. Knew his pain, anger, and resentment ran deep. But she also knew that Spencer Harris (though he'd certainly contributed to Brooks's misfortunes and pain) wasn't the sole cause.

Brooks had been dealt a bad hand in life. He'd experienced pain and loss like so many other people Jo had met—even worked with—over the years . . . including herself. And if he continued down the path he was taking—if he continued searching for closure by inflicting pain or exacting revenge on someone else rather than dealing with the anger that tormented him on the inside, he'd never find peace or be satisfied with anything or anyone. Including her.

Blinking back tears, she slowly stood and, moving quietly so as not to disturb Cheyenne, went into the bathroom, shut the door, and washed her face. She patted her face dry with a hand towel and looked in the mirror, frowning at the dark shadows under her eyes and her strained expression.

She wanted to give Brooks the answer he hoped for. She certainly didn't want to walk away from him. But . . . she couldn't stay. She couldn't continue to blindly support him in a quest for vengeance and power that she knew would never bring resolution to his pain. But maybe, just maybe, she could persuade him to see her side of things. Help him understand why she was making the decision she was and, hopefully, persuade him to join her.

After showering, Jo dressed in jeans and a T-shirt, left a note for Cheyenne letting her know she'd be back soon, then exited the room quietly. She walked to the other end of the hall, glancing at the closed doors of Frankie and Earl's room as she passed. Once she reached Brooks's door, she raised her fist, hesitated briefly, then knocked.

Moments later, the door opened and Brooks, his dark hair disheveled and his expression looking as stressed as she felt, stepped back and swept his arm toward the interior of his suite as though he'd been awaiting her arrival.

"I just had a fresh carafe of coffee delivered," he said, striding across the suite to the sitting room area. He, like her, was dressed casually in jeans and a T-shirt, and his hair was damp and disheveled as though he'd just emerged from a shower, but his strong hand shook slightly as he picked up a white ceramic carafe and poured coffee into a mug. "You take sugar and cream, right?"

Her lips curved. "You've noticed?"

He paused in the act of pouring cream, glanced back at her, and smiled. "Yeah." He resumed adding cream, then sugar and stirred, murmuring softly, "I've noticed everything about you."

She stood still, her breath coming more rapidly as he walked toward her, holding out the mug. Aromatic steam rose from the rim and mingled with the masculine scent of his aftershave, the heady combination enticing her senses. "Thank you."

His fingers lingered on hers as she accepted the mug. Then he moved away, returning to the small table in the sitting area, pouring a cup of coffee for himself and gesturing toward one of the two chairs at the table. "Please, have a seat."

She did so, settling into one of the soft chairs and watching as he did the same.

"So," he said, cradling his coffee in both hands as he faced her across the table. "Have you thought things over?"

"That's all I did last night." She sipped her coffee, her lips trembling against the rim of the cup. "I couldn't sleep."

"Neither could I." His dark eyes roved over her, sadness pooling in them. "You're not staying, are you?"

She remained silent and sipped her coffee again, then asked softly, "If you found out you only had one month left of life, what would you do with it? How would you spend it?"

He frowned, an exasperated expression crossing his face. "Jo—"

"Please," she said, evoking their private joke. "Humor me?"

The displeasure in his eyes faded but he clenched his jaw, then said, "I'd certainly want to live it to the fullest."

"I'd hope so." She set her mug on the table and leaned forward, resting her arms on the table. "My time is the most valuable asset I have. I don't want to spend one day of it doing something I don't believe in." She looked down, interlocking her fingers and squeezing to still the tremors running through them. "When I started teaching, I loved it, and I had such high hopes for the future. I really thought I could make a difference and I truly believe I did for a while." She glanced up, meeting his eyes. "But over time, things changed, and I didn't feel as though I were in the right place anymore. I lost my joy in it and I felt like a pawn. I didn't want to believe it, but after I finally accepted that I needed to move on . . . that there was something better waiting for me somewhere else, I was able to picture a different future. One where I regained control of my life again."

Brooks reached out and covered her hands with his. "Jo . . . I—"

"Do you remember when we first met? The busted lip I sported?" Smiling ruefully, she lifted her hand and tapped her bottom lip. "It took getting socked in the mouth by some kid for me to let that place go. That's how devoted I was to teaching—to a career that was offering me nothing but pain and degradation in return for my time and dedication." She placed her hand on his wrist, feeling his pulse beat softly against her thumb. "Natasha— the student that hit me—she was in an argument with another student and just couldn't let it go. As a matter of fact, she was always fighting with everyone who crossed her path. So many of us at that school tried to help her, tried to coax her into turning her life around but the thing was, no matter what we did, she never made the choice to commit to change. And that was one thing we couldn't do for her—that had to come from her."

She leaned closer, squeezing his wrist and hand. "You could spend every moment of your life from this point forward strategizing, putting together plans, and pursuing some form of retribution against Spencer Harris and never find what you're looking for. I suspect what you're really looking for isn't something you'll ever receive from him."

His mouth tightened and he stared down at their joined hands. "And what is it you think I'm looking for?"

"A way to make the pain go away," she said softly.

"You have so much already, Brooks, and none of it is making you happy. Hurting Spencer isn't going to erase the bad memories you're carrying or give you back the time you lost with your parents. But you do have a choice in terms of how you spend the time you have ahead of you." She reached out and cupped his cheek, drifting her thumb over his strong jaw, the dark stubble on his cheeks rough against her skin. "Choose to let this feud with Spencer Harris go and come back to Lone Oaks Crossing with me. Put him—and the regrets—behind you and start over. Build a new life that makes you happy with me and Cheyenne. With Frankie and Earl. With the kids you've been helping at Dream House. You're not alone, Brooks. Come home to Lone Oaks and start fresh."

He was quiet for a while, holding her gaze. Then he turned his head, took her hand in his, and kissed the center of her palm. "I wish I could, Jo. But I can't."

Heart breaking, Jo closed her eyes, memorizing the feel of his lips against her skin and the deep throb of his voice. "Okay." She stood, walked around the table, and leaned down, brushing a tender kiss across his mouth. "You know where I'll be."

"Jo."

She paused on the way to the door and glanced back at him. "You won't have any trouble finding a trainer now." She smiled. "Everyone'll be lining up for a chance to work with Another Round—and you—in one way or another."

He was standing now, his lean cheeks flushed and chin trembling. "You're really quitting?"

Wet heat trickled down her cheeks as she nodded. "Sometimes that's the only way to move forward. And it's the hardest—not the easiest—thing to do. To let go of what's not healthy or not working. It's the right choice for me. I don't feel guilty about that anymore. I'm on a new path now—have been for a while. One where I can make a difference in Cheyenne's life and help her find her way in a loving home. Maybe do the same for other kids at Dream House who need support in a way that a traditional school can no longer provide. One where I can spend my days with my family, taking care of Earl, supporting Frankie, and choosing how I spend my time on my own terms. A life that's safer and more joyful than the one I had before." She walked to the door and opened it, saying over her shoulder as she left, "I just wish we could have traveled that path together."

Packing was easy but later that morning, after leaving Brooks's hotel room and returning to her own, breaking the news to Cheyenne was much more difficult than Jo had anticipated.

"What do you mean we're going back to Lone Oaks?" Cheyenne scowled at Jo as she laid her suitcase on the bed in their hotel room, opened it, and began filling it with her belongings. "Another Round just won the Derby. Frankie said that means he has a shot at the Triple Crown and that Brooks'll probably take him on to the Preakness race."

Jo walked over to the dresser, opened a drawer, and scooped out her clothes, then went back to the bed and tossed them into her open suitcase. "Brooks is taking Another Round to the Preakness, but we won't be accompanying him."

Confused, Cheyenne narrowed her eyes, tilted her head back, and skimmed her gaze over the ceiling as though an explanation dangled from the heavens. "I don't get it. Another Round just won. He's going on to the

Preakness with Brooks, and we're going home? But . . .
you're Another Round's trainer. You can't just leave him
in the middle of a competition."

Jo returned to the dresser, opened a second drawer, and
withdrew the pants she'd placed there two weeks earlier,
then tossed them in the suitcase, too. "I can and I will."
Sighing, Jo walked around and sat on the edge of the double bed, facing Cheyenne, who stood beside hers. "Look,
I'm not going to explain every detail of my decision, but
I will share with you that I'm not interested in accompanying Another Round to the Preakness—or to any other
race, for that matter."

Cheyenne slumped onto the edge of her bed, facing
her. "But why?"

"Do you remember when I told you what to expect
here at the Derby and that I'd been here before?" Jo
asked.

Still scowling, Cheyenne nodded.

"The horse I trained back then—Sweet Dash—we
took him on to the Preakness after he won the Derby, and
things didn't turn out so well for him there. He had an ac-
cident on the track and we ended up having to put him
down." She rubbed her eyes, the strain of the morning
catching up to her. "Up to that point, we'd had great luck,
you see? And we thought our luck would just continue on
forever. We didn't think about stopping. About taking our
win and our healthy horse back home where he could be
safe and happy. We would still have had a world-renowned
thoroughbred to flaunt." She shook her head. "I don't
want to take that risk with Another Round. I don't want to
be a part of taking the chance that Another Round's luck
may run out. Plus, my agreement with Brooks to serve as
his trainer only involved getting Another Round to the

Derby and, hopefully, helping him secure a win. I've done that. So now, it's time to go home."

"But . . ." Cheyenne looked down and dragged her bare feet across the carpet. "I thought you guys were, I don't know, like together or whatever."

Jo blinked as her face heated, unsure of how to respond.

Cheyenne looked up, studying her face. "I mean, I'm right, ain't I? You like him? And he likes you?"

"Well . . ." Jo shrugged awkwardly. "Yeah. We like each other well enough."

Cheyenne rolled her eyes. "Oh, come on. I ain't dumb. I can see how it is. Y'all like-like each other."

Despite the awkward tension, Jo laughed. "Okay. We like-like each other."

"But you're still leaving?" Cheyenne asked. "Just like that? Leaving him here on his own with Another Round?"

"Brooks is a grown man," Jo said firmly. "He can take care of himself, and believe me, he'll have more choices than he could imagine when it comes to hiring another trainer for Another Round." She stood, walked to the end of the bed, and resumed packing. "I'm not discussing my relationship with Brooks, but I will tell you this much. He and I just want different things right now. We're choosing to go in different directions. That may change in the future, but for now, it doesn't look like it's going to happen."

Silence fell between them. The only sounds were Jo's shoes stepping softly across the carpet as she continued packing, retrieving toiletries from the bathroom, and returning her foundation and lipstick to her makeup caddy while Cheyenne watched her in silence.

Then Cheyenne stood and, fidgeting with the hem of

her shorts, eyed Jo hesitantly. "So . . . what is it you want that Brooks doesn't?" Her gaze skittered away as Jo faced her. "I mean, what are you wanting to do besides train Another Round?"

Sensing the cautious tone in Cheyenne's voice, Jo stopped packing and sought her eyes, holding her gaze. "I want to go back to Lone Oaks Crossing and take care of the horses we're boarding. I want to get Earl home so he can rest, watch the horses graze under the sun on the back deck, and enjoy the spring weather. I want to work with Frankie to start renovating the main house and updating our stable so that we can build a new business for Lone Oaks Crossing and maybe invite more people in need to stay with us. And I want to get you settled back into your daily routine, help you study for your exams and get great grades, and explore what you want to do with your future." She spread her hands. "After all, your grades are excellent right now and you'll be starting your sophomore year after summer. If you decide to continue taking classes online, you'd be able to stick to your current schedule and still work with the horses every day."

"After summer?" Cheyenne's brows lifted, her eyes widening. "You mean . . . you're going to let me stay at Lone Oaks Crossing even after I finish my community hours?"

Jo smiled gently. "I'm not 'letting you.' I'm inviting you to stay with me, Earl, and Frankie at Lone Oaks Crossing for as long as you want. It'd make me happy for you to call Lone Oaks Crossing your home."

Cheyenne's chin trembled. "Y-you mean you want me to stay for good? Like . . . as part of your family?"

Jo crossed the room and nudged Cheyenne's chin up, meeting her eyes. "As far as I'm concerned, whether you decide to stay at Lone Oaks Crossing or not, you're already a part of our family. We'll always be here for you."

Two big tears rolled down Cheyenne's cheeks and a smile broke out on her face, lifting her cheeks and lighting her eyes. "I'd like that." She threw herself into Jo's arms, pressing her cheek to Jo's neck, her hot tears damp against Jo's skin. "I'd like that a lot."

Jo, blinking back tears of her own, hugged her close, then smoothed her hand over her hair. "Does this mean you're not going to give me any more grief about us going home now?"

Cheyenne laughed, her slight frame shaking against Jo before she eased away and dragged the back of her forearm over her wet cheeks. "Yeah. I'm okay with going home." She narrowed her eyes. "So long as you let me ride shotgun? I'm sick to death of the back seat."

"Always the negotiator." Jo laughed, then nodded. "I think we can handle that."

Two hours later, after Jo had shared her decision with Frankie and Earl, she, Cheyenne, Earl, and Frankie were all packed. They carried their bags to the parking lot and began loading them in Earl's truck.

"I see y'all are getting a head start on the trip back."

Jo, standing by the tailgate of the truck, hefted the last bag into the back, then glanced over her shoulder. Brooks stood a few feet away, his hand shoved in the pockets of his jeans as he surveyed the packed truck.

"Yeah," she said. "We wanted to hit the interstate before the heaviest traffic."

"Hey, Brooks?" Cheyenne left the passenger side of the truck and walked over to Brooks, hesitating a couple feet away from him. "Will you . . . will you tell Another Round 'bye for me?"

Brooks smiled. "Of course. I'll even give him a hug for good measure."

He held Cheyenne's gaze for a moment, and when she didn't move, he removed his hands from his pockets and spread his arms. Immediately, Cheyenne ran over, threw her arms around his waist, and pressed her cheek to his chest. He hugged her, smoothing one strong hand over her hair and dropping a kiss on the top of her head.

"I'm gonna miss you, kid," Brooks whispered, his voice barely discernible above a car passing by through the parking lot. "Take care of the horses for me, okay?" He looked up, his eyes meeting Jo's. "And Jo, too, all right?"

Cheyenne nodded against his chest, then pulled away, scrubbing the heels of her hands over her wet cheeks. "I-I will."

With that, she darted back to the truck, opened the passenger door, and climbed inside.

"Good luck at the Preakness," Earl said, walking over and hugging Brooks. "And be careful on the road."

"I will." Brooks smiled as Frankie jogged over and wrapped him in a bear hug, too. "Y'all be careful on the road, too. Give me a call when you make it back safely, okay?"

"Of course." Frankie patted his chest, then walked with Earl back to the truck, saying over her shoulder, "If you need us, you know where we'll be."

Moments later, the engine cranked and Jo stood by the tailgate a minute longer, holding Brooks's sad gaze and absorbing the vibrations of the metal bumper against her palm. Then she pushed off the tailgate, walked over, wrapped her arms around his waist, and pressed her cheek to his chest just as Cheyenne had.

His heart pumped rapidly beneath her cheek, each strong beat coming in time with the shallow breaths rasping between her lips. "I'm going to miss you."

His lips, soft and warm, pressed against the top of her head, and his big hands tightened around her back, pulling her closer. "No more than I'll miss you."

The catch in his normally steady tone made her heart squeeze. She lifted her head from his chest, rose to her tiptoes, and pressed her mouth to his. He kissed her back, his mouth moving with slow tenderness against hers until she reluctantly pulled away.

"Everyone's waiting for me," she whispered brokenly. Forcing a smile, she blinked back the tears that threatened to fall and repeated Frankie's words as she walked away. "You know where we'll be."

CHAPTER 15

One and a half weeks later, Brooks stood near the dirt racetrack at the Pimlico Race Course in Baltimore, his hands in his pockets and his eyes on the track.

The chirps of birds enlivened the warm, morning air as Another Round galloped around the track while traffic sped by in the distance. Engines roared sporadically amid the rustle of trees, the pounding of hooves, and the quiet chatter of a nearby tour group viewing Another Round's morning training session. The atmosphere was infused with a vibrant blend of admiration, anticipation, and excitement that should have stirred a sense of pride in Brooks. Instead, he found his gaze straying from what should be his sole focus and caught himself staring blankly at the highway in the distance, his attention lingering on the cars, trucks, and SUVs as they disappeared from view.

You know where we'll be.

Jo's words had stayed with him every day and night since she, Cheyenne, Frankie, and Earl had driven off in the direction of Lone Oaks Crossing, leaving him, Nancy, and Lee to proceed to the next destination of the Triple Crown on their own. He'd known it would be difficult to continue the journey and undertake the next competition without Jo, but he hadn't realized exactly how difficult it would be.

"He looks like he's having a tough time out there."

Nancy's voice tugged him out of his regretful daze and he refocused on Another Round, studying the thoroughbred's movements as the horse continued around the dirt track.

"His time is good," Nancy continued, "but it looks like something's off out there." She turned her head, shielding her eyes against the sharp rays of the morning sun as she squinted up at him. "Don't you think so?"

Reluctantly, Brooks nodded. " 'Fraid so."

Another Round had performed well but not at his peak ability, and it hadn't escaped his owner's notice that the thoroughbred seemed a bit tense—on edge, even.

"He's still adjusting to the track," Brooks said. "And to his new surroundings. It's expected that he'll take a couple days of workouts to settle in."

Though he wasn't sure if that would turn out to be exactly true. It was clear Another Round missed Jo and Cheyenne's presence. The thoroughbred's normally outgoing and friendly personality had been lackluster and standoffish of late. Even Lee had commented on Another Round's change in demeanor, stating he thought the horse seemed a bit morose.

"Of course," Nancy agreed. "But . . . we've already been here three days and I haven't seen much improvement. He still seems uptight." She shrugged. "I suppose he's feeling the tension in the air, too." She waved an arm toward the other thoroughbreds being groomed, walked, or prepped for their training. "Considering the competition warming up and the small crowds already touring the grounds to catch a glimpse of the horses, we can't blame him. Another Round's probably feeling the pressure more than we are."

"More than likely." Brooks glanced around, taking in the tour groups strolling around the racetrack, their laughter and chatter mingling with the noise of nearby traffic. "Things are very lively here. I used to love coming to Pimlico, but everything seems different this time around."

Nancy laughed. "Yeah. You own a Derby winner. Everyone wants a piece of you."

Brooks tried to smile. "I wouldn't go that far."

"I would." Her laugh faded. "And it seems like everyone else is more excited about your win than you are."

Brooks remained silent for a moment, considering this. Nancy was right that he was not as enthusiastic about his win as he'd imagined he would be. All he could think about was Jo and Lone Oaks Crossing.

"Brooks?" Nancy was studying him, a concerned gleam in her eye. "Things haven't quite been the same since Jo left, have they?"

"No." Brooks cast a reassuring look in Nancy's direction. "But I don't want you to think that you haven't done a fantastic job, because you have. Without Jo and Cheyenne, we just aren't the same team we were." A sad smile rose to his lips. "Or without Earl and Frankie, for that matter. It feels like a huge part of us is missing, and I imagine Another Round is feeling the same way."

Nancy nodded. "I won't argue with you there." She fell silent, watching Another Round gallop around the track and hit the home stretch. Soon, he was done with the workout and the pony horse and rider joined Another

Round and Lee to escort them back to the stable. "So, what do you want to do?"

Brooks frowned. "What do you mean?"

"What do you want to do about Another Round?" she asked. "I could spend some extra time with him this afternoon. Let him out for a while and give him a chance to walk out his nerves?"

Brooks straightened as Another Round and Lee drew closer. "No. I doubt that would do it." He lifted his hand, motioning for Lee to draw Another Round to a halt. "Nice workout, Lee."

"Not as good as it could be," Lee said. "He's holding back. Seems keyed up still."

"I know," Brooks said. "You and Nancy have been working your butts off lately. Why don't y'all take a break? Go get some lunch, relax, and explore the place for a while. I'll cool Another Round down, give him a bath, and get him settled."

Lee hesitated but dismounted, then handed Brooks the reins. "I appreciate it." He walked toward Nancy, then paused and glanced back at Brooks, his expression drawn. "I can't tell you with any degree of confidence that he'll shoot out of that gate on race day."

Brooks held his gaze, recognizing the underlying fear lacing Lee's tone. If Another Round wasn't sturdy and confident on his feet at the gate, there would be a much higher chance of his making a mistake or panicking. Neither of those conditions was ideal on a racetrack packed with other powerful thoroughbreds jockeying for position. Brooks and Nancy had been able to see Another Round's tension; clearly, Lee had been able to feel it during the ride.

"How much do you want this?" Lee walked back toward Brooks and lowered his voice. "It's always a gamble putting a horse on a track, but I can tell you now that the odds are worse, given Another Round's behavior lately. Is this win worth it to you?"

Now, holding Another Round's reins, Brooks looked up and eyed the thoroughbred beside him, his gaze drifting over Another Round's thick neck and muscular body, then returning to the horse's soulful eyes. "Don't rush through your lunch," he said softly. "I'm going to spend some time with our winner here."

Brooks walked Another Round across the grounds, stopping to give him water and allow him to cool down slowly. Afterward, he led Another Round back to the stables, removed his tack, and began washing him down.

The change in pace and scenery seemed to soothe the tension in the thoroughbred's body. His ears and posture relaxed, his stance grew calm and confident, and he leaned into Brooks's hands, searching for his touch and responding to his soft words of encouragement and praise.

"That feels good, doesn't it, buddy?" Brooks sprayed cool water over Another Round's back, washing away the pleasant-smelling soap he'd used to bathe the thoroughbred. "You were craving some downtime, weren't you?"

Another Round ducked his head and nuzzled Brooks's arm with his nose as if in agreement.

Smiling, Brooks moved farther along Another Round's powerful frame, spraying the cold water over every inch of him until his coat was shiny and clean. "There." He turned off the water and tossed the hose aside in exchange for a large, soft towel. "Now, I'll dry you down, get you a good supper, and put you to bed for a few hours. How's that sound?"

"Sounds like it'd be a better offer coming from a good-looking woman," a familiar voice drawled from behind.

Brooks paused in midmotion and glanced over his shoulder.

Spencer stood a few feet away, his hands in his pockets and his eyes on Another Round, a surly grin on his face. "Don't you have people for that, Brooks?"

"At times I prefer to roll up my sleeves and help out." Brooks narrowed his eyes at the other man. "Not that I'd expect you to understand that."

Spencer's grin widened. "Yeah, I heard you lost over half your entourage. I haven't seen Jo around lately. Lost another trainer, have you?"

Brooks faced Another Round again and resumed drying the thoroughbred, remaining silent. No doubt Spencer was already well aware of Jo's departure and had decided to stop by to gloat.

"It's unfortunate experiencing that kind of loss so close to a competition," Spencer continued. "Not that you'll have any trouble finding a trainer—or an entire new team—now that you've got a Derby win under your belt."

"What is it you want, Spencer?"

The sound of footsteps drew closer as Spencer walked over and stood in front of Another Round, eyeing the horse. "I just came to wish you well. Isn't that what a friendly competitor would do?"

"A respectful one, for sure," Brooks said through clenched teeth. "But you've never been either of those things."

Spencer shrugged. "I'm a businessman, first and foremost, Brooks. I don't consider it my obligation to be friendly when doing business."

"Or fair." Brooks walked over to the other side of Another Round and began drying his neck with the towel.

"You take more pride in stealing from people than you do in earning what you own."

"I don't steal." Spencer's tone hardened. "I simply take advantage of opportunities as they arise. As every effective businessman does."

Brooks rubbed the towel more quickly over Another Round's back. "There's taking advantage of opportunities and then there's exploiting other people's weaknesses. You've always had a tendency to do the latter rather than the former."

"It's not my fault that some people don't know when to stop."

"Like my father?" Brooks stopped drying Another Round and glared over at Spencer. "You certainly exploited his weakness. Stole everything from him that he held dear."

Spencer returned his stare for a few moments, then said, "I'm not a bad guy, Brooks. And no matter what you may think, I didn't deliberately target your father." He crossed his arms over his chest and tilted his head to the side. "I was only a few years older than you at the time. The business that transpired was mainly a deal between my father and yours. I was simply there to assist in the closing of it. There's no need for you to carry a grudge against me."

A mirthless chuckle rose from Brooks's chest. "The past is too dirty for you to paint rosy, Spencer. Tell yourself whatever helps you sleep at night, but you and I both know the truth. You were as much an instigator back then as you are now. Just like you tried to be several months ago when you threatened Rhett and then Jo." Another Round was dry now. Brooks tossed the towel aside and faced Spencer. "Problem is, you underestimated me and Jo."

Spencer's jaw clenched, but a stiff smile spread across his face. "That, I'll concede. See how friendly a competitor I can be, Brooks?" He stepped closer, a more congenial tone entering his voice. "As a matter of fact, that's one of the reasons I came to speak to you. I have a business proposition for you."

Brooks laughed. Man, the absolute absurdity of it all. The bastard had some nerve.

"Yeah," he drawled, "because you're the type of person I've always wanted to do business with. I'm not the kind of man you are, Spencer."

"Just hear me out." Spencer followed Brooks as he walked around to the other side of the thoroughbred. "You've done really well for yourself establishing Original Sin. You've brought a lot more business to town, created an innovative tourist destination, and have local investors salivating at the prospect of tossing money your way after your recent win." He spread his hands. "I've got the connections, and now you've got the clout. It makes sense for us to merge our businesses and form a partnership."

"It makes anything but sense," Brooks said. He smoothed his hand over Another Round's head, neck, and back, searching for any damp spots he might have missed. The thoroughbred's muscles flexed under his touch and the horse's eyes followed Spencer, some of the earlier tension returning to Another Round's posture. "Whatever you're offering, I'm not interested."

"Why not hear me out at least? There's a lot to this deal that would benefit you. Probably more than you imagine."

Brooks continued smoothing his hands over Another Round's back. He had no difficulty imagining just what Spencer planned to offer. A murky partnership, probably.

One in which Brooks would be presented with what appeared to be a fantastic deal, when all the time, Spencer's primary motive would be to keep Brooks under his thumb. To have a controlling interest in the business Brooks had built from the ground up with next to nothing—no name, no money, and no connections. Spencer would eventually lay claim to it all in the name of this partnership. And, as a bonus, he'd be able to control every move Brooks made.

Brooks supposed it went both ways though. Merging his business with Spencer's would afford him the opportunity to be privy to Spencer's moves as well. He'd have much more access to Spencer's dirty doings than he could have on his own. And what was that saying? Ah, yes. Keep your enemies closer . . .

"Think of the possibilities," Spencer continued. "With your spectacular bourbon and Derby winner and my successful casino ventures and quality thoroughbreds, we'd have a leg up on all the competition in our area."

Brooks walked to the front of Another Round and rubbed his forehead, trying to ignore the sound of Spencer's voice.

"Come on, Brooks. Is this really what you want to spend your time doing? Washing down horses, chasing down trainers, and spending every waking moment busting your tail to score a win when you could be paying someone else to do it for you?"

Brooks's hand stilled against Another Round's head. The thoroughbred's dark eyes locked with his, seeming to peer deep. "What did you say?"

An exasperated sound left Spencer's lips and his boots crunched across the ground as he moved closer. "I said, is this how you want to spend your time?"

Brooks smoothed his thumb over Another Round's forehead gently, leaning closer, concentrating on the horse's soft breaths against his chest. He thought of Lone Oaks Crossing. Of the routine Jo had taught Cheyenne. He thought of the striking picture Another Round always made in the pasture behind the main house as Cheyenne groomed him every morning at daybreak. He thought of Earl and Frankie, sipping coffee on the back deck, as they watched Cheyenne's progress with pride. He thought of Jo, staying close to Cheyenne, watching her every move, supporting and protecting her as she learned. He could see the smile on Jo's face now, the way her eyes would light up as she saw Cheyenne grow into a stronger, more confident young woman with a mature head on her shoulders.

He thought of spending his days—every day—just like that. Enjoying every moment of every hour at Lone Oaks Crossing with Jo and the warm, welcoming, camaraderie of the little makeshift family they'd built over the past few months. And he thought of the future . . . of the lives they could change—equine and human, alike—for the better, in the peaceful home he had grown to love as much as he loved Jo.

It was all there waiting for him, just as Jo had said. All he had to do was set his anger and resentment down, leave them here with Spencer and walk away.

"Yeah," he said softly. "This is exactly how I want to spend my time."

He took Another Round's reins in his hands and led the thoroughbred away.

"Brooks!" Spencer shouted after him. "Just think it over. The possibilities would be endless."

"They already are," Brooks called back. He glanced

up at Another Round and patted his neck. "Let's get you brushed and fed, boy." His smile grew. "You can sleep on the way home."

"Jo! Take a break and come over here!"

Jo, standing in a field behind the main house at Lone Oaks Crossing, turned off the HVLP paint sprayer she held, and glanced over her shoulder. Earl waved from where he stood by the white fence of the adjacent pasture, beckoning her over with a wide smile on his face.

A smile rose to her own lips. Since their return to Lone Oaks Crossing almost two weeks ago, Earl had made impressive strides in his recovery—even more so than he had prior to their trip to Churchill Downs. The trip to the Kentucky Derby and subsequent win had done Earl a world of good, but it was the return home to Lone Oaks Crossing that seemed to have really kicked his rehabilitation into high gear.

After they'd said goodbye to Brooks in Louisville, Jo, Cheyenne, Frankie, and Earl had endured a sad, quiet drive home. But Earl had been the first to perk up when they reached the farm, announcing how glad he was they had returned and how eager he was to get a good night's sleep in his own bed. The following morning, he had risen early, along with Jo and Cheyenne, and had met them in the kitchen for breakfast with Frankie. Earl had been eager to get back into the daily routine.

Every morning thereafter, he rose early, ate breakfast, and walked to the stables with Jo, Cheyenne, and Frankie to attend to the horses they were boarding. He aided Cheyenne in the grooming routine, telling humorous anecdotes and giving sage advice. He and Cheyenne had shared several laughs during their time working together and soon, their friendship had blossomed along with Cheyenne's skill with the horses. Clearly, Earl delighted in spending time with Cheyenne and Cheyenne basked in his caring attention.

This morning, Earl had risen early as usual, joined Cheyenne in the stables, and helped her groom one of their new arrivals. Benny (short for Benjamin The Great) had arrived at Lone Oaks Crossing one week ago. The thoroughbred was a retired racehorse in need of a permanent home. Earl, who'd been almost as eager as Jo to open a new rehab retreat at Lone Oaks Crossing for retired racehorses, had welcomed the thoroughbred with excitement. Benny had taken to the daily routine at the farm quickly and possessed a friendly personality reminiscent of Another Round.

Jo looked down at her boots and dragged one toe across the thick bluegrass. A painful ache still throbbed in her chest at the thought of Another Round and Brooks. The past couple weeks without them had been difficult, to say the least. She'd been surprised at how quickly and easily Brooks had slipped into their daily routine at Lone Oaks Crossing . . . and her heart. Even though every morning started the same as it had over the past several months, she still felt as though something was missing. Lone Oaks Crossing simply wasn't the same without Brooks and Another Round.

They'd be at the Pimlico Race Course in Baltimore by now, preparing for the Preakness Stakes. And if they won, they'd progress to the Belmont Stakes at Belmont Park in New York. Who knew where they'd end up after that? Or if Another Round would make it safely to the finish line of each race? Or if Brooks would ever decide to set his feud with Spencer aside long enough to return to Lone Oaks Crossing and her?

It had been hard to walk away from Brooks . . . and it was turning out to be even harder to let go of her hopes for his return.

"Jo!" Earl shouted again. "Come take a look. You gotta see this!"

Jo pulled in a strong breath, rolled her shoulders, and began walking across the field toward the pasture. Heart aching or not, today was too gorgeous a day to wallow in misery. Spring had fully sprung at Lone Oaks Crossing. The trees bordering Brooks's property were lush with leaves, the bluegrass underfoot was thick and healthy, and the morning sun cast a golden glow over the green landscape, lending it a nostalgic appeal.

No. She smiled as she drew closer to Earl and noticed the pride in his expression. Her sadness over Brooks's absence would have to wait. Right now, Earl was happy, Lone Oaks Crossing had found new life and Cheyenne was thriving. At the moment, that was all that mattered.

"It's about time you took a break," Earl said as she joined him at the pasture fence. "You've been painting that new paddock fence all morning."

Jo laughed. "It's not even noon yet, Earl. I'd hardly say I've been painting all morning. Besides, I'm anxious to get that paddock fenced and ready for horses." She lifted her chin toward the center of the pasture, where Cheyenne and Frankie stood with Benny, stroking his neck and back and speaking sweetly to him. "Frankie said someone stopped her in town just yesterday. She mentioned they're anxious to send over more retired racehorses that need a place to stay until they're adopted. The more space I make, the sooner we can take them on."

Earl nodded. "Just don't overdo it. An extra day or two of delay won't make that big a difference. You need to enjoy what you're doing and take breaks when you need them. That's one of the reasons you left that old job of yours, wasn't it? To slow down? Life moves at a healthier pace out here if you let it." He pointed at Frankie and Cheyenne. "Like them. Take a look at that kid. She's caught on so fast, I'd say she was about born for this. And she takes her time and enjoys it."

Jo watched as Cheyenne held out her palm, called Benny, and waited patiently as the thoroughbred strolled over and nuzzled his nose against her hand.

"There," Earl said, a broad smile breaking out on his face. "These new horses are taking to her like bees to honey."

Jo laughed. "That they have. I've noticed she's grown a lot more comfortable acquainting herself with new arrivals on her own. She used to shy away from horses she didn't know, but she's overcoming her fear a little bit more every day."

"All of them." Earl's hand moved, sliding over the top fence rail to cover hers and squeeze gently. "That's your doing. You gave her a home, love, and purpose. She's like a different kid altogether from when she first arrived here."

Cheeks heating, Jo leaned over and kissed his temple. "That wasn't just me. That was all of us." She watched Cheyenne and Frankie work with the new thoroughbred silently for a few minutes. "I'd say Frankie has done as much, if not more, work with Cheyenne than I have."

Earl grinned, his eyes roving over Frankie. "That she has. You know . . . I've been thinking of asking her to stick around."

"Frankie?" Jo glanced up at him and narrowed her eyes, searching his expression. "And what does that mean exactly?"

"Well . . ." He shifted uncomfortably beside her. "You know."

Jo smiled wider, a giddy feeling fluttering in her middle. "No, I don't know," she teased. "Explain it to me." She nudged him gently with her elbow. "Go on."

Earl slapped her elbow playfully, then grumped, "You know what I mean, girl. It's about time I did the right thing by her."

Jo slid her arm around his elbow and leaned against him, saying softly, "And you love her."

Earl fell silent, a sheen of moisture gathering in his eyes as he looked away, blinking rapidly. "Yeah. I love her something fierce. Always have."

Jo followed his gaze, watching Frankie as she hugged Benny's neck then laughed, the joyful sound echoing across the grounds. "Then why have you waited so long to commit to her?"

"Just scared, I guess." His voice trembled. "After losing your grandmother and your mother, I was alone and angry. It broke my heart, I guess you could say."

Jo bit her lip. "And me. I'm sorry I left you, too."

"No." Earl wrapped his arm around her shoulders and squeezed her close, kissing her forehead. "You have a life to live, and you were determined to do it your way. Still are. Thing is, I should've been living all that time, too." He looked down at her, tears collecting on his lower lashes. "All I could think about when I lay in that hospital bed, unable to talk and hardly able to walk, was how much time I had wasted. How much of it I just let go of, not staying in the moment, not finding meaning in every second possible. I just let it pass without notice." He looked back at the pasture, his smile returning as his gaze settled on Frankie again. "I'm not doing that anymore. I got you here, I got Cheyenne, and now it's time to get Frankie here, too—on a full-time, permanent basis, I mean. Then I'll feel like I have my family together." He met Jo's eyes again, a fierce pride in his smile. "A new family. A stronger, healthier one so we can enjoy every second of every day together."

Jo hugged him again and clasped his hand in hers. The moment was almost perfect except for one thing. Brooks wasn't there to share it.

She swallowed hard past the tight lump in her throat and smiled anyway, savoring the moment with Earl, watching Cheyenne and Frankie work with Benny in the pasture, and mentally making plans for the future retreat she planned for Lone Oaks Crossing.

After a while, Cheyenne and Frankie walked Benny across the pasture toward them.

"This one's a winner, too," Cheyenne said, her face flushed with excitement and the warmth of the spring sun. "How long is he staying with us?"

Jo shook her head. "I don't know. As long as we let him or until he's adopted, I imagine."

Cheyenne lifted her chin, a broad smile appearing. "I'll adopt him."

Jo smiled. "I think we could make room for one more around here, if your heart's set on him."

"It is." Cheyenne practically jumped in place. "Oh, it is."

"But," Jo stated firmly, "it'll be your responsibility to take care of him. And I'll still expect you to complete your other chores and keep your grades up."

Cheyenne jogged over to the fence, hopped up onto the bottom rung, and pecked a kiss on Jo's cheek. "Thanks, Jo. You won't regret it, I promise."

"Then start proving it now," Jo said, smiling. "Take him back to the stables, get him in a stall, and give him something good to eat."

"Yes, ma'am." With that, Cheyenne grabbed Benny's reins and led him toward the stables, chatting to him the whole way. "Did you hear that, boy? You're gonna stay. And you're gonna be mine."

Frankie laughed, following in Cheyenne's wake. "I'll stick with the kid for a while and make sure she gets her chores done." She flashed a smile in Earl's direction. "It's a beautiful day. When I get back to the house, I'll cook us up some lunch and we can sit out on the deck and eat together. Soak up some of this beautiful sun. What d'you think, Earl?"

Earl chuckled. "I think I'll go inside, get the steaks out of the freezer, and start defrosting them. Then I'll set up the grill on the deck and we can cook together."

Frankie seemed happy with that. "Hey, I ain't gonna argue with having a helping hand in the kitchen."

She followed Cheyenne and Benny to the stables as Earl headed toward the main house.

"Want to come inside and take a break?" Earl asked over his shoulder.

"Not yet." Jo shoved off the fence and started walking back toward the new paddock. "I'm going to spray some more paint on that fence first; then I'll join you."

One hour later, Jo had finished spray painting another section of the new paddock fence. Sweat beaded on her brow and her cheeks burned as though she'd gotten a bit too much sun. Exhaling, she set down the spray gun, ran the back of her hand across her forehead, and leaned back, stretching her tight back muscles. Her muscles ached, her arms were heavy and tired, but just the sight of the progress she'd made filled her with sweet satisfaction.

The delicious aroma of sizzling steak and charcoal lingered on the spring air, wafting past Jo's nose. Earl, Frankie, and Cheyenne were all on the back deck now, working around a grill Earl had set up, and Jo's heart squeezed at the sight of them laughing, an unexpected pang of grief shooting through her as she imagined Brooks standing there as well, just as he had on so many occasions over the past few months.

Eyes burning from more than just the sting of sweat, she stretched her arms overhead, rolled her shoulders, and walked away, stealing a few moments to hide her grief before joining them. Today was a good day and she wouldn't ruin it.

She slowed her steps across the bluegrass and closed her eyes, tilting her head back and enjoying the cool whisper of the spring breeze over her sweat-slicked skin. It was peaceful here, with the birds chirping and the tall grass rustling in the breeze, but heavy steps across the ground and a quiet snuffle prompted her eyes to open and focus on the oak trees in the distance.

And there, between two strong oaks, Brooks emerged, leading Another Round across the grassy field toward her.

Jo stopped in her tracks, her breath catching at the sight of Brooks's muscular frame, striding purposefully across the field, his dark eyes fixed on her and a slow smile spreading across his face.

She stood frozen in place as they drew close, her heart kicking against her ribs. "Wh-what are you doing here? You're supposed to race in a couple days."

Brooks stopped a few feet away from her, grinning

wider as Another Round continued forward, nudging his broad head against her waist, seeking her attention and affection. "Well, this guy here got to missing you and let me know it was time to come home. I was feeling the same, so I decided to pack up, call it quits, and leave the race and everything that went with it behind." He chuckled as Another Round pushed closer to her, nudging her back a step. "And, seeing as we're back in town now, we thought we'd pay you a neighborly visit."

Jo stumbled once more under Another Round's insistent nudging then steadied herself and hugged the thoroughbred's neck, pressing a kiss to his forehead. "You're not my neighbor."

The happy light in Brooks's eyes died. "What do you mean?"

Jo patted Another Round's neck, eased around him, and walked the few feet between her and Brooks, only stopping when the toes of her boots met the toes of his. She tilted her head back and looked up at him, her eyes searching the dark depths of his, her smile growing so big her cheeks ached with happiness. "You're not my neighbor," she whispered. "You're family. And I'm glad you finally came home."

Brooks shook his head slowly, his bright smile re-emerging. "Lord, I'm glad you said that."

He wrapped his arms around her and drew her close, lifting her to her tiptoes and covering her mouth with his. The tender pressure of his lips parting hers and the warm, intoxicating taste of his kiss was all too familiar . . . and so very missed! Her skin tingled with pleasure and her blood rushed, the surge of emotions swirling inside her evoking a heady sensation that left her feeling almost dizzy when he lifted his mouth from hers.

She missed his kiss immediately, but the separation was more than worth it to hear his next words.

"I love you, Jo," he murmured softly against her cheek as he nuzzled her ear and glided his cheek against her neck. "My time is the most valuable asset I have, and I don't want to spend another second of my life without you in it."

Heart fit to burst, she whispered, "Well, you're in luck. Because I love you, too, and we have all the time in the world."

EPILOGUE

"I'm sorry this is going to happen to you, but you deserve it."

Jo's brows rose as she backed away from Brooks, laughter bursting from her lips at the mischievous grin on his handsome face. "What are you doing, Brooks? What are y—oh, good grief!"

Another eruption of laughter broke from her lips as he tugged her against him, wrapped his arms around her, and fell backward into a brightly colored pile of fall leaves they'd finished raking only minutes earlier.

"Brooks!" she gasped, laughing, as she tumbled on top of him, his strong hands settling her gently against him. "We just finished raking these up."

His dark eyes, warm with love, gazed up at her. He stroked his hand over her long hair as he murmured, "And I just couldn't resist rolling you in them."

Blushing, she grinned. "Isn't that something you're supposed to do in hay?"

He looked up, considering this, then made a face. "I suppose you're right, but since there's no hay around, I had to improvise with something else that was readily at hand." He winked. "Besides, doesn't matter where we are . . . I can't resist you."

Which, Jo admitted silently as she leaned down and kissed him, was the honest truth.

Two years had passed since she'd stood in this same field and watched Brooks emerge from the tree line bordering his property, leaving the racetrack and his feud with Spencer Harris behind to join her at Lone Oaks Crossing. She'd been overjoyed at his return and all too eager to join her life with his. It had only taken a few dates and many, many stolen kisses during each workday on the farm before Brooks had finally proposed and a mere fraction of a second before she'd accepted.

Three months later, Lone Oaks Crossing hosted its first double wedding as she and Brooks had happily celebrated the same wedding day as Earl and Frankie. The celebration couldn't have been more perfect. Cheyenne had served as maid of honor for both Jo and Frankie at a small ceremony witnessed by their closest friends. There'd been cake—and kisses—for days, and Jo had never been happier.

And Brooks . . . well—she grinned as she kissed him more deeply—he hadn't been able to keep his hands off her. She snuggled closer to him, a tender pleasure blooming right where the slight swell of her soft belly pressed against his lean hips, her lips curving in a smile as she thought of the secret she'd only just discovered this morning. She'd tell him tonight.

Excitement bubbled up within her, sending a delicious shiver through her. Their little family was growing. Would they have a boy or a girl? A daughter with her blue eyes and stubborn chin? Or a handsome son with his dashing features and gentleman's soul?

"Mmm." His sensual mouth moved gently against hers. "You think they'll miss us if we sneak off for a little while?"

"I doubt i—"

"Yes! I'd notice!" Two turquoise boots shuffled across the carpet of fall leaves and stopped inches from them. Cheyenne glared down at them, her hands on her hips—but her lips twitched and there was a humorous glint in her eyes. "We just finished raking these things up and here y'all go mussing 'em up. It'll take forever to get them back in a decent pile again."

Brooks's broad chest vibrated against hers as he chuckled. "Nah. We'll have 'em up in a jiff. Besides, you better be extra special nice to us, or we won't take you for your first driving lesson."

Cheyenne's demeanor changed instantly. "Whatever you say, parental units." Smiling, she held up her hands and backed away, then spun on her heel and strolled toward the back deck of the main house. "Wallow around in the dirty leaves all you want. Just call me to help finish raking them back up when you're done."

Jo stared after her, her mouth falling open. "It's amazing what a sixteen-year-old will agree to do at the prospect of earning a driver's license."

"She's a go-getter," Brooks said. "Just like her mom."

"Mom," Jo repeated softly, still staring after Cheyenne, her heart fit to burst with the joy growing inside her. "I'm her mom . . ."

And in eight months, she'd be a mom to a brand-new baby created by the love she and Brooks shared.

One week after their wedding, they'd asked if Cheyenne wanted to be an official part of their family, and when she'd eagerly accepted, Jo and Brooks had initiated adoption proceedings and embraced her as their new daughter.

Brooks had consolidated his business and property with Earl's and rebranded Original Sin as an extension of Lone Oaks Crossing. Though she, Brooks, and Cheyenne lived next door, they spent most of their time at the farm with Earl and Frankie, working with the new horses that continued to arrive for boarding or rehabilitation, and supervising the foster children from Dream House that they invited to intern in the stables. Lee and Nancy had rejoined them at Lone Oaks Crossing as well. Lee, eager to begin a new career as a trainer, had begun interning with Jo, and Nancy had partnered with Earl and Cheyenne to oversee the daily operations of the stable.

She and Brooks had a beautiful home, a beautiful daughter, and a beautiful life that would only get better.

"You're a great dad," she said softly, tracing his lower lip with her finger.

"And you're a great mom," Brooks said as he tucked a strand of hair behind her ear. He continued staring up at her, his dark gaze roving over her face. "Man, you're beautiful—inside and out. The most gorgeous woman I've ever known." He brushed his lips along her cheekbone, temple, and forehead. "You know, Earl told me once that what I had on the other side of those Oaks was a dream and that I should hold on to it tight." Cradling her face in his hands, he smoothed his thumbs over her cheeks and whispered, "He was wrong. My dream was right here—on the other side of that tree line. And I never plan on letting you go."

She smoothed his hair from his brow and glided her fingertips over the stubble lining his jaw. "Good. Because I'm never letting you go either."

He smiled. "What do you say we let our daughter hang out with Frankie and Earl a little while and stay here a bit longer? Just you and me?"

"I'd say," she whispered as she kissed him, "there's no place I'd rather be."

Don't miss ONE IN A MILLION from Janet Dailey!

CHAPTER 1

Summer had arrived early. It was barely the end of May, but the season already promised to be a scorcher. The Texas plains sizzled under a blazing sky. Heat waves shimmered above the scrubby yellow landscape. A rattlesnake, coiled in the shadow of a mesquite, stirred, then slithered into the deeper cool of an empty badger hole.

Mirages swam like water over the narrow asphalt road that branched off Highway 277 and led to the Culhane Ranch and Stables. But Lila Culhane knew better than to be fooled by these, or by mirages of a different sort, like the illusion of a solid marriage.

Lila had paid the investigator she'd hired and tucked the damning evidence into her purse. The only remaining question was when and how to use it. Did she want to keep Frank? Did she want to punish him? Or maybe both?

The AC was blasting air from the vents of Lila's white Porsche 911 Carrera, but the silk blouse she wore still clung like glue to her skin. When she reached up to brush back a lock of tastefully streaked blond hair, she could smell her own sweat. She stank like an oil-rig worker.

At thirty-eight, she was no longer the teen queen who'd won the Miss Idaho pageant nor the Vegas showgirl who'd lured a rich Texas rancher away from his middle-aged wife. But she still looked good. She'd kept her figure and taken care of her skin. She'd given him everything he wanted in bed; and for the past eleven years of their marriage, she'd been one hundred percent faithful to the bastard.

She'd even shared his passion for horses—at first, as a way to catch his attention, then later as a genuine enthusiast. Either way, she'd given Frank no cause to be sneaking around.

Lila's hands tightened around the steering wheel. Frank deserved the worst punishment she could give him. But first she had to take care of her own needs.

Too bad about that prenup she'd been forced to sign. Without it, she could hire a lawyer and take him to the cleaners, just as his first wife had done. But no such luck. If she were to divorce Frank, she'd probably end up living in a two-room flat and driving a ten-year-old Chevy.

In the distance, through the blur of heat waves, she could see the stately white house and the vast horse complex—the covered arena, the stable with its fifty-four stalls and attached treatment facility, the breeding shed, the round pen for breaking horses, and the well-watered paddocks where spring colts frolicked under the watchful eyes of their dams. The distant pastures were dotted with black Angus cattle, an important cash source that enabled Frank to focus on his real passion, working with the champion quarter horses he bred, raised, and showed in reining and cutting competitions.

Even before they were married, Lila had understood

that the horses were Frank's first love. For eleven years she'd settled for second place in his heart, learning to understand the sport and cheering him on at every reining event. But now everything had changed.

Lila ran a hand over the back of her neck. Her palm came away slicked with moisture. *Damnation*, but she hated this infernal heat—almost as much as she hated Frank.

What she craved now was a dip in the pool behind the house, followed by an ice-cold mojito under the shade of the pergola. But that wasn't likely to happen. Not as long as Frank's daughter, Jasmine, was staying in the house awaiting a call from her phantom Hollywood agent.

Jasmine had made the pool and patio her own little kingdom. She might tolerate a visit from her father or her brother, Darrin. But when Lila was around, Jasmine radiated pure, seething hostility. The great house was her castle. As Frank Culhane's daughter, she was its princess; and her stepmother was the wicked queen.

Lila sighed as she swung the car off the road and up the long driveway, bordered with drooping magnolias. Frank and his daughter had always been close. If Jasmine knew about Frank's affair, she was probably cheering him on.

Back in her upstairs bedroom, Lila gazed out the window that overlooked the pool. Visible from below the roof of the pergola, she could see a pair of suntanned legs and manicured feet adorned with electric blue toenails. The princess had staked out her territory. And a swim wasn't worth the price of dealing with her sidelong glares and verbal jabs.

Lila still craved the mojito. But she would drink it in

her private office, after a shower. Seated at her desk, she would rake over Frank's betrayal, until she'd worked up enough rage to do what had to be done.

The covered arena stood thirty yards back from the rear of the house, with the attached stable beyond. Jasmine had angled the lounge chair to give her the best view of the cowboys doing chores and riding her father's blooded performance quarter horses. Here on the ranch, with nowhere to go and not much to do, it was the best live entertainment to be had.

Not that she was complaining. Most of the cowboys were either kids or old hands, but some of the men were handsome enough to stir her interest. Jasmine took pleasure in devouring them with her eyes—and if they caught her watching, what was the harm? They enjoyed the game as much as she did.

In the past, she might have done more than watch. At thirty, she was wiser and more discreet than in her younger years. Still, now and then, a man would show up who was hot enough to dampen her panties—like that tall, dark-headed trainer who'd hired on since the last time she was here.

Jasmine had done her homework. Roper McKenna was the firstborn son of the scab-knuckled family who'd bought the small ranch fifteen miles from the Culhane property. In the two years since their move from a Colorado cow town, the McKennas had remained outsiders, ignored by their wealthy Texas neighbors. They drove old cars and trucks, bought their clothes at Walmart, and were never invited to barbecues or joined for neighborly chats.

The McKennas were all right. They just weren't what

you'd call quality folk. It was almost as if they were invisible—except for the one thing that set them apart.

The four younger McKenna siblings—three brothers and a sister—had taken the national PRCA rodeo scene by storm, winning every event from barrel racing to bull riding. They'd even appeared on the cover of *Sports Illustrated*.

According to an article Jasmine had Googled, Roper's bronc-riding career had ended years ago with a spectacular wreck at the National Finals Rodeo in Vegas. Sidelined for months, he'd taken a job at a stable, exercising high-strung show horses. That was when he'd discovered a natural gift—a way of fostering trust between horse and rider that produced winners in the arena and brought in prize money for wealthy owners like Frank Culhane.

Jasmine shifted in her chair, shading her eyes to get a better view of the cowboy who'd caught her fancy. She knew that Roper was good at his job—otherwise her daddy wouldn't have hired him to train his precious horses. But truth be told, Jasmine wouldn't have cared if Roper couldn't swing his leg over a horse's rump. The man was so hot that she could feel the sizzle all the way across the yard.

This afternoon, Roper was riding Frank's retired champion American quarter horse, One in a Million. Over the years, the big bay roan had competed in showing and cutting events for prize winnings of over a million dollars. But his real value to the ranch lay in his prowess as a stud. Since his retirement from the show arena, the winnings of his colts and fillies and their offspring had totaled more than four million dollars. A straw of his frozen semen sold for more than a thousand, his IVF embryos with eggs from a champion mare went for several times that. His fee for a live breeding was listed in the EquiStat Stallion Registry at $10,000, although live breeding was rarely performed here at the ranch. If Roper had his way, the dangerous practice would cease entirely.

At the age of thirteen, One in a Million could still perform the strenuous spins, patterns, and sliding stops that had made him a champion. But the demands of the arena were judged too risky for his aging body. He was given a special diet and exercised every day to keep him healthy and fit for the breeding shed.

A smile curved Jasmine's lips as Roper loped the stallion around the arena. The horse still had his elegant moves. The speed it took to win might have tapered off. But the man was a master, putting the great horse through his paces with subtle moves of his hands, knees, and feet. She wouldn't mind getting a closer look. But the timing was wrong today. There were too many people around. Roper would be tired and wanting to finish his work. And today, after a hard swim in the pool, she was a stringy-haired, red-eyed mess.

Roper usually arrived at work early in the morning. That would be the best time for her to take a stroll and bump into him—purely by chance, of course.

She laughed, imagining the surprise on his handsome face. She'd tried more than once to catch his eye. So far, he'd seemed unaware of her. But Jasmine knew her way around men, and she knew how to get herself noticed. She looked forward to the challenge.

It was a long-standing custom for the Culhane family to eat dinner together every Friday night. The tradition had started two generations ago when a giant oak tree on the ranch was felled by lightning. Frank's grandfather, Elias Culhane, had declared the strike an act of God, sliced a long, diagonal section of the trunk and had it made into a table for the family dining room. It had been Elias—a preacher's son—who'd given orders that hereafter, his descendants should sit down at the table and share a weekly meal in peace, harmony, and love.

Nobody crossed Elias, not even decades after his death. But over the years, peace, harmony, and love had become a joke. And the table had become more of a Friday night battleground.

Wearing a yellow sundress, with her fiery hair twisted into a high bun, Jasmine surveyed her family around the table. Not a bad-looking bunch. But in other respects . . .

"Hey, sis, what have you heard from that fancy agent of yours?" Darrin, her brother, was seated across from her. "Is Ron Howard still begging you to come and star in his big movie?"

Butthead. Always was, always would be. And as usual, he knew right where to jab. "I'm still weighing my options," she said. "How's that Supreme Court nomination coming? Any word from the president?"

"Good one, sis." Darrin was four years older than Jasmine. Redheaded like his sister and their mother, he kept an office in the house he rented in the nearby town of Willow Bend, but the ranch had always been his home, just as his destiny had long since been carved out as the Culhane family lawyer.

"Actually, Jasmine, your brother has a point." Simone, Darrin's petite blond bride, was from Dallas oil money via finishing school. "Get real, honey. You're never going to make it as a movie star. Find yourself a job—or better yet, find a man who'll take care of you and give you some babies to raise. You're not getting any younger."

Jasmine caught the amorous glance that passed between the newlyweds. *Heavenly days, was Simone already pregnant?*

Anxious to change the subject, Jasmine spoke to her father, who sat at the head of the table.

"Daddy, have you chosen your horse for the Run for a Million?"

Frank Culhane speared a second slice of prime rib, taking his time to answer. He was a strikingly handsome man—his body fit, his hair thick and streaked with silver. A respected trainer and champion rider, he was still winning cash prizes at reining events. This past March, at the Cactus Classic in Scottsdale, he had qualified to be one of sixteen top riders in the biggest reining event of the year—the Run for a Million, to take place later that summer at South Point Arena in Las Vegas.

"It's too soon to decide," he said. "The Run for a Million won't happen until mid-August. There's plenty of time."

"Come on, I know you, Dad," Jasmine teased. "Give me a hint. Is it Million Dollar Baby?"

He shrugged. "Can't say. You know the drill. I'll be taking three horses to the competition, two of them as backup. I probably won't make my final decision until the night of the competition. Meanwhile, I'll be riding in two other events. That should help narrow down the choice."

Yes, Jasmine knew the drill. She'd grown up in stables and arenas where both her parents were competing for prize money. Not all Jasmine's memories were happy. Sometimes the tension between her parents would get so heavy that she could almost taste it in the air. Maybe that was why, although she was a capable rider, she'd never wanted to compete.

In reining events, each rider chose the horse to show. And there were rules. A horse could be shown by its owner, a family member, or an employee. A trainer without a suitable horse could lease one from an owner or ride a client's horse. Prize money would be split between the owner, the rider, and usually the runners-up.

"When are you going to retire, Dad?" Darrin asked. "You'll be the oldest rider in this year's competition. Isn't it time you stepped back and let the next generation take over?"

"Some of your trainers are good enough to win," Jasmine said. "Look at Roper. When he rides, it's as if he creates a mind link with the horses. Put him on a winner and he could make some serious money for the ranch. When are you going to give him a chance?"

Frank chuckled. "After I win the Run for a Million, I'll think about it. But don't talk to me about retiring. I'd rather die in the saddle than in a rocking chair or, heaven forbid, in some blasted hospital bed. Give me my horses and the thrill of competing for a prize. For me, that's heaven."

"I understand, Dad. But you're not as young as you used to be. We want you to take care of yourself."

Jasmine did understand, although she knew better than to speak the truth. Frank enjoyed being the center of attention. He didn't want anybody stealing his thunder in the arena—especially a younger employee who was probably a better rider than his boss. And Frank wouldn't be too keen on sharing the prize money either, or having his best trainer quit for a better offer.

One person at the table hadn't spoken. Lila sat at Frank's left, toying with the food on her plate. She was a stunning woman, tall and elegant, her stylishly streaked hair tied back with a silk scarf. Usually she held her own in the weekly dinner table conversations. But tonight she appeared troubled.

Whatever was wrong, the bitch deserved it, Jasmine told herself. She had hated her stepmother from the moment she'd set foot in the great house and started redecorating. At first, Lila had tried to make friends with her husband's daughter. But there could be no forgiveness for the woman who'd destroyed her parents' marriage. After the first few months, Lila had abandoned her overtures and settled for cold civility.

The tension had eased when Jasmine left for L.A. to pursue acting and modeling work. But when she came home between gigs, it was as if she'd never been away.

Frank finished his pecan pie and stirred in his chair. "I'm going down to check on that mare who's about to foal," he said, turning to Lila. "If she's in labor, I'll stay with her, so don't wait up for me."

"Fine." The word was spoken with no change in Lila's expression. "Try not to wake me when you come in."

"I won't. I know my girl needs her beauty sleep." He pushed his chair away from the table and stood. "'Night, all. If I'm not here in the morning, don't come looking for me. I'll just be with the mare or having coffee with the boys."

"Do you want some company, Dad?" Jasmine asked. But Frank had left the room. In the kitchen, she heard him say a few words to the cook. Then the back door opened and closed as he headed outside. Never mind, Jasmine told herself as she excused herself and left the table. It was early, but she could read or watch TV for a while, then get a good night's sleep. Tomorrow morning, if she managed to catch up with Roper McKenna, things could get interesting.

As she washed her face and brushed her teeth, Simone's words echoed in her memory.

You're never going to make it as a movie star . . . Find a man who'll take care of you. You're not getting any younger.

Jasmine tried to shrug off the comment. Simone always seemed to be putting other people down. But what if she was right? Not about the man, of course. Jasmine's marriage, at twenty, had been an eleven-month nightmare that had included an early miscarriage. She wasn't in a hurry to try again, if ever. But the part about never making it as an actress had stung. True, she hadn't been offered even a small movie part in more than six months. Even TV commercials, once her bread and butter, had dwindled to two or three a year. The agent call that never seemed to come had become a family joke.

She couldn't live here and be Daddy's baby doll forever. Maybe it was time she put on her big-girl panties and looked for other options.

But not tomorrow. Tomorrow, what she needed was a distraction—a tall, dark, and gorgeous distraction.

At 5:00 on Saturday morning, Roper pulled his battered Ford pickup into the Culhane Stables employee lot. After swigging the last of his coffee, he put the mug into the cup holder and climbed out of the truck to start the workday.

At any given time, there were between fifty and sixty horses on the Culhane Ranch. They belonged to Frank or to clients who paid to have their horses trained and boarded here. Some of the brood mares were pregnant or nursing foals. The other horses were required to be ridden every day.

The quarter horses currently in competition were usually trained by Frank. The rest of them—about forty animals, including the senior stallion, One in a Million—were Roper's job. He decided which ones should be passed down to the assistant trainers. The rest were trained by Roper himself. By the time he'd exercised them all and put them through the turns, patterns, and slide stops of a reining display, the sun would be low in the sky.

Roper whistled an off-key tune as he strode toward the stable. The first rays of morning were painting the sky above the distant hills. Birds trilled from the pastures. A Mexican eagle flashed white-tipped wings as it swooped down on a rabbit in the yellow grass.

Roper liked his job, for now at least. Frank was a decent boss, and the pay was good. But he missed the clients and horses he'd left behind in Colorado, and he missed the freedom to compete. Frank had hired him on the condition that he focus strictly on training and forget about entering contests. Roper had needed a good job close to home. Even more urgently, he'd needed an introduction to the big-money events. For now, he'd accepted the limitation. But he knew that he was good enough to hold his own in reining and cutting. Next year, he vowed, he'd be out there proving it. All he needed was knowing the right people and having the right horse.

As he entered the stable by the front door, Roper decided to start the day with a sharp dun mare at the far end. He would work his way forward, saving One in a Million for last. Riding the seasoned older stallion would be a relaxing way to end the day.

As usual, he was the first one here. By the time he'd wrapped the mare's legs and saddled her, the stable hands and grooms had shown up—youngsters willing to shovel manure, haul feed, and rub down horses for their chance at a dream. They were local kids who lived in town, unlike the cowboys who tended cattle and slept in the bunkhouse.

Roper left the stall door open for the cleaner and rode the mare out of the barn into the spacious training arena. The dun mare was a client's horse, three years old and in the early stages of training. Roper warmed her up, then started on circle patterns. She was smart, her hooves steady on the deep layer of sand, loam, and sawdust.

By now the sun was coming up. Giving the mare a pat and a moment's rest, Roper found himself gazing toward the rear of the Culhane mansion. The patio was empty, sunlight sparkling on the surface of the pool. There was no sign of Frank's glamorous daughter yet, but then, it was early.

He was aware that she watched him, but they'd never spoken. He didn't even know her first name—but that didn't matter because if they were to meet, he would address her as Miss Culhane, and he would keep his hands off her. If ever there was a shortcut to professional suicide, it was fooling around with the boss's daughter—or worse, his wife.

Enjoy your day, Miss Culhane, he thought. *You may be beautiful and sexy as hell, but I've been burned before, and it's not going to happen again.*

With that, he put the mare through one more pattern and rode her back inside, where the grooms waited to hose her down and put her away. His next horse was waiting, saddled, wrapped, and ready.

Dressed in jeans, boots, and a white shirt open to the third button, Jasmine strode down the corridor that separated the facing rows of stalls. The activity at the far end gave her hope that her timing was good. With luck, when Roper finished his ride, she'd be there to meet him. They wouldn't be alone. That couldn't be helped. But she had her story—and as the boss's daughter, she could expect him to be agreeable.

As he rode in from the arena and swung off a filly, she stepped forward. Only then did he appear to notice her.

"Miss Culhane." He tipped his hat. His eyes were dark gray, like clouds before a storm. His voice was cold to the point of indifference. "Is there something I can do for you?"

She gave him her most winning smile. "I know you're working, so I won't take much of your time. I'm just hoping you might be willing to do me a favor."

"That depends. You've got five minutes to tell me about it. But no promises. I'm on the clock."

"I understand." She nodded, tilting her face at what she knew to be a flattering angle. "I promise to be on the clock, too. Cross my heart." Her fingertip traced an *X* across her chest, its path meant to draw his gaze downward to the hollow between her breasts.

"I'm listening," he said. "Go on."

"I've enjoyed riding in the past," she said. "I wouldn't mind trying it again. But it's been a few years, and I've forgotten most of what I used to know. I could use your help in choosing a horse, and riding it—it shouldn't take long, and you'd be paid extra for your time, of course. Come by tonight, after work, and we can talk about it— maybe over dinner. There's a nice steak house in Willow Bend. What do you say?"

She'd at least expected some interest. But his expression was as icy as ever. "Miss Culhane, I work for your father. You should take this up with him, not me. If he wants me to help you, as part of my job, fine. If not, you'll have to find another way. Now, if you'll excuse me, I've got horses to exercise."

Turning away, he mounted the waiting stallion and headed back toward the arena.

The three grooms—two boys and a girl—had unsaddled the filly and were leading her to the wash station. The grooms had pretended to ignore the conversation, but they'd probably heard every word. Jasmine's face burned with humiliation.

Fine, she told herself. If Roper expected her to ask her father, that was just what she would do. Frank usually said yes to whatever she wanted. Soon she would have Roper McKenna at her beck and call. And he would learn to like it.

She hadn't seen her father this morning. But he couldn't be far. He'd mentioned sitting up with a mare in labor or sharing breakfast coffee with some of the cowboys. Finding him should be easy enough.

Taking her time, she walked back along the double row of stalls. The last stall on her right belonged to Frank's prized stud horse, One in a Million.

As she came closer, she noticed that the stall gate had been left open a few inches. Maybe Frank had stopped by to spend a few minutes with his old friend. That should put him in an agreeable mood.

"Dad?" Her voice echoed strangely in the space below the rafters. From over the top of the stall gate, she could see the stallion. Usually the calmest of horses, the big bay roan was snorting, tossing his head, and showing the whites of his eyes. She couldn't see her father anywhere, but something was upsetting One in a Million—and he was telling her the only way he could.

Her hand felt cold as she slid the gate farther open and

stepped into the stall. At first, she could see only shadows. Then her foot bumped something solid. Looking down, she gasped.

Her father lay sprawled facedown in the straw.

He wasn't moving.